AF226417

The Mentoris Project
Barbera Foundation, Inc.
P.O. Box 1019
Temple City, CA 91780

Copyright © 2017 Barbera Foundation, Inc.
Cover photo: Tony Baggett/istockphoto; Met Museum/Artist-Jacob D. Blondel/Gift of Mrs. James Bradley Cook, 1967
Cover design: Suzanne Turpin

More information at www.mentorisproject.org

ISBN: 978-1-947431-35-5

Library of Congress Control Number: 2017959824

All net proceeds from the sale of this book will be donated to Barbera Foundation, Inc. whose mission is to support educational initiatives that foster an appreciation of history and culture to encourage and inspire young people to create a stronger future.

The Mentoris Project is a series of novels and biographies about the lives of great men and women who have changed history through their contributions as scientists, inventors, explorers, thinkers, and creators. The Barbera Foundation sponsors this series in the hope that, like a mentor, each book will inspire the reader to discover how she or he can make a positive contribution to society.

Cannon to the right of them,
Cannon to the left of them,
Cannon in the front of them
Volley'd and thunder'd
Storm'd at with shot and shell,
Boldly they rode and well,
Into the jaws of Death,
Into the mouth of Hell
Rode the six hundred.

Charge of the Light Brigade
Alfred, Lord Tennyson, 1854

Contents

Foreword

First and foremost, Mentor was a person. We tend to think of the word *mentor* as a noun (a mentor) or a verb (to mentor), but there is a very human dimension embedded in the term. Mentor appears in Homer's *Odyssey* as the old friend entrusted to care for Odysseus's household and his son Telemachus during the Trojan War. When years pass and Telemachus sets out to search for his missing father, the goddess Athena assumes the form of Mentor to accompany him. The human being welcomes a human form for counsel. From its very origins, becoming a mentor is a transcendent act; it carries with it something of the holy.

The Mentoris Project sets out on an Athena-like mission: We hope the books that form this series will be an inspiration to all those who are seekers, to those of the twenty-first century who are on their own odysseys, trying to find enduring principles that will guide them to a spiritual home. The stories that comprise the series are all deeply human. These books dramatize the lives of great men and women whose stories bridge the ancient and the modern, taking many forms, just as Athena did, but always holding up a light for those living today.

Whether in novel form or traditional biography, these books plumb the individual characters of our heroes' journeys. The power of storytelling has always been to envelop the reader in a vivid and continuous dream, and to forge a link with the subject. Our goal is for that link to guide the reader home with a new inspiration.

What is a mentor? A guide, a moral compass, an inspiration. A friend who points you toward true north. We hope that the Mentoris Project will become that friend, and it will help us all transcend our daily lives with something that can only be called holy.

—Robert J. Barbera, President, Barbera Foundation
—Ken LaZebnik, Founding Editor, The Mentoris Project

Prologue

CHARGE AND CHARGE AGAIN

Aldie Gap, Virginia—June 17, 1863

One, two, three. Stop. He pivoted on his boot heel. One, two, three. His head bumped into the down slope of the tent. He stopped and scowled at the tent wall. Sweat trickled down his lower back. Would no one ever invent a tent that wasn't either oven hot or freezing cold? It felt like he'd spent his entire life in military tents, first in northern Italy, then in the Crimea, and now here in Virginia. He ought to know by now that a man couldn't pace in a military tent, not even a colonel's field operations tent. He stood still, hands clenched by his side, reviewing the morning. Once again his temper got the better of him. He should have been more careful. While he was confined to quarters his men were out there fighting at Aldie Gap. They'd die, some of them. His men. He could hear horses and yelling and the boom of artillery, along with the higher-pitched sound of mine balls. And the gunpowder, its scent on the morning breeze like an evil flower. And he wasn't there. He felt his nails dig into his palms. If he'd just kept his mouth shut he wouldn't be under arrest right now.

When would he learn? Of course Parnell would make the best lieutenant colonel. He had more cavalry experience than anyone in the Union Army, himself included. He'd been one of the few Hussars to come back from that ill-fated charge at Balaclava. What had the poet called it? The Charge of the Light Brigade, that's what it was. The Union Army didn't have one man brave enough to make that charge or good enough to survive it. And still they wouldn't give Parnell the promotion that would make him Louis's second in command. But he should have gone about his protest more carefully. On the continent, a colonel and the son of a count might speak frankly with a general, but not in America. He shouldn't have charged into Pleasanton's tent in a temper and he shouldn't have said what he had. He'd handed the General an excuse to take his weapons and place him under arrest. It didn't matter that Pleasanton was wrong, only that he was his commanding officer. Pleasanton. There was a misnamed fellow if ever there'd been one. The Cavalry Corp's commander hated foreigners and thought they ought to be removed from the Union Army. And he had no trouble saying so at every opportunity, even after their great cavalry victory at Brandy Station.

Although in truth, the Union Army seemed to specialize in fools for generals. Most of them didn't know a thing about war, neither how to move troops nor how to fight. Oh, they'd been to school, knew all about books and battlefield theory, but only a simpleton thought that sort of thing had any meaning when it came to the mud and blood of war. They certainly didn't have the sense to treat experienced soldiers with respect. General Gregg was no better and no worse than most of them, making regimental decisions based on personal preference, not military capability. Why, he'd put his own brother in command of Louis's brigade on no better recommendation than ties of blood.

Louis heaved a sigh that was half growl, pulled his one chair away from his camp desk and sat. After that trouble in January he'd promised Mary he'd be more careful. Still, it made him angry that he had to be careful. In a fair world he'd be one of the generals. No one in this country had his experience in war. Why should a man whose best qualification was that he was a general's brother get bridge command and not himself, a man on his third war?

Northern elites hated the Irish and Gregg was from one of those old Calvinist families that thought so highly of themselves. People like that didn't like Italians much more than the Irish. What they really hated were Catholics, regardless of where they came from. As if a man's religion mattered on the battlefield. He had fought with Muslim Turks in the Crimea and they'd been as dependable and skilled as the French or British.

He pulled open the top drawer of his small desk and removed a piece of paper. He'd write to Kilpatrick and explain. Judd Kilpatrick was Irish. He knew what sort of men Gregg and Pleasanton were. Louis dipped the pen in the inkwell and then paused, cocking his head toward the tent door. A horse snorted and stamped, so close it sounded like it was in the tent. Louis heard the thump of a man dismounting and he grinned. He'd recognize the jangle of those particular spurs anywhere. They were particular to the British Hussars.

"Stand aside, man."

Louis heard a scuffle outside his door, then the wooden framed canvas door swung open.

William Parnell stepped inside, his bushy beard preceding his high forehead in a manner that suggested he was in an awful temper. "For the love of Mary, what are you doing sitting on your arse? There's fighting to be done." Parnell grinned at Louis before his face turned serious. "You've got to come. The men won't move without you. "

Louis reared back his head and stared at Parnell. "I've been arrested and confined to quarters, Major. You were there when it happened." Poems were written about the Light Brigade's bravery but Louis had seen it for himself. Parnell had been one of the few men to make it back that great and terrible day. He had been British Army and one of the things the British excelled at was troop discipline.

Parnell shook his head and stepped toward the door. "The men. They attacked and were routed. Lieutenant Colonel Taylor is dead, shot through the head. The men won't go back. Not without you. You want them all cashiered? Or worse? Hung?" He pushed open the door. "Let's go. *Now*."

Louis thought for a second. Poor Taylor hadn't been lieutenant colonel for a day before he'd been killed. Louis knew that his men needed him. And a real leader took care of his men. He buttoned the top two brass buttons of his navy blue cavalry tunic and buckled his belt. Then he reached for his saber, which he always leaned against his desk when off duty, but his hand slapped empty air. He remembered. He'd surrendered it to General Gregg at dawn, along with his Sharps carbine and Colt revolver.

Parnell's face fell. He shook his head again. "I forgot about your weapons. I'll tell the men. They can't expect you to go into battle empty-handed."

Louis pulled his kit bag out from under his camp cot, shaking his head. "Hold on." He thrust his hand into the bag and brought out a six-shot Remington revolver. "It's almost useless except in a close fight. So we'll have to get close." He shoved the revolver into his belt.

He stepped out the tent door and ran into the pimply-faced private who stuck his head in the door.

The boy blushed deep red. His mouth gaped at the sight of Louis and he looked past Louis for Parnell. "Major, I'm supposed to be guarding the Colonel. I'll get in trouble for sure if this door is open." The boy pretended he couldn't see the colonel standing before him, clearly disobeying orders.

"Then you best close the door," Parnell barked. "Colonel, are you sure?"

Louis snorted, breaking the illusion. "You came to get me, didn't you Parnell? Private, you'll just have to say I over-powered you and escaped." He pushed past the private. "I see you brought my Red." Louis slapped his chestnut horse on the shoulder and said, "Once more into the breach, dear Red." The horse snorted in agreement. Louis laughed as he heaved himself up into the saddle. He looked down at Parnell, still standing in the tent doorway. "See there, Parnell. Even Red thinks I should go."

Parnell shook his head and grinned. "And people say the Irish are hot heads." Parnell mounted his horse and spurred him forward. Louis followed, laughing as he went. In their wake Louis could hear the young private swearing.

Louis surveyed the 4th New York Cavalry. They were both a pitiful and a glorious bunch. Of the nearly eight hundred men he had recruited, just over half were still alive, the rest fallen to sabers, bullets, cannon fire or bloody flux. The Cavalry Corps, along with a great portion of the Army of the Potomac, crossed the Rappahannock a week ago, pushing hard under the scorching sun through the gap in the mountains at a tiny town called Aldie. They were in a race, trying to cut off General Lee before he got his army to Pennsylvania. Aldie sat at a crucial crossroads of the Ashby's Gap Turnpike and the Little River Turnpike, but it wasn't much of a town, so food was in short supply. The punishing heat and lack of water hadn't done the horses any good either. The water at Bull Run Creek this morning had been a muddy mess, more frogs than wet. Thank goodness the Little River, where they'd made camp, had water in it or half the horses would be dead. So here they were, in a fight for the Gap.

"Men," he bellowed as he rode down the line. "Remember Kelly's Ford!"

A cheer rose from the cavalrymen. Though the newspapers said the Union Army lost Kelly's Ford, the men who'd been there knew otherwise. It had been a fine day for the cavalry, full of slashing sabers and clashing horses. Louis was proud of his ragtag regiment. He accepted all men, regardless of their country of origin or their religion. Not like other regiments, who only wanted American-born Protestants. He had Germans, Frenchmen, Hungarians, one Spanish fellow, and a handful of Italians.

"That fox Lee intends to take his war north, to Pennsylvania. And Jeb Stuart's cavalry to help him." Louis stopped Red so he stood at the center of the cavalry line. "Will they go forward?"

"No!" The men cried back. "No!"

Louis wheeled Red around. He raised his arm high, then slashed it downward as if he had his saber in his hand. Red sprang forward. The 4th New York followed hard on his heels.

They rode like men possessed. Sabers flashed, blood flew. People said the Confederate cavalry man Jeb Stuart was the best the country had ever seen. After today people would know that wasn't true.

Louis rode back and forth across the field, exhorting the men. Yellow grass bent, then crushed into dust with the press of hooves and boots. Red screamed, slashing with his forelegs at fallen men in grey. The organized charge turned into a melee.

Louis rallied his men. They pushed forward, up the hill with the Confederate artillery. Cannon balls exploded around them, sending clumps of dirt everywhere, each as hard as a rock. Dust and smoke in the air made it hard to see. Through the grey Louis saw Parnell engage a grey-uniformed cavalryman, sabers flashing. Parnell didn't see the other Reb on his flank. Louis raised his arm, then remembered his hand was empty. If Parnell died because that fool of a general had taken his saber he'd punch the man in the nose despite the consequences. Louis kneed Red forward. The second man never saw Louis and Red's charge. They crashed into him, knocking him right off his horse. Red stomped on the man whose head split like a melon dropped off a wall.

Parnell slashed at his opponent, sinking his saber deep in the man's neck. A great gout of blood gushed from the man before he slumped and slid off his horse. He pulled back his sword, wheeling to meet the men behind him. Parnell's sword came around, right at Louis. Red dodged. Parnell's sword came up. It swept past the tip of Louis's nose, hitting only hot wind.

The two men grimaced at each other, each only too aware of how close they'd come to death. Louis looked across Parnell to the fallen man, now still on the ground. The fellow's sword lay with him, still gripped in his hand.

"I'll get it, sir," Parnell hollered as he moved to dismount. Off to the left a cannon ball exploded.

"Leave it," Louis screamed. He wheeled Red in a tight circle. Time to regroup, he thought. "Retreat," he bellowed. He muscled Red around, pulling hard at the horse's head and spurring him back the way they came. The men followed. They rode back down the hill and into the trees, where Confederate cavalrymen were loath to follow. Louis turned and checked over his shoulder. Parnell was back there; he could see the Irishman's grey horse. Louis breathed out a great gasp of air. A great commotion of thundering hooves and jangling metal sounded to the west. Red wheeled and Louis again reached for his missing saber, grabbing at nothing. He swore in Italian. A small group of men in dark blue uniforms broke through the trees. Lieutenant Estes, aide to General Kilpatrick, rode at their head.

Louis grinned as Estes pulled his horse to a stop before him. Estes grinned back, then saluted. "The General wants you." The young man pulled his horse around and dashed back the way he'd come, his men hard on his heels. Louis followed Estes and the others through the trees to Kilpatrick's temporary headquarters. Parnell went with him like he always did.

General Kilpatrick was a small scrap of a man, like a lot of the Irish, and no more than twenty-five years old. The two often shared a drink and told stories, some of them truer than others. A lot of American military men didn't care for Kilpatrick, calling him Kill-Cavalry behind his back, but that was because they didn't understand how to use cavalry soldiers in an army. Most generals thought cavalry were good for no more than patrols and surveillance, but Judd Kilpatrick understood the real strength of a cavalry unit was in the mayhem and fear a good offensive cavalry action could inspire. Men died in attacks like that, but men died of the bloody flux lying in camp too and no one complained about that. Louis thought the men who objected to the pugnacious little general really did so because he was Irish. And fearless.

Kilpatrick jerked his chin at Louis, his voluminous side-whiskers waving in the breeze as he did. "Cesnola, you got a talent for trouble. It's why I keep you around. If the brass are fussing about you, they can't be fussing about me." Kilpatrick frowned. "Gregg put you under arrest."

Louis shot a glance at Parnell. Parnell shrugged.

Kilpatrick swept his arm out, gesturing at the field of battle below. "And yet I saw your charge."

Louis nodded. He could hear the screams of men and horses, the shots of rifles, the boom of the cannon. Men were fighting and dying while he stood here like a schoolboy in trouble for pulling a girl's hair. "Sir, the 4th is crucial to Pleasanton's battle plans, is it not?"

Now it was Kilpatrick's turn to nod.

"The men refused to attack without me." Louis said, resisting the temptation to explain further.

Kilpatrick looked at Parnell.

"It's true, sir. The new lieutenant colonel took a bullet in the first charge. They wouldn't go again. The Colonel's their good-luck charm."

Kilpatrick chuckled. He looked back at Louis. "So you defied the order of a superior officer and charged into battle."

"Yes, sir."

"Without your weapons."

Louis shrugged and gestured at the pistol, still tucked in his belt. "I had a pistol, sir."

"But no saber. Nor carbine."

"No, sir." Kilpatrick would have been apprised of the arrest of one of his colonels within the hour of the event.

"Colonel, I've seen a number of brave actions in this army, but nothing like yours today." He nodded into the distance, then pointed. "The Rebs are dug in at the top of that hill, behind the fence. We need that hill. And your men will follow you."

Kilpatrick turned to face his aide. "Estes, I hate to ask, but could you loan this crazy Italian your saber?"

Estes grinned widely. "Glad to, sir." He unbuckled his belt and handed it and the sheathed sword to Louis. "Give 'em hell, Colonel."

Louis took the saber in his right hand. What had just happened?

Then, as if what he'd done was not at all remarkable, Kilpatrick looked over his shoulder at an older man behind him. "Oh, and Sergeant, find the Colonel a carbine, would you? He's going to need it."

Twenty minutes later, Louis rode into the clearing that held the men of the 4th New York. One of his captains saw him first and let out a cry. "Huzzah!" Someone else hollered, "The Colonel's back."

"And he's got a sword!"

"And a rifle," came another voice. After that it got noisy as men laughed and talked.

Parnell rode alongside Louis, a broad grin on his face. "Shall we?"

Louis called his men to attention and gave them their orders. They charged out of the trees and across the small valley toward the hill like men with the devil at their backs.

Three times the 4th charged the hill; three times they were beaten back. By late afternoon, they were exhausted and back in the trees. Louis handed Red off to one of his captains and walked among his men, offering words of encouragement and praise as he went. His uniform was so wet with sweat he felt as if he could take it off and wring it out. Near the end of his circuit, Parnell found him.

He looked his major in the eye. "Remind you of anything?"

Parnell shook his head. "Not even close. Balaclava was a hundred times worse than this. It was a hopeless waste of life."

Louis wordlessly laid his hand on Parnell's shoulder. Sometimes he forgot how young his friend was. Sometimes he forgot how young *he* was. He'd been in three wars before his thirtieth birthday.

"I am worried about the horses." Parnell understood that in the matter of cavalry offensives the health of one's mount made all the difference.

Louis looked over at the makeshift corral. "They're in a lot better shape than a month ago. Thank the Blessed Mother for spring grass. They've got one more charge in them."

The men mounted up again. The light was failing as they rushed out of the trees and toward the hill a fourth time. They made it across the valley before the Confederate artillery boomed.

Louis laughed out loud. He'd be willing to bet the enemy thought they'd had enough for one day. Louis charged up the hill, his men behind him. They were halfway up the hill before the Rebel cavalry rode out to meet them. Sabers flashed in the failing light. Horses screamed in terror and anger. Louis slashed his saber right and left at the grey-clad men in his way. Red never slowed his surge upwards. They crested the hill to see Confederate foot soldiers and artillerymen in flight.

Louis wheeled Red to face his men. Behind him the Rebel cavalry was in disarray. Where was this great cavalier, Jeb Stuart? On the right, a knot of three Confederates surrounded one of his men. Louis couldn't see who but it didn't matter. He wrapped Red's reins around the pommel, squeezed with his knees to keep Red still, and pulled his Sharps carbine. He sighted down the barrel, aiming at one of the men in grey. Just as he squeezed the trigger Red staggered and his shot went wild. Something struck Louis in the head.

They fell together, he and Red. Time slowed down. They fell and fell and fell. He hit the ground with his shoulder, then Red landed on him with a great, shattering whoomph. For a second he thought he'd never breathe again. He gasped and his breathing came back. He yanked at his leg. It was pinned beneath Red, who lay as unmoving as a dead thing.

Louis didn't want to look. Didn't want to know. Of all the deaths he'd lived through in his life, it was the horses that were the worst. Because they hadn't had a choice. Because a cavalryman was supposed to keep his horse safe before himself. He lifted his head. His eyesight blurred. He wiped at his eyes, his hand coming away red with blood. At least he could see. He looked at Red's head. Nothing. He tried to lay his hand on Red's shoulder. Blinding pain shot through him. He turned his head and quietly puked up what little was in his stomach. It felt like he'd been shot in the shoulder. He turned his head carefully and looked again. It was near dark now, but it looked like there was a bullet hole in his uniform, at the shoulder. Blood didn't show on navy wool. He tried for Red's body again, this time more carefully. He laid his hand upon the horse's neck. Nothing. No echo of a great, beating heart, no quiet rise and fall of respiration. The poor beast. He'd been a gallant mount. Louis lay in the dark, mourning the death of his horse. Then something struck the back of his head, knocking his chin down onto his chest. His teeth rattled and he was gone.

For a time it was dark. When he opened his eyes it was still dark. He tried to lift his head, but a wave of dizziness told him it was a bad idea. He turned his head, careful not to lift it from the cold ground. The stars were out, bright as any clear spring night. He couldn't feel his leg. Probably what came of having a half-ton of cooling dead horse lying on it for hours.

He lay there in the dark, with only his dead horse for company. How had it come to this? How did the second son of a Sardinian count end up near dead on a battlefield thousands of miles from home? What would his mother say? He lay there in the night thinking about the answers to those questions while he waited for rescue or capture. Whichever came first.

Part I

Chapter One

NO SOONER MET

Rivarola, Italy—1844–1846

Luigi pulled at his collar, hating its starchy constraint. Mother caught his movement from the corner of her eye, turned her head infinitesimally and frowned. Then she redirected her gaze to the front of the church. Luigi gave his collar one more tug and looked up at the shiny black casket not more than six feet from him. He was supposed to be sad, but he wasn't. Not even one little bit.

He'd hardly known the man. Father stayed away from them for months at a time, living down the valley in Turin with his friends and his whores. Mother pretended not to know. Not knowing unpleasant realities was Mother's specialty. And she never stood up for her sons when he did come home. He would charge into the house like a bull into a herd of cows. Everything displeased him. Then he'd pick one of his sons, most often Luigi, and punish him for some infraction, real or imagined, it didn't matter which. One day he'd grabbed Alerico by the arm and punched him square in the chest. Alerico, who was three years older than Luigi, had shoved the old man hard enough to push him into Mother's blanket chest. From behind a chair where he'd been hiding Luigi watched his father stumble and go down. When Alerico walked away Father let him go. That's when he learned what his father really was: a bully. And Father Pietro said all bullies were cowards. Luigi bided his time, waiting for the moment when he could fight back like Alerico.

And then the day came. Father staggered into the kitchen where Luigi was eating a bowl of wide noodles bathed in oil, anchovies, and garlic.

"Come here now, boy," Father bellowed, swaying to stay on his feet. He had a riding crop in his right hand, which he smacked against the side of his leg.

Cook took one look at Father and scuttled out the kitchen door.

Luigi watched her go. He didn't blame her. He stared at his father in disgust. It was just lunchtime and already the old man was drunk.

"Young pup, you do as you're told." The riding crop swished through the air but hit nothing, not even the table.

Luigi looked regretfully at his pasta bowl. Cook really did make the best Tajarin. But Luigi had been growing and he was almost as big as his father. It was time. He pushed his bowl away from him, took a deep breath and then threw himself out of his chair with a great clatter. By the time the chair hit the wall behind him he'd hit his father, barreling head first into the old man's alcohol-softened gut. Just like Alerico, Father fell. Luigi fell with him, but he let go and was scrabbling back up as soon as his father hit the floor.

Luigi learned two things that day. First, speed and sobriety were more important than size or age in a fight. Second, when a boy knocked his father down he was no longer a boy.

Father sent him away to the Jesuit school in Ivrea after that. He'd driven Luigi to the gates of the school and handed him over to Father Pietro. "You can have him, and good riddance," Father told the old Jesuit. Father Pietro tucked his hands into his robe and looked down his long nose at Father. "You intend him for the priesthood then?"

Father nodded, then remounted his horse and rode away, leaving Luigi without a backwards glance.

The Ivrea Jesuits lived in a huge stone fortress that was always cold, no matter how warm the day. Luigi lasted in the place for just over a year. Some parts of his Jesuit experience had been quite pleasant. He enjoyed learning, so he particularly enjoyed the Jesuits' emphasis on literature and language. He loved Dante and Shakespeare in equal measure. In his time at Ivrea, Luigi learned the rudiments of Greek, Latin, German, and English. He'd already learned French and Italian at his mother's knee because she, like all gently reared Piedmontese, spoke the two languages almost interchangeably. His favorite days in school were they ones where they acted out plays, from ancient Greek dramas to more modern Italian works like those by Francesco Ongaro. None of the priests approved of Ongaro's liberal politics, but they enjoyed his humorous plays. Luigi liked the plays that called for sword fights, even if they did use only wooden swords. He also enjoyed playing his flute on stage. The boys made fun of him for his choice of instrument, but he loved his flute. Unlike most instruments, you could tuck a flute into a pocket and take it anywhere. No, the education at Ivrea had been fine. More than fine really, though Luigi would never admit that to either of his parents. The problem was that he didn't want to be a priest because priests didn't have adventures. Father Pietro said Luigi lacked self-restraint. Luigi just wanted to be treated like the other boys, the regular boys. While most orders of the priesthood only took students studying for the priesthood, the Jesuits educated a great number of the sons of the nobility with the aim of returning them to society. Sons headed for the priesthood were treated differently, more stringently, than the boys who would eventually return home to join the family business.

Luigi hated the constraints of being an acolyte. He was moved from place to place with quiet dignity. *Quiet dignity? What fun was there in that?*

One day he received yet another summons to Father Pietro's austere office. He went expecting a gentle but stern lecture on his failings. Instead the Jesuit handed Luigi a letter, his face impassive as always. Luigi noted that the wax seal imprinted with the family crest was broken. He looked at the seal. "Oppress Resurgent." Oppressed, He Rises. He looked up at Father Pietro, feeling unsure. Father made a waving motion with his hand, the black folds of his robe quietly rustling with the sudden movement.

To Emmanuelle Pietro Paolo Maria Luigi Palma di Cesnola,

My son, I regret to inform you that your father has been killed. You will come home for the funeral and remain home, ending your tenure with the Jesuits.

Your Mother,
Countess Eugenia Rica di Casstelvecchio Palma di Cesnola

Luigi held the letter very still, aware that Father Pietro was watching him. It was just like Mother to send such a short, unemotional message and yet release him from this terrible exile.

She was not a lady to be trifled with, stern and rigid in her ideas, but she was a much better parent than her husband. Luigi wanted to throw the letter in the air in joy. He wanted to whoop and caper about the room but he did not. Even he knew one did not rejoice in a parent's death in front of a Jesuit priest. Instead he returned to his room, packed his bag, took his horse from the stable where it had been since he arrived thirteen months earlier and rode home. The funeral took place the day after Luigi arrived.

Mother tapped Luigi on the shoulder, bringing him back to the present. He lurched to his feet, conscious of the ache in his knees as he did. How long had he been kneeling? Alerico and four of Father's friends from town stepped forward to hoist the coffin to their shoulders. Luigi stood to join them. He had to because his younger brothers were too small. When Mother asked him to do his duty as a pallbearer his first impulse had been to refuse. Then it occurred to him that he'd be doing it for *her*, not his father who'd been so foolishly drunk he'd allowed himself to be run down in the street by a pair of runaway horses.

They carried Luigi Mauricio Palma di Cesnola into the churchyard and past a herd of tumbledown, lichen-covered headstones. Though it was early summer and sunny, the day was only warm, the sort of weather one might take advantage of with a hike and a picnic. This far north, in the Piedmont, surrounded by the snow-capped Alps, they rarely had uncomfortably warm days. Not like down south, towards Rome or even Sicily. Luigi loved the Piedmont. It was a place of extremes and its people were strong.

Luigi watched two old men lower his father's casket into a dark, damp hole. He sighed, wishing he'd known his father before he'd become a drunkard. Once, long ago, he'd been a revolutionary along with Uncle Alerino. The two brothers left

Rivarola when they were not much older than Luigi was today. They'd gone to France to fight for the revolution. His father had almost died on the long march back from Russia in the winter of 1812. When Luigi was little his father used to tell stories and the one Luigi remembered most vividly was the one about how Father and Uncle Alerino caught and roasted rats for dinner.

After that, Father and Uncle fought in the Piedmontese revolution, the one back in the 1820s with the Carbonari. When that revolution failed, Father and all the other Carbonari were excommunicated and ordered imprisoned but they had managed to escape to Spain. A few years later, Father applied for and received a papal dispensation and was allowed to return to Rivarola. The Pope viewed Father's older brother Alerino as one of the movement's leaders and would not pardon him. Uncle, now living in Greece, lived under a death sentence to this day.

One of the two old men took up a shovel, then looked expectantly at the parish priest. The black-clad Franciscan stepped forward and said a few words. Well, more than a few words. In Luigi's experience, no priest ever said two words when a hundred would suffice. The priest chanted and they chanted back. Finally it ended. Mother stepped forward with her sons lined up behind her. Luigi watched as they each dropped a scoop of dirt into the hole. When it was his turn he bent, grabbed a handful of moist, dark loam and squeezed it into a tight ball. He held his hand out over his father's grave and opened his fingers. As he did he vowed to never ever be like his father. He would not be a failed revolutionary, bitter, and abusive to his family. He would fight for things that mattered and he would not sell himself for safety and drink. He would not waste his life and leave a widow and children behind to fend for themselves.

He walked away from the grave. Like his father when he had dropped Luigi off at the Jesuit school, he did not look back.

Abrielle, Abrielle, Abrielle. Luigi paused and shot a look over his shoulder before hastening up the path. The Castello Abrielle Roxanna Balbo. She was perfect in every way. Her hair was the rich, soft brown of the finest honey, her eyes dark and always sparkling with fun, framed by two perfect half-moon arches of eyebrows. And she was a Balbo, so not even his mother could object to her. Her uncle Cesare was both an intellectual and a revolutionary, and most importantly a man who had figured out how to navigate between revolutionary and papal politics without upsetting either side. And the Balbos were an old Sardinian family. Mother had gone to convent school with Abrielle's mother, Agneta, though Agneta had married a handsome young count while Luigi's mother had married a man forty years older than her, for all that Father had also been a count.

Luigi had known Abrielle since childhood. Like his brothers, she had always been there. But a year ago he began to see her differently: she had begun to glow in his mind. The more time they spent together the more he loved her. No one paid them any mind because everyone thought they were too young for love.

Luigi knew better because Shakespeare knew better. Romeo and Juliet had been young. He'd copied passages from the play and given them to Abrielle. Once she'd given him some lines from *As You Like It*. He never forgot them. "No sooner met, but they looked, no sooner looked than they loved." Sometimes he played her arias on his flute. Or read her poetry. And month after month no one seemed to notice they were in love. That would all change soon.

Luigi stuck his hand in his pocket. Yes, her latest note was still there. He resisted the temptation to take it out and read it again. It was so short that he had memorized it the first time he read it. "*Meet me at the Castello at 3. Come alone. A.*"

Last Sunday afternoon he had asked Abrielle to marry him. Oh, he knew they were both too young, but they loved each other too much to wait. Romeo and Juliet waited and look how that turned out. Well, maybe they hadn't waited, but their unhappy ending was reason enough to seize this moment. Once engaged, he would finish military school. In two years' time they would both be sixteen and of an age to legally wed. In the meantime, everyone would know they belonged to each other.

He hurried up the path, breathing out short puffs of air against the climb. The Castello Cesnola had once housed Palmas, but that had been long, long ago. Mother often told the story of how the castle had been built eight hundred years before by one of his ancestors. The man had been a Spanish adventurer who pledged himself to the Savoys and was granted a large parcel of land that became the Palmas' home. The Spaniard built the castle with Savoyard funds to guard the mountain pass against rivals. By the 1600s, the House of Savoy had grown to such a power in the region that the area no longer required a castle fortress in Rivarola. The Palmas moved to a much more comfortable villa in the valley and the old fortress fell into disrepair. Now covered in moss and vines, surrounded by wild flowers and chestnut trees, it was a popular place for family outings and lovers' trysts.

He crested the hill and approached the Castello. Off in the distance a bird sang. Just in front of him was a looming rock wall, interrupted by a large stone arch that led to the interior. He stepped through the arch and into the Castello, looking up as he always did. The absence of a roof always surprised Luigi, though he had played in this space since he was old enough to climb the hill. He glanced around, then smiled so widely that he thought the corners of his mouth might reach his ears.

Abrielle sat on a stone just ahead of him, the sun shining on her in a way that made her glow like an old Roman coin his mother kept in her jewelry box. He hurried toward her, then stopped, puzzled. These last few months she always ran toward him when she saw him. It was one of the things he loved most about her—her impetuous enthusiasm for life. But this afternoon she sat on her stone, unmoving. She did not return his smile.

His stomach rolled over in unease. Part of him wanted to go back the way he had come so he would not have to hear what his golden girl would say.

Last week she had refused to give him an answer to his proposal. She had held his face in her soft hands and said, "I must ask my parents for permission. You understand, don't you?"

He did. Abrielle was a good girl, from a good family. He was from a good family. Oh, sure, he got in trouble occasionally, but nothing major. And however much his father might be regarded as a failure, he had been a noble and a count. And there was no shame in being a second son in a family as old and distinguished as the Palmas. He understood she wanted to ask permission and he had been sure the answer would be yes. So sure. Their mothers were friends, weren't they?

He approached her, knowing in his heart that he'd been wrong. He stopped two, maybe three steps away from her.

She bit her lip, shook her head, and then burst into tears. Luigi couldn't help himself. He swept her into his arms. He felt her tears hot on his shoulder, seeping through his linen shirt like tiny drops of acid. After less than a minute she stopped and withdrew from him. He didn't know that he would never hold her again.

"So the answer is no," he half whispered.

She shrugged her soft, round shoulders. "It's worse than that."

He waited.

She took a deep breath. "I'm to marry your brother Alerico and be the new countess."

Luigi wanted to scream, to cry out to the open blue sky above him. Alerico had never even looked at his Abrielle. Never once. All he cared about were his dusty old books. He'd been reading while Luigi had been outside riding with Abrielle. He'd been reading while Luigi danced with Abrielle at parties, while they'd hiked this very hill. Boring old Alerico had never made daisy crowns for her hair. And *he* got her? Because he was first born and the Count?

"When?"

"The first Sunday after my sixteenth birthday. We have more than a year before that. We can meet in secret. I love you." She sniffed, but did not start crying again.

He steadied himself. She loved him. But she had no more choice than he did. She would be Alerico's wife one way or the other. He had no right to make her miserable, not if he loved her. He made up his mind.

"Alerico is a good man. He's kind and gentle. He'll be a good husband to you. You should spend the year with him, not me."

Before she could see his tears he turned and walked away. For the second time in his life he did not look back.

He lay on his bed for two days, thinking and praying. Why had God given him this great love only to take it away? He asked God, but God had no answer. Mother had his meals sent up to him but he couldn't eat. He felt dead inside, hollow and empty. On the morning of the third day of his self-imprisonment he rose from his bed, washed himself, and dressed. He tried to put on his funeral suit, thinking it would suit the way he felt, but it no longer fit. He'd grown too much the last two years. He reminded himself of the family crest. "Oppressed, he rises." Luigi went downstairs to speak to his mother.

He knew she knew. She had to. Father had been dead for over a year so she must have arranged the marriage between Abrielle and Alerico. And certainly Abrielle's mother would have told her about Luigi's proposal to her daughter. She knew. That's why she'd had his meals sent up to his room.

Mother was sitting on the back veranda, taking her morning espresso in the dappled sunshine. She sat down her tiny coffee cup at his approach. "I am glad to see you up and about, my son," she said quietly.

He bowed at her and then took a seat next to her. Whenever he saw his mother he experienced a moment of surprise. The mothers of his school friends looked like mothers, stout, sturdy ladies in black mantillas and heavy gold jewelry. His mother looked barely older than a school girl. She'd been forty years younger than Father when they married and was the local beauty. Father had been old and impoverished, but he had the title and that title made him a good match. Like Alerico, Luigi thought bitterly.

She looked him over. "I know you are disappointed, but you should have known."

He resisted the urge to yell at his mother. She did not tolerate emotional displays and would send him away if he raised his voice. He sighed again. "It's because I'm a second son, isn't it?"

"Of course," she agreed. "Abrielle is from a good family, a prosperous family. Her dowry is immense. I regret to say your Father was a poor money manager and the estate needs money."

Luigi raised his chin and looked his mother in the eye. "I thought you brought money when you married Father. And look how he treated you." He wanted her to know that he knew she'd been sold, just like Abrielle was about to be sold.

"It is the way of the world, Luigi. I wish you were more practical. You have a romantic streak like your father and uncle."

"But couldn't I marry Abrielle for both romantic *and* practical reasons? Her dowry would become ours regardless of which son she marries." As soon as he said the words Luigi heard how stupid they were.

She shook her head sadly. "It's the title and you know it. Your brother is already Count Palma di Cesnola and your Abrielle will be countess when she marries him. And, more importantly, her son would be a count some day. That's what her family wants."

He slumped his shoulders in defeat. It was a defeat he'd known was coming.

She poured a tiny cup of coffee and pushed it over to him. "Luigi, today you feel as if you could die. You will get over this." She held up her hand to stop his denial. "You will. You are strong. Not like your brother Alerico. If God had willed it, you would have been the first born. Alerico is the family intellectual. He would make a better priest than count. You, my son, are brave and bold and strong, in both body and mind. You will love again because you're a survivor. Which makes me think it is a good thing Alerico is first born and not you. He's a house cat, Luigi. He will be happy staying here in this small, safe place for the rest of his life. You would shrivel and die for you are a tiger who cannot be caged. Like your father, you need adventures. You need to see the world and conquer it. If you married Abrielle you'd leave her, over and over again, like your father left me. You would break her." She left unsaid: *like your father broke me.*

Luigi took a sip and stared into the distance. Part of him wanted to argue with her, but the larger part of him knew she was right. He was stronger than his brother. He was larger, though Alerico was two years older than him, and he could ride and climb and jump far better than Alerico. And he was handsome. He had thick auburn hair like his mother, but he was tall and broad like his father. Abrielle wasn't the first girl he'd kissed. He'd just thought she'd be the last.

Then he steeled his resolve and asked Mother if he could transfer from his current school to the Military Academy at Cherasco. Mother looked at him with understanding. "It's fifty miles or more away. You'd have to board there full-time."

He nodded. Cherasco was south of Turin, a good two days' ride away. Mother could be a hard woman sometimes. He supposed she had to be. He waited, watching her face for a sign.

She sighed. "I suppose it's for the best. I'll have to find the money."

He tried to smile but could not.

He left before the week was out, riding out of the villa gates on his favorite horse at dawn. This time he did look back, fixing the place in his mind. He knew it would be a long time before he had the courage to return.

Chapter Two

GONE TO WAR

Northern Italy—March–May 1848

The leather heels of Luigi's riding boots made a most satisfying thunk on the stone hallway floor. He was filled with purpose. The Colonel could hardly say no with Milan under attack. He knocked on the door to Colonel Milleti's offices, using a bit more force than was generally considered polite. He dropped his right hand to his side and relaxed his fist. It wouldn't do to appear overexcited.

The Colonel's aide-de-camp, Second Lieutenant Ignatius Revel, opened the door. The two young men grinned at each other. Though Revel had graduated from the school last May and was now a junior officer in Sardinia's regular army while Luigi was a lowly underclass man with two years of schooling still to finish, the two were friends of a sort. Revel had that effete wispiness so common among the nobility, but he'd introduced Luigi to the best taverns in Cherasco. Not that Luigi drank much. He'd vowed to not end up like his father, drunk and disappointing to everyone who knew him.

Revel waved Luigi into the Colonel's anteroom with a grin. The Second Lieutenant knew exactly what Luigi was up to because they had discussed it the night before. "Let me see if he's got a moment."

Minutes later Luigi found himself standing before Cherasco Military Academy's headmaster, Colonel Milleti. The Colonel was a heavyset man with a magnificent white mustache that made him look like a shaggy old dog. The Colonel was actually quite a nice man, or at least as nice as any man in charge of 125 sons of the Italian nobility could be. Luigi saluted his colonel, then assumed parade rest position.

Milleti picked up a single piece of paper and peered at it before looking up at Luigi. "I'm glad you're here. I'd be glad to accede to your mother's wishes and allow you a brief leave to go home."

"Leave?" Luigi heard his voice squeak in surprise. Was something wrong with Mother? Was she sick? He really should have visited her at least once in the last two years. He cleared his throat and tried again. "My mother needs me to come home?"

"For your brother, Count Palma di Cesnola's wedding. Of course you should be there."

Luigi felt his stomach do an uncomfortable little flop. He'd managed to forget that his brother and Abrielle were to be married when she turned sixteen. He hardly ever thought of his one and only love anymore. Not more than once or twice a day.

He shook his head. "That's not why I'm here, Colonel. I've come to ask permission to enlist in the Sardinian Army."

"Ahhh, I should not be surprised. There's been a regular parade of students into my office to ask the same. I've said no to each of them."

"But sir," Luigi began.

The Colonel held up his right hand. "Tell me, young man, do you trust the king?"

"He's my king, sir. If he says we're to fight the Austrians then I want to fight the Austrians."

Luigi knew what Milleti was really asking. In the last few years, King Carlo Alberto's policy toward Austria and Italian independence had changed. For decades he'd sided with the Austrians: when the Spanish revolted against them and again when the Portuguese did the same. Why, he'd even signed death sentences in absentia for both Mazzini and Garibaldi for their part in the Young Italy movement. They and their followers wanted a unified Italy and a constitutional monarchy, but the king stood against them. But then the old pope died and the new one, Pius IX, officially objected to the Austrian occupation of Italy as a whole and the Papal States in particular. King Carlo Alberto suddenly became a liberal, siding with the new Pope and the revolutionaries against the Austrians. Why, he'd even approved a constitution for Sardinia.

"Hmmm." The Colonel shifted in his seat, then tapped the folded newspaper that sat on the left side of his desk. "You may be right. Certainly it's not for me to disagree with the king. With Sicily, Venice, and now Milan in revolt, the king must know that Sardinia would do well to seize the main chance. This may be Italy's chance for independence. I think our king understands that, however sympathetic he is to the old ways and to that rotten Corsican usurper Napoleon."

"Yes, sir," Luigi said. Where was the Colonel going with this?

"I have your file here." The Colonel tapped a folder on the desk before him. "I had Revel pull it when I was considering giving you leave for the wedding. You're a model student. First Lieutenant of the Fourth Student Regiment, I see."

"Yes, sir." His military designation was only a school rank, with no power outside the Cherasco Military Academy, but he was proud of it nonetheless.

The Colonel flipped open the file, his mustache quivering as he peered down at it. "Says here you've top marks in engineering, topography, cartography, physics, and ethics. And you've mastered six languages? Can that be right?"

Luigi nodded. Languages had always come easy to him. "I'm going to be a professional soldier. A cavalry officer, I hope. My Uncle Alerino once said that a good military man should be a linguist because he never knew where he'd be fighting, or for whom."

Miletti smiled. "That's right. You're the son and nephew of the revolution-inclined Palma brothers, aren't you?"

Luigi nodded. "The king banished my Father and his brother after the 1821 Revolt, but then he pardoned Father."

"And your uncle?"

Luigi frowned. "Still in Greece, sir. But if this war goes well maybe the king will let Uncle come home."

The Colonel snorted. "Kings are tricky creatures, but I suppose a boy can dream." He stared at Luigi's paperwork, then closed the folder and tapped it with his forefinger. "I see you're not of age."

"No, sir. I'm still fifteen. That's why I've come to ask your permission."

"Seems a shame to keep you out of the war just because you're underage. I've got eighteen-year-olds that aren't half the student you are," the Colonel said. He stroked his silver mustache, then once again tapped Luigi's file. "I am granting you temporary leave to enlist in the Sardinian Army. I'll write you a letter of recommendation for the Queen's Brigade. I've got an old friend in command there that'll take care of you. Since you've not graduated you'll have enlisted rank, not officer, understand?"

"Yes, sir. Thank you, sir," Luigi sputtered.

"Son, there's glory in dying for a good cause but I'd just as soon you stayed alive and finished your schooling once this war is done." The Colonel pushed himself up out of his chair, straightened himself, and saluted Luigi. Luigi saluted the Colonel back and left the room, a large grin splitting his face. Revel laughed when he saw him and wished him well. Once out in the hall, Luigi jumped up in jubilation. Here came an adventure! It almost made up for not marrying Abrielle. Almost.

Luigi packed one bag and rode east for the Sardinian Army encampment wearing his school uniform. In his front coat pocket he had the Colonel's letter of introduction. His new commander, a colonel for the 9th Infantry Regiment, made him an under-corporal. Two days later, they marched on Milan, King Carl Albert at their head. The King rode right by Luigi on his way to the front of his troops. He looked like a tired professor on a borrowed white charger, but still it was thrilling to see him. Country boys didn't run into kings every day.

Before they arrived at Milan's gates, the Milanese people revolted against the Austrians, driving General Radetsky's forces from the city. The Sardinians arrived just in time to chase the great Radetsky's army through the countryside. The Austrians retreated to the four fortresses that made up Milan's outer defenses: Legnago, Verona, Mantua, and Peschiera. Their retreat was sufficiently rapid and disorganized that they didn't destroy any roads and bridges in their wake, making pursuit all that much easier.

The 9th followed the part of the Austrian Army that made for Peschiera, trapping the Austrians inside the fort. Luigi felt more than a little disappointed that the war had so far been nothing more than chasing a retreating army. On foot, he and the other enlisted men marched all day, from dawn to dusk, eating the dirt the horsemen before them kicked up. The cavalry and infantry moved so fast that they left the artillery regiments behind. They laid siege to Peschiera, which turned out to be pretty boring, too. The first three days of the siege they did no more than surround and guard the fortress, penning the Austrians inside, waiting for the artillery units to bring up the siege cannons. The fact that the fortress stood on a small island in the Mincio River made the job easy. On the fourth day, the Sardinians' siege artillery rolled up to Peschiera and began bombarding the fortress day and night. At first it had been terribly exciting, but it quickly became both dull and irritating. Luigi discovered that one thing common to soldiers everywhere. Cannon fire, even when it wasn't the enemy's, was nerve wracking and exhausting.

Luigi made friends with a group of boys, none of them any older than he. Most of them were privates and peasants, boys who'd enlisted not for glory, but for the pay. They quickly found out that, with not much to do, their commanding officers paid them little attention. To alleviate their boredom, Luigi took to leading his cadre of boy soldiers out on expeditions around camp. They stuck their noses into everything, learning who would share food, wine, and songs. They had free run of the camp, and could swim and fish in the river as long as they went upstream far enough to be out of range of the Austrians' guns. Sometimes Luigi played his flute and the boys sang or danced. He hadn't known going to war would be such fun.

On the sixth day of the siege, they found an old row boat and used it to inspect the fortress walls during lulls in the artillery shelling. Luigi, who'd grown up with the Castello in his backyard, had the boys pay particular attention to the base of the fortress. Castles and forts always had tunnels for bringing goods and people in and out. They also had smaller tunnels for sewage. Of course the engineers with the Sardinian army knew that too, but they didn't get as close to the fortress as the group of boys in the small boat. So the boys found a small tunnel the engineers missed. They took the intelligence to Luigi's colonel, who gave them all an extra ration for their dinner that night.

And so, before his first month in the army was over, Luigi had his first promotion, from under-corporal to corporal, all because he'd led the expedition that found a tiny sewage outlet.

While the 9th laid siege to Peschiera, across the Rivoli plateau, outside Verona, the King led the Sardinian Army against the Austrians in the Battle of Santa Lucia. Radetsky prevailed, driving the Sardinian Army back and holding Verona. King Carlos Alberto retreated and led his army to Pescheria, where their combined forces forced the Austrians inside the fort to surrender at the end of May, less than seven weeks after the siege began.

Luigi was standing at the edge of the crowd when the Austrian commander left the fort and offered surrender to the king. Up close, the king was even less impressive looking. He was pale, like a man not entirely well, grey haired, and had a long neck and a pointy chin that made him look like a fox. Seeing him Luigi was reminded of the king's nickname, Carlo the Hesitant.

The successful siege of Peschiera turned out to be the high point of the war for the Sardinians. While they'd been strangling the

Austrians at Peschiera, General Radetsky moved his Army towards Mantua. Before the Sardinian forces could come to their aid, the Tuscan Division suffered defeats at Curatone and Montanara. The Tuscan soldiers took the twin defeats as a reason to return home, with whole companies sneaking away under cover of darkness. Worse still, the Pope withdrew his army, after which the Sicilian Army also bowed out. The failures of the Tuscan, Papal, and Sicilian Armies left the Sardinians alone in the field of battle, with only twelve thousand men. With no one to fight, Radetsky turned his entire army toward the Sardinians.

Luigi heard rumors in the camp that the Pope had pressured King Ferdinand of Sicily to withdraw from the field, fearing that Sardinian military success would lead to Sardinian control of any new Italian state that might result from the war. Luigi couldn't believe his ears when he heard it. He'd been a huge fan of the new Pope ever since the man's ascension, believing he championed liberty and independence for all Italians. Instead Pius IX seemed to care only about seizing power for himself and the Papacy. It was an opinion one heard quite a lot around the Sardinian encampment. It seemed terribly cowardly to Luigi.

The Austrians and the Sardinians spent June circling around each other, jockeying for position on the Rivoli plateau. The Austrians finally attacked one cloudy morning at the end of July, driving a wedge that separated the Sardinian Army into two smaller, weaker forces. The 9th found themselves in the southern force, along with the king and his command. For days they did nothing. True to his name, the king was hesitating again, though to be fair they were vastly outnumbered and outgunned.

At dawn on the morning of the 25th of July, they were ordered to attack. The 9th charged through the grey mist. All around them guns boomed, sabers rattled, horses screamed. Even at the back of the battlefield Luigi saw and heard plenty. More than plenty. The battle shifted to and fro. Sometimes they pressed the Austrians, sometimes the Austrians pressed them. Luigi stayed with the boys of the 9th. Mostly they tried to stay out of trouble. Once an Austrian soldier made it back to where they were. He was covered in blood and running as if his life depended on it. Luigi lowered his rifle, ready to shoot, but the man ran right by them like they weren't there. Mostly the little band of privates, led by a fourteen-year-old corporal, found injured men and dragged them off the battlefield. Before long they were covered in mud and blood, but it felt good to do something that helped.

By late afternoon, it began to rain. The battlefield turned into a mire of sloppy mud, tinged pink with blood. Both armies withdrew, leaving the field clear. There were men and horses littered across the field like nothing Luigi had ever seen. No class he'd taken at the military academy prepared him for the sheer butchery of it all.

By evening, rain poured out of the sky in cold sheets of misery. Each regiment, each man, took cover where they could. Luigi spent that night under a supply wagon with his group of boys. They huddled together for warmth, though even under the wagon they were all so wet that the cold found every part of them. At about dawn the rain ceased and Luigi started to feel warmer. At first he thought it was the sunshine, but by mid-morning he was burning with fever. Two of the privates hauled him out of from under the wagon and into the camp hospital. When he awoke he thought he'd caught a cold. Then the fever and chills got worse, a cycle of burning and shivering that he thought would kill him. It turned out he'd caught that scourge of military encampments everywhere: typhoid fever. Of course he didn't find out until much later. Camp doctors were too busy sawing off arms and legs and sewing men up to bother much with one feverish fourteen-year-old corporal. When they finally got to him they put him in isolation. Then other soldiers joined him as the typhoid spread through the army.

While Luigi lay in hospital, King Carlo Alberto surrendered rather than continue the battle. Radetsky benevolently allowed the Sardinians to keep their arms and horses. A week later, the two men signed an armistice ending hostilities. The war for Italian Independence was over and the Austrians were as firmly in control of Italy as ever.

Chapter Three

REVOLUTION AND REVERSAL

Piedmont and Lombardy —February–March 1849

By the time the Army packed up the hospital and moved back to Turin, Luigi was covered in rose-colored itchy spots. The rash wasn't as bad as the diarrhea. His bowels seemed to have lost their ability to function and whatever the nurses put into him ran right back out. Rice didn't work, nor the thin, polenta-like gruel they kept spooning into him for reasons he never understood. By fall, he looked like a skeleton with skin and he was too weak to feed himself or get out of his cot. That's when he caught pneumonia. Or maybe the coughing and wheezing were a part of the typhoid. The doctors couldn't seem to agree and Luigi didn't think it mattered much either way.

He lay in bed, day after day, hurting from his eyeballs to his toes. He caught himself wishing for death, but fought the feeling. He would not die. He had more to learn but maybe this was the end of his adventures. If his first foray into war had taught him anything it was that war was not an adventure. Or maybe it was. There had been some awfully good days, but it wasn't only an adventure. It was dirty, boring, brutal, and awful.

And wonderful, thrilling, and full of meaning. He loved the comradeship of being in camp with military men and he didn't mind the tents and bad food. The battles were unbelievably frightening, but fear taught a man things. What he'd learned was that everyone was afraid. Everyone was repulsed. That a soldier went to battle, not because he was so brave he had no fear, but in spite of his fears. A soldier embraced fear and death and fought anyhow. For his country, for independence or freedom from occupation, but mostly for his friends.

By Christmas, he was on the mend. The nursing sisters let him sit outside in the weak winter sun a few hours each day. He felt well enough to feel rootless and purposeless. Some days he played his flute, glad both for its music and the fact that he still had it, the one constant in the shifting panorama that was his life. When he wasn't playing he sat and thought. Should he go home? He didn't want to because Abrielle would be there, the new Countess Palma di Cesnola. He couldn't go back to school either. He wasn't strong enough and it was the middle of the term anyway.

He was sitting on his favorite bench, his face turned up to the sun, when Sister Maria Agneta brought him a visitor. It was an older man, well past his prime, but still hale and fit. His silver mustache brought to mind Colonel Milleti, though this man was considerably older and wearing a Major General's uniform.

Luigi struggled to his feet to salute this unknown general.

"At ease, son," the man said. He sat on the other half of the bench, waving at Luigi to join him. When they'd settled he introduced himself. "General Georgio Ansaldi, commander of the 17th Brigade."

Luigi could only stare at the man. He had immensely broad shoulders and kindly blue eyes that clashed with his military bearing and the grandeur of his uniform, which was blue with red trim, epaulettes, and turn backs. He carried under his arm a black hat of prodigious size, topped by a red-feathered plume.

"You're Mauricio Palma's boy, aren't you?"

Luigi nodded. This magnificent man had known his drunken father?

Ansaldi nodded, then leaned forward, hands on his knees. "Your father was a good man. He saved my life once, a long time ago."

"Really?" Luigi couldn't hide the note of disbelief in his voice.

"Yes, yes, he did." Ansaldi paused, as if remembering. "We were both at Waterloo. On different sides. He fighting in Napoleon's army, while I'd enlisted in the Prussian Army. We were both injured, but I more gravely than he. It rained before the battle, days of hard rain. I was shot, came off my horse, ended up in a ditch full of water. I almost drowned but your father pulled me out. Dragged me under a tree. When I asked him why he said he recognized a fellow Italian when he saw one. He never did say how, but I'd be dead if weren't for your father."

Luigi didn't know what to say. The man he knew had been a father mostly in absentia, coming home from war long enough to leave another son in his wife's belly. In retirement, he'd been a drunk and a bully. Luigi regarded the General with care. "If you say so, sir," he said meekly.

The General cuffed Luigi lightly upside the head. "I do, you insolent pup. I owe your father a great debt that I can never repay. But I *can* take care of his son. What's this about you being a corporal?"

Luigi shrugged. Something about the way Ansaldi asked the questions told him that the General didn't approve.

"You're the son of one count and the brother of another. And your commander says you're brave. And smart. Italy is going to need men like you. There's going to be war. More war, I should say."

Luigi smiled at the General. "I'll fight until the Austrians are gone from our land, sir."

Ansaldi grunted and sat back. "I'm sure you would, son, but Italy doesn't need corporals. It needs leaders. You have to finish at the Academy and enter the army as an officer. If you're like your father, you'll be a general one day."

Luigi frowned. "I can't go back now, sir. The term is half over and Sister says I'm not well yet." He dropped his head, embarrassed at his weakness.

"No shame in being sick, son. Typhus, cholera, malaria and all manner of diseases plague every army that ever marched. Now listen, here's the plan."

Luigi straightened up, feeling something in his heart lighten.

"You'll finish your convalescence here, then join me at my staff office as one of my aide-de-camps. It will be light duty. Next fall, you'll go back to the Academy. When you've graduated you'll return to my regiment as a junior officer. And then I expect we'll turn those damn Austrians out of the country."

Before Luigi could reply, the General abruptly stood up. "I'll expect you at my headquarters in a month's time. I'll leave the particulars with the hospital administrator." He turned and walked away without another word.

Luigi could only gape at the old warhorse as he strode across the hospital's courtyard garden. What had just happened? He'd gotten his future back, that's what. All because his father may not have been the monster he had thought him to be. Luigi smiled up at the sun and focused all his energy into getting well.

≈

In late January, Luigi left the hospital and joined General Ansaldi's staff at his headquarters outside Turin. Although theoretically the Kingdom of Sardinia, which included the Piedmont, had signed a peace accord with the Austrians, Italy was far from peaceful that winter. Rome erupted into a revolution before the holidays, when the Pope's liberal administrator for the Papal states was assassinated. The Austrians reacted to the unrest by disarming the Pope's Swiss guards and surrounding the Papal palace. This caused rioting in the streets. The people drove out the Austrians and demanded that Pope Pius approve a constitution. Luigi thought it served old Pius right. If he'd backed the Sardinian Army the summer before instead of running away like an oath-breaking coward, they might have driven the Austrians out of Italy then.

In February, both Rome and Tuscany declared themselves Republics. Romans pillaged and burned Catholic churches, convents, and palaces while the Tuscans ran their king off entirely. Then the Pope fled Rome in the middle of the night, turning up later in Sicily. The Tuscan king tried to forestall the revolution by declaring himself in alliance with King Carlo Alberto, but his people were having none of it. Leopold II of Tuscany joined Pius IX in exile.

At Ansaldi's headquarters, each piece of news was greeted with agitation and excitement, particularly when Leopold declared for Sardinia and the Piedmont. Ansaldi's headquarters saw a flood of telegrams containing news of the violence erupting all over Italy. As February turned to March, Ansaldi made weekly visits to the king's residence in Racconigi, a half-day's ride south of Turin, riding out one day and returning the next. As Ansaldi's aide-de-camp, Luigi rode with the General and often sat in on his meetings with the king, taking notes for the General as needed. He could hardly believe his luck when he'd first sat in the same room as the king, but had soon found out that meetings with kings were just as boring as any other meetings.

The king could not decide what to do, either about the revolutions in Tuscany and Rome or the Austrian occupation. His chief fear seemed to be that the Piedmontese would revolt just as the people had done in Tuscany and Rome and drive him off his throne. Ansaldi and the other generals tried to steer the king toward another war with Austria on the principle that Austria was so busy fighting revolutions all over Italy that the Kingdom of Sardinia might be able to drive them out of the Piedmont.

Finally, in the second week of March, the king decided. Luigi had been dozing in an uncomfortable straight-back chair against the outside wall of the meeting chamber when he heard Ansaldi's distinctive shout. He jerked up his head and glanced around the room. Everyone was on their feet shouting and cheering—everyone, that is, but King Carlo Alberto and even he looked happy.

It took a few minutes for Luigi to figure out what had happened, but he covered his confusion by joining the celebration. The King had allowed himself to be convinced he should denounce the armistice with Austria and prepare for war.

They marched to battle with startling rapidity, pushed by the Austrians' almost-immediate response to the news that the Armistice was over. Radetsky took his army out of Milan and marched Southwest, towards Turin. Days later, the Austrians conquered and occupied Mortara.

The Sardinian Army marched hard and fast, stretching out on the road to Milan for miles and miles. Luigi rode near the front with the General. Just behind them rode a regiment of Sicilians, led by a dashing young colonel. Luigi often dropped back to ride with Colonel Fardella's men, finding them entertaining storytellers with a seemingly inexhaustible supply of grappa. They spoke a variant of Italian they called Siculo that Luigi could not resist learning. His interest in the Sicilians and their language brought him to Fardella's attention.

Fardella was only thirty months older than Luigi, who couldn't believe there was even such a thing as a twenty-year-old colonel. The Sicilian was young, but he'd played a prominent role in Sicily's revolution the previous year, which had thrown out the Austrians and given constitutional power to their own king. And like Luigi, he was the son of a count, from a noble family whose estate was on the western coast of Sicily, outside a small town called Trapani. He was also immensely optimistic about their chances of success.

"My king, you see," Fardella explained, "has been inspired by your king with regard to constitutions and parliamentary power. And so I think, when I see that your kingdom is about to go to war, that I will take my men to help. And my King, Ferdinand the Second, he said for me to go and help. So here I am." He threw his arm in the air with a flourish and yelled out encouragement to his men. They responded with a resounding cheer.

Luigi laughed out loud at the Sicilian's ebullience. Northerners tended to be more circumspect and controlled than these Sicilians. It took only a few days for Ansaldi to notice Luigi's deepening relationship with the Sicilian contingent and so he made Luigi his staff attaché to the Sicilians.

They met the Austrians at Novara, north of Mortara and west of Milan, in the heart of the Lombardy region on the fourth day of their march. The two armies immediately clashed. Ansaldi kept Luigi with him, running messages to and fro across the battlefield. By late afternoon, it was clear the battle was going poorly for the Sardinian Army. They were outnumbered almost two to one. Also, the Austrians had considerably more discipline than the Italians. Part of the Sardinian problem was that their support units from other parts of Italy turned tail and ran at the first evidence of Austrian firepower. It was like a replay of last year's war, but all rolled up into one disastrous afternoon.

Luigi begged General Ansaldi to let him to go the front. He wasn't so foolish as to think he'd be any help up there, but men were dying while he stood safely by in the General's tent. It was personally shameful.

Ansaldi pointed out that generals did not go to the front because that was no way to direct a war and generals needed aides. The old man slapped Luigi rather forcefully between the shoulder blades and said, "There's no shame in being here with me, Corporal."

So Luigi missed the first half of the battle, but he did not miss the second half.

By nightfall, the Austrians had pushed them back, out of Navarra, back the way they'd come. They fought on through the night. Ansaldi refused to move his headquarters and as a result Luigi's wish to see the frontline eventually came true. Well after midnight, a wave of Austrians, their white pants grey and red with mud and blood, broke through the Sardinian line. Luigi watched in amazement as General Ansaldi, who was certainly too old to fight, drew his saber and charged into the melee. Luigi drew his own saber and charged after his general, sparing a moment of regret for his musket, which stood abandoned in the corner of the General's tent. An aide-de-camp didn't carry messages behind the lines with his firearm at his side.

Ansaldi ran straight at one of the Austrians, his sword blazing in the artillery flashes. The Austrian, who was young and as broad as a wild boar, swung at the general. Ansaldi parried, then thrust his saber into the man's belly. The man fell, clutching his belly and screaming. Luigi was no more than six feet behind the general when Ansaldi wrenched his sword from the man's body and turned, ready for his next opponent. He didn't see the grenadier that charged him on his left flank. Luigi did.

He saw the general turn his back on the charging Austrian and rushed forward. The Austrian grenadier was so intent upon the general that he didn't see Luigi until he crashed into him. Afraid he'd fail with the sword, Luigi launched himself at the man like a human cannon ball. Down they went into the muck, tangled up together, the grenadier on top. They wrangled around in the dirt, but the Austrian had a good twenty pounds on him. He straddled Luigi and then sat up and grabbed Luigi by the neck. Luigi felt the man's thumbs dig into his windpipe, cutting off his air. And then he remembered his dagger, the one he usually used to open sealed messages and cut his meat. He groped for it, fumbling at the cross belt on the front of his uniform. The man squeezed harder and Luigi's vision dimmed around the edges.

Then it was in his hand. His little dagger, last used to peel a mid-winter orange. He pulled it out of its sheath and stabbed its four inches of steel into the man's side. The grenadier's grip on Luigi's throat loosened. Luigi took a large, gasping breath and stabbed again, harder this time. Then from the corner of his eye he saw a boot fly through the air. The boot connected with the

Austrian's head with a horrible thump. The man crumpled to his side, away from Luigi, who was gasping in the mud.

General Fardella loomed above him. He held his hand out to Luigi and pulled him to his feet. "Sorry to interrupt your fight, son, but I think it's best we get your general out of here right now."

Luigi looked around. They'd been completely overrun by the Austrian Army, the fighting no longer in orderly columns but broken down into a chaotic melee. In the middle of it, Ansaldi's saber flashed and clanged. Luigi looked at Fardella in amazement.

Fardella grinned at him. "He's quite something for an old man, isn't he? Let's go save him from himself."

They waded into the melee and made an alley for the General's retreat. Once back near his tent, the General looked around and shook his head. He frowned like a man considering a bad glass of wine, then mounted his horse and signaled to his men to retreat. By dawn they were five miles down the road.

Not content to merely defeat the Sardinians at Novara, Radetsky chased them north toward the Alps. He drove them hard, allowing the fleeing army little time to forage or sleep. Two weeks after the battle, they were exhausted and starving. Finally at Borgomonaro, at the northern edge of his kingdom, the king called his army to a halt.

Luigi was resting outside Ansaldi's tent when the General came back from meeting King Carlo Alberto. He called his aides and staff together.

"Men, I have three important announcements. First, the king has surrendered his army to the Austrians." There was a moment of silence. The surrender wasn't a surprise, but it was disappointing nonetheless. "Second, the king will abdicate his throne in favor of his son Victor Emmanuelle."

At this the men erupted into shouts of protest. The king hadn't always been popular, but the last few years he'd shown a commitment to Italian independence that his men appreciated and respected. Moreover, he hadn't just sent his army to war while he hid in his fancy castle south of Turin. No, he'd gone to war at their head and he'd been at the front of the battle, close enough to the danger to receive a wound of some kind—gossip varied from a slight gash to a total amputation of his arm.

Ansaldi held up his right hand for quiet. "The Austrians insist upon it, men, as punishment for breaking the peace. I'm sure they think the son will be more amenable to their regime. His mother is Austrian and he's married to an Austrian princess. I think they've got a surprise coming."

Luigi had seen and heard the Prince in meetings at the king's palace. Victor Emmanuel was his own man. And unlike his father, who'd been forced against his will to agree to a constitution to forestall a revolution, the son approved of and encouraged constitutional and parliamentary government.

The men talked amongst each other for a few minutes before Colonel Fardella raised his voice. "You said three announcements, General. If you don't mind me asking, what's the third?"

The general smiled at Fardella, his mustaches twitching like two mice wrestling on his face. Fardella smiled back, his expression more like a satisfied cat. Luigi thought they looked like they were up to something nefarious.

Ansaldi reached for a small medal case on the table before him. "Colonel, I'm glad you asked. One among us acted with uncommon bravery at Navarra and his heroism did not go unnoticed." Ansaldi paused and looked around the room.

Luigi noticed that most of the men seemed to be as amused as the General was.

"Corporal Palma, step forward," Ansaldi barked.

"Me?" Luigi felt his voice go all squeaky. His face flushed with heat, but the officers in the tent didn't laugh at him. He walked around the table to stand in front of his general.

The general opened the slim wooden box.

"For bravery above and beyond the call of an aide-de-camp and enlisted man, I honor you, Corporal Palma, and commission you a Lieutenant in the Sardinian Army."

The officers began to clap.

Luigi stepped forward and took the box from Ansaldi.

The General clapped Luigi on the shoulder and leaned forward. "You saved my life, Lieutenant Palma. Just like your father. I am twice indebted to your family." Then he kissed Luigi three times, alternating cheeks. They'd lost the battle, the war, and their king, and yet Luigi had never been so happy.

Chapter Four

CAVALRY LESSONS

Pinerolo, Italy—1853–1854

He wiped his brow, thankful the Baudenesca forest offered a bit of shade on this side of the ride. They were cantering over the broad grass track that circled a tiny outcropping of acacia trees to warm up before taking the course that ran through the woods. He'd learned to ride when he was no more than six years old and before he came to the Pinerolo Cavalry School he thought he was a fairly accomplished rider. He'd found out differently. The school challenged man and beast in ways Luigi could never have imagined.

Volotare gave a soft nicker as he cantered smoothly along the path, clearly enjoying the afternoon as much as his rider. Luigi patted the chestnut gelding's neck. He was a Calabrese horse, part thoroughbred, part Andalusian, and part Arabian. He had the pretty dished face and muscular neck of his Arabian ancestors and the long, straight back of a racing horse. Like all Calabrese, Volotare jumped like he was born to it. The school gave each student three horses and they were allowed to bring one of their own. Luigi knew there were horses at home for the taking but he hadn't been able to bring himself to ask.

Not that he was still heartbroken about Abrielle. He wasn't. His new lady love, Carolina, was showing him what a real woman should be. Abrielle had been a child, a school boy crush, no more. Carolina, on the other hand, with her passionate kisses and sultry voice, was all woman. More importantly, he now realized that his love of Abrielle had been doomed from the start. The staid life of a country noble was not for him, which was why he didn't want to ask Mother or Alerico for a horse. Legally all the horses, in fact *everything*, belonged to Alerico. Luigi had gone to war and been decorated for bravery. He left home and achieved glory for the family name. Why, he'd been such a good student that after graduation the Academy offered him a teaching position. First he'd been the youngest lieutenant in the Sardinian Army when he was sixteen and then the youngest teacher ever hired by the Academy at nineteen. And what had Alerico done? Married a rich girl and had a baby with her. And had the good fortune to be born first, instead of second. No, he would not ask Alerico for anything. Ever.

They turned south, riding along the east side of the wood. One more loop and they'd go in, down the twisting paths, over the jumps, going faster and faster. For right now though, they cantered along, resting the riders who'd already had four hours of lessons this morning. They were also warming up horses, each of whom was out for the first time that day. He'd ridden Baree, a sturdy Neapolitan bay mare, this morning. She was smaller and less showy than Volotare, but she was utterly unflappable in the ring, even with all the other students and horses and shouting in-structors. She didn't jump as high as Volotare but her short back and heavy hindquarters made her excellent at the sharp turning maneuvers crucial to cavalry training. As pretty as Volotare was, and even though he flew through the air like a gigantic red bird, Luigi thought if he had to take one of his three assigned horses to battle he'd take Baree. Sardo, his third horse, was resting today, which was fine with Luigi. Each horse worked two of every three days, which was a lot, but the school conditioned horses for the Sardinian, Tuscan, and Roman cavalries as much as it trained cavalry officers. While Volotare and Baree had been at the school for almost two years, Sardo was new, three years old and a stallion. He was Sardinian Anglo-Arabian and half a hand taller than Volotare, but without the gelding's experience or Baree's steady ways.

He clucked at Volotare to quicken his pace. Luigi reveled in the gelding's response. He'd been right to leave teaching for Cavalry school. At first being Assistant Instructor had been exciting, but mostly it had been gratifying to be asked. But teaching was not for him. Not after the rigors of war. So he left the school and returned to Ansaldi's regiment. The old general, as fond as Luigi as ever, remembered their talk from five years before, when the sick corporal confessed he wanted to be a cavalry man. Ansaldi put Luigi up for the Pinerolo Cavalry School. The school was the finest in Italy, maybe the top cavalry training school in Europe. Luigi knew that with Ansaldi's recommendation and his own family name there was no chance the Pinerolo would reject him, but the acceptance letter had nevertheless made him as happy as the day Ansaldi made him a lieutenant.

Ahead of him the line of riders and horses turned into the trees. They trained in three "rides" of twenty men each and were in the saddle two hours each morning and two more in the afternoon. In between and after they attended classes on equine management, cavalry history, and tactics and leadership. His "ride" worked at the school's inside riding ring each morning and rode out each afternoon. Volotare took the curve into the woods like a steam engine, barely slowing down. Luigi let him. The most important thing they'd learned at Pinerolo was to not interfere with the horses overmuch. The school's technique was to let each horse be as natural as possible, to trust the horse's instinct to find its own balance and to know when and how to stop, turn, and jump. Luigi's job was to stay on the horse.

To help the horses learn to trust themselves, the riders were supposed to keep their hands quiet and their seats still. This required Luigi to entirely relearn his riding technique. His childhood instructor had been English and the English style was a considerably more busy, controlling style. The English probably got more out of their horses, but they also ended up with more nervous animals.

Learning a new seat had been excruciating. The English system used a long stirrup, which allowed the rider to stand slightly over the saddle for trotting. Pinerolo used a short stirrup, one no longer than the length of a forearm. This forced the knees up quite high, a position that made Luigi want to shift back in the saddle. His instructors yelled at him repeatedly until he corrected that mistake, forcing himself to sit in the middle of the saddle with his knees well up, his lower legs far back and his heels down. The only thing that distracted him from the pain in his thigh muscles was the agony of his lower back. Day after day, hour after hour in the saddle, holding that seat made his back muscles ache like he was an old man in rainy weather. He'd finally gotten used to it, but the first month at school he'd lain in his bed sleepless for hours, his back too sore to sleep.

Infantry men disdained cavalry soldiers for riding in battle, as if it were easier and made for softer soldiers. Privately, Luigi thought something like that himself when he'd been a sixteen-year-old infantry corporal. Now he knew better: no one was stronger or more agile than a cavalry man.

As they entered the trees, Volotare shifted to a gallop. He charged down a dim, shady path that was none too smooth. Volotare didn't mind it a bit, but Luigi did. He'd ridden this course several times and it still made him nervous. It wasn't so much the course itself, but the speed at which they took it. Their instructor, a gruff cavalry captain who sat on a horse like he'd been born on one, set the pace, playing a dangerous game of follow-the-leader through the underbrush.

The path was strewn with obstacles. The first was a fallen log. Luigi felt Volotare gather himself. He barely lifted his seat out of the saddle and kept his body back, a jumping position at odds with what he'd learned as a child. The horse sailed over the log, took three long strides and sailed again, this time over a small stream. Never once did he break stride or slow down. They took a steep path up a hill, each turn a near-blind corner, until they achieved the summit. A castle ruin stood there. Up the stairs Volotare plunged, the horse in front of him striking sparks off the stone with his shoes. Up they lunged, fifty steps, then they were out, in a small grassy courtyard. Volotare charged across the small flat in four bounds. Before Luigi could catch his breath they were galloping down a steep slope. Luigi kept his hands still, resisting the impulse to pull back the reins and slow the horse. He'd done that the first time he'd taken this course and been vigorously chastised by the instructor. And then, as if the stone steps hadn't been bad enough, at the bottom of the hill Volotare leapt off a six-foot drop, landing on the road. The big horse made the hairpin turn and plunged down a narrow track that led down hill, through a thick stand of trees that made the path as dark as night. At the bottom of the slope lay yet another six-foot drop, this one with a stream at its base. Luigi resisted the impulse to throw himself off the horse in sheer terror. Instead, he held on, kept his seat, and let Volotare do his job. The gelding took the jump like he'd done it dozens of times before, which Luigi thought was probably true.

Luigi took a moment to miss Baree. She did as well as Volotare on this path, though being considerably smaller she was slower and closer to the ground and thus considerably less frightening. Last week Sardo refused the jump and almost unseated him. Even the gruffest instructors were kind about falls, on the principle that learning to ride meant learning to fall, but Luigi had seen the pitying looks students gave a fallen rider and he strove to avoid that indignity as much as possible.

They burst from the wood out onto the wide grassy track again. The captain slowed his horse to circle the track once more before heading back to the stables. Luigi breathed a sigh of relief. He didn't think that ride would ever be anything but terrifying, but he was learning that he could do it over and over again and survive. That was, he supposed, the point. Who knew when he'd have to take a ride like that in war, with the enemy hot on his heels, guns booming and the threat of death all around. He smiled to himself just thinking about it.

Luigi walked slowly, being careful not to stumble on the cobblestones that lined the streets of Pinerolo. Unlike Turin, which had modernized in the last few decades, with new buildings, gas streetlights, and modern restaurants and hotels, Pinerolo was still essentially a medieval town, built on a hill with a massive stone fortress at the top. The Cathedral Pinerolo, where Luigi attended Mass each Sunday morning, was almost a thousand years old. Luigi enjoyed its ancient simplicity, though it lacked the multi-colored stained glass windows of newer churches. He certainly wasn't going to church tonight. Far from it. He'd stopped for an hour or so at a taverna, one frequented by the cavalry students, and shared a bottle of wine with Tomas, Frederico, and some of the other fellows.

Mostly he spent the evening waiting for it to be late enough to visit his lover. His heart quickened at the thought of Carolina. Her passionate kisses were as intoxicating as her beauty and intelligence. Her married state was her only flaw, but thankfully her husband was often away.

He had met her months ago, not long after he arrived at the school. The experience had been revelatory. He'd loved Abrielle, or he'd thought he had, but he'd never done anything more than kiss her. Theirs had been a childish love, pure and chaste and romantic.

Unlike many of his fellow students, he'd never visited any of the ladies who made their living on their backs. His friends sometimes laughed at him, but he didn't see why a military man couldn't also be a gentleman. Gentlemen didn't use women for sport or take advantage of the wretched creatures who followed any army camp, willing to trade their bodies for a crust of bread or a couple of lire. Not to mention the disease. Men caught all manner of diseases from the camp followers, from lice to the clap. Luigi wanted no part of that. A man who found himself infected could guarantee that he'd infect his wife one day, thus ruining a good woman's life for no better reason than her husband's ungoverned lust. Mother had spoken to him about this before he left home six years ago. It had been an excruciatingly embarrassing talk, but he'd taken her words to heart.

He'd managed to control his manly urges until Carolina. At twenty-two she was two years older than him and wise in the ways of love. The Pinerolo Cavalry Academy had dances on the second Saturday of each month, both to entertain the local nobility and military officers and their wives and to teach the students the social arts. Luigi's instructor maintained that the best Cavalry officers were as light on their feet as they were in the saddle and so required the students of his "ride" to attend the dances. Luigi hadn't wanted to. He hated dancing. Having gone to military school when he was fourteen and to war when he was sixteen he'd missed those crucial years when men learn how to talk to ladies. But the Captain gave him no choice, so he'd gone to the stupid dance.

He'd been standing against a wall, holding a small glass of warm, over-sweet punch, feeling out of place when he saw her across the room. It was if the room went dark and a spot of light shone only on Carolina. She was dancing with an older man, one of the Colonels at the local garrison. She was tall for a woman and slim. Unlike Abrielle, who had been all honey-colored sunshine, Carolina was dark haired and dark eyed, all mystery and intrigue.

Luigi waited until the music stopped before approaching her. He bowed to her and asked, "May I have this dance?"

She'd snapped open her emerald green fan, a lace confection that matched her dress, and fluttered it below her dark eyes. "Why, you bad thing," she'd said, her words coming out in a low, sultry tone that surprised him. "My dance card is full and we've not been introduced." She stepped back and looked him up and down. "But my, aren't you a pretty thing!"

Luigi bristled a bit at this. He knew he was handsome. He was young, tall, lean, and muscular and he had a head full of wavy auburn hair. But he wasn't pretty. Girls were pretty. He turned to go, unwilling to be made a fool of by this gorgeous creature, but just then the music started again.

"Lieutenant, you asked me to dance." Her voice came out low and husky again. He turned and brusquely took her in his arms, feeling stupidly awkward. She had no right to make him feel that way. He gripped her tightly and glowered at her all during their dance. Weeks later, one evening as they lay in bed, she told him she'd enjoyed it, his forceful embrace and stony anger.

He called upon her the next day, having quizzed his friends about her. She was married to a brigadier general currently stationed in Milan. Luigi knew it was wrong to call upon a married woman but he couldn't seem to stop himself. She was all he could think about, even while his riding instructor yelled at him in the ring the next day. He couldn't help himself. He visited her every chance he could. When he wasn't with her he wished he was. It was excruciating and glorious at the same time.

Luigi knew it was wrong. She was a married woman. But she needed him and he couldn't get enough of her. She told him her marriage had been arranged and her husband was cold and distant. He left her alone for months at a time. He didn't love her and she so very much wanted to be loved.

Luigi didn't know what he thought would happen. He had some vague ideas that her husband would die and that he would marry Carolina. Recently he'd been thinking about running away with her. He would lose everything, everything but Carolina. She was worth it.

Of course it ended badly. Such affairs always do.

～

After nine months at the cavalry school Luigi graduated third in his class. General Ansaldi came to the ceremony and then showed him his new orders.

Lieutenant Luigi Palma di Cesnola joined the First Squadron of the Sardinian Army's Light Cavalry regiment under Colonel De Savoiroux. The Squadron was nicknamed the "Navarro Cavalry" because it had so many veterans of that last battle of the war. It was peace time, but they patrolled the borders of the Piedmont, always on the lookout for renegade Austrians or other brigands. When he wasn't on patrol, he acted as regimental riding instructor, particularly to the mounted artillery units where most of the enlisted men had little or no experience with horses. Luigi did well and was promoted to captain after six months in the Navarro Squadron. There was even talk of sending him back to Pinerolo the following year as an assistant instructor. Luigi didn't really want to go back to teaching, but he also knew that the instructor positions at Pinerolo came with automatic advancements in rank. He planned on being the youngest cavalry colonel in the history of the Sardinian Army.

They were stationed at Turin, close enough to Pinerolo that Luigi could visit Carolina at least once a week, arriving after dark and departing before dawn. One early morning, well before Luigi had even begun to consider dressing and riding back to the squadron, Carolina's bedroom door opened. An older man, tall and greyhound thin, stood in the doorway. The ensuing scene was chaotic and loud.

The general had not been pleased to find a twenty-two-year-old cavalry captain in his young wife's bed. Worse still, Carolina denounced Luigi, insisting he'd taken her against her will. She threw herself at her husband, sobbing about how he'd saved her from Luigi's unwanted advances. The old man pretended to believe her.

Luigi's heart broke for the second time. He would never forget how Carolina had turned on him, how she'd thrown him away like a torn handkerchief. He swore it would never happen again. Love was pain and betrayal and he would have no more of it.

A court marshal should have followed, but General Ansaldi prevailed upon the Judge Advocate to allow Luigi to resign his commission instead. Luigi suspected that no one in the officer corps believed that the general's bride had been an unwilling victim. But she was a General's wife and Luigi had to go.

And so in October 1854, Luigi found himself standing on a street in Turin, his career and life in utter ruins. He had no idea what he would do. Hire himself out to another army, he supposed. He certainly couldn't go home. He'd thought he was so much better than his older brother, such a model to his two younger brothers, but he was nothing now, nothing but a disgrace. He looked up and down the street, suddenly aware that no one was paying him the slightest attention. A man passed him with a hand cart of fall cabbages, and then a wagon went by, its bed full of round yellow squashes. Neither man spared Luigi the slightest glance. Outside of military headquarters no one knew or cared that he'd disgraced himself. He squared his shoulders and set out walking. He'd fallen before and he supposed he'd fall again. The key was to pick yourself up and get on with it. Wasn't that the family motto anyway? Oppressed, he rises. Maybe, but first he'd get a drink.

Chapter Five

CHARGING THE CRIMEA

Sicily and Balaclava, Crimea—1855–1856

A knock sounded at his door. Luigi heaved himself off his bed, a move that caused his stomach to lurch in a most unpleasant manner. He opened the door to find his landlady scowling at him. She handed him a letter and left, clomping down the stairs in a manner that managed to convey her disapproval. He placed the letter on his tiny table and flopped back into bed. Whatever it was, it could wait. Each day he rose from his bed, looked around his depressing room and swore he'd sober up enough to apply for a position in the Sicilian army.

When Ansaldi signed his discharge papers he reminded Luigi that their old friend Fardella had a place in the Army of the two Sicilian states. Luigi took the hint. He went back to his old school and bought the Neapolitan mare, Baree. He briefly considered making an offer for Volotare, but decided against it. The gelding was fearless and flashy, but he'd have been considerably more expensive than Baree and, if Luigi ended up fighting for the Kingdom of Sicily he was sure Baree would be a better war horse. Though if he thought about it, he mostly wanted her because he was done with flashy, high-spirited females. Only steady, dependable ladies from now on.

He rode south, stopping briefly in Rome to see the Basilica of St. Peters. On the road he drank a fair bit, which didn't make him feel better. It made him feel like he was becoming his father, but did help him temporarily forget the way Carolina had forsaken him when he needed her. He wondered if that's why his father had drunk so much. Had he too suffered from a broken heart?

He kept riding south until at last he reached Reggio Calabria, at the very tip of Italy. From there he took a ferry across the water to Messina in Sicily. As he suspected, Baree didn't mind ocean travel one bit. He doubted Volotare would have been half so sanguine when the waves rose to three and four feet high and the boat rocked like it was about to tip over. He stayed in Messina just one night and then took a road across the island to Palermo, marveling at the wild countryside. This far south it was so different, so much drier and somehow wilder than home in the north. From Palermo he made one last push, west to Trapani and the Fardella estate. Luigi didn't think a soldier like Fardella would be home, but he was sure his family would know where he was.

The good news was that Fardella's family *did* know where he was. The bad news was that when he knocked on the door and asked for Fardella he was taken to an older woman who burst into tears when he repeated his question.

"Enrico is in trouble," she wailed. "He has gone a long time ago."

Luigi patted the lady on the shoulder awkwardly, surmising she must be Fardella's mother. She cried for a few minutes more before stopping abruptly. She wiped her eyes with a lace-edged handkerchief she pulled from the sleeve of her black dress and told him the story.

"Enrico, he came home from up north and made war on the Bourbons here at Trapani. They drove out the invaders and my boy became a big man in the new government's army. His older brother Vincenzo was elected president of the Parliament." The old lady beamed at Luigi in pride. Then her face fell. She wrung her handkerchief and continued her story. "The Bourbon invaders, they come back with a bigger army. And the cowards here, they all run and my boys were put on a list of those to die. They had to leave Sicily. They go to England, where they stay and never visit their mother, who grows old and lonely."

Luigi's heart fell at the news. When she spoke of the Bourbons she meant the Piedmont's old enemy, the Austrians. They'd driven the brothers all the way to England? He'd known the revolution had gone badly in Sicily but he hadn't known that the Fardellas had been up to their eyeballs in it.

He left the old lady with a heavy heart and no will to go back north the way he'd come. Instead he and Baree took rooms at a boarding house in Trapani. Well, *he* took a room. Baree got a stall in the stable down the street. They rested, drank, and grew fat. Well, he drank and she grew fat. He wrote the General, telling him about Fardella. He also wrote his mother so she'd know where he was. He had some money saved and figured he could live in Trapani for a few months before he had to go back to the Piedmont and beg his brother for a place on the family estate.

He awoke again at mid-day, thirsty and hungry. He splashed cold water on his face, noticing his room was cold again. He kept forgetting to use the tiny coal stove. He'd expected Sicily to be warm in winter, but it wasn't. Oh, it wasn't cold like the Piedmont and it certainly never snowed, but it rained all the time and while a man could go around in shirtsleeves during the day the nights called for a good, sturdy coat. On his way out the door to find a tavern he remembered the letter his landlady delivered the day before. He tucked it into his front pocket so he'd have something to read while he ate.

In spite of the cold he sat outside, enjoying the fact that one could do that in late February in Sicily. He ordered a bottle of red wine and plate of Pasta alla Norma. He ate the thick noodles in tomatoes, fried eggplant, and ricotta cheese far too often. They didn't have eggplants up north and he'd discovered an almost unquenchable passion for them. Better eggplants than women. So far, an eggplant had never betrayed him.

While he was waiting for his meal he tore open his letter. It was short, one piece of paper and half a page of writing.

February 4, 1855

To Lieutenant Luigi Palma di Cesnola,

I am hoping this letter finds you in time. King Victor Emmanuelle and his prime minister Cavour have ordered a Sardinian Expedition to the Crimea under General Ferrera La Marmara. They intend to curry favor with the French and British in the hopes that after this war those nations will help us against the Austrians. Let us pray that this plan will come to fruition.

It is time for all good Sardinian soldiers to join the expedition. I am pleased to report I have been charged with organizing the Reserve Brigade. I am also pleased to tell you that half of this Expedition will be made up of regular Sardinian Army and the other of new volunteers. My reserves shall be entirely volunteers.

I order you to meet me in Genoa by April 1st. On that day or soon after 18,000 men and 5,000 horses will sail for Balaclava. You must be with us. My reserves have no cavalry for you to command. You shall be my aide-de-camp. Come my friend, my wished-for-son and fight with me once more.

Ansaldi

Luigi checked the letter's date. The letter had taken almost three weeks to find him. His mind spun frantically. It would take him at least a month to get to Genoa and then only if the roads were clear and Baree's health held out. He'd need perfect luck. Luck, which had eluded him of late. Then he remembered. There was a boat between Palermo and Genoa, a rickety thing more like a ferry. He'd heard it took ten days, sailing along the coast with land always in sight in case it sank. And Baree didn't mind shipboard life. If the worst happened they could swim. He went to take a sip of his wine, then pushed the glass away. He was done with that. Instead he gobbled his pasta, tucked his letter into his coat pocket, and went back to his room to pack.

They sailed out of Genoa on April 5th: Four frigates, three corvettes, and five brigantines. The flotilla also included eight paddlewheel steam boats and three screw-driven steam frigates. The seas were relatively calm. The steam ships arrived in Balaclava on May 9th and the sailing ships five days later.

When they arrived, the war was nearly two years old. Luigi hadn't paid any attention to the newspapers in Sicily but the four weeks shipboard provided plenty of time for Ansaldi to educate him. On the face of it the British and French went to war against the Russians in support of the Turks, who objected to the Russian demand to control all the Orthodox subjects of the Ottoman sultan. In reality, both England and France wanted to prevent Russia from taking Turkish territory on the Black Sea. Control of the Black Sea would gain the Russians easy access to the Mediterranean and greater control over those waters. Ansaldi explained to Luigi that one of the only things that kept the Russian bear from dominating the rest of Europe was its dearth of deep-water ports from which to sail a navy. Without a strong navy, Russia couldn't set the terms for its own trade, take territory from other European nations or gain a foothold in North Africa. In short, given its immense size and military might, Russia's status as a land-locked nation was all that kept it from making England and France one of its holdings. The Ottomans stood between Europe and Russia, but the Ottoman Empire was the "sick man" of Europe. The great European powers would do almost anything to prop it up in order to thwart the Russians.

Luigi didn't care so much about the politics of it all. What he cared about was the opportunity to prove himself in a Sardinian military force, even if he was a volunteer and not regular army. Before the Sardinian Expedition left Genoa they heard the Russian czar had died. Luigi worried the war would be over before they got there, but the new czar, Alexander II, declared he would continue the war until Russia was victorious. Luigi heaved a sigh of relief.

They disembarked at Balaclava, site of the famous Charge of the Light Brigade the previous fall. Now an occupied city, Balaclava crawled with men from every European nation. Luigi delighted in the polyglot of languages, practicing his English, French, German, Sicilian, and Turkish in turn. He and Ansaldi worked dawn to dusk setting up an Italian camp and organizing the volunteers. The city was, quite frankly, a depressing ruin.

Everywhere there were bombed buildings and soldiers huddled around fires, trying to stave off the Russian spring, which did not seem to be much warmer than the Russian winter.

A week after they arrived, a warm wind began to blow, causing a thaw that turned the frozen ground into a thick glop that stuck to everything from boots to wagon wheels. Everywhere there were sick men. Instead of treating the ill in Balaclava, the British Army shipped sick men across the Mediterranean to hospitals in Turkey. There was much talk in camp of a woman with the unlikely name of Nightingale who ministered to the sick over in Scutari. According to camp gossip, the lady worked miracles at the hospital there, shifting the death rate from "certain death" to "you'll live" in a few months. Luigi wished he could sail across the water to meet this paragon of women. It would be nice to meet a lady who did something meaningful with her life.

They were in Balaclava for less than two weeks before the main fleet of British, French, and Italian ships set sail for Kerch, a tiny city that sat on the strait between the Black Sea and the Sea of Azov. Luigi watched over sixty ships sail out of Balaclava harbor and wished he was on one of them. Sadly, the Reserve Brigade was left behind. Days later, a telegram came to Ansaldi's headquarters proclaiming Allied victory in Kerch.

With the strait under control, the fleet sailed across the Sea of Azov to Taganrog. Luigi didn't understand the significance until he and Ansaldi examined a map. The Sea of Azov sat behind the Black Sea. Taganrog lay on the far northeast end of the Azov, on the River Don. Having taken Kerch and the Bosporus Strait, the Russians could no longer resupply their troops in the Crimea by ship. And with Sevastopol besieged, the Russians had to resupply the city by land. But, if the Allies took Taganrog then they also took the Russians' best source of food and military supplies, no matter how the Russians moved them.

Luigi stood next to General Ansaldi on the battlement of one of Balaclava harbor's defensive fortifications one fine day in late May, watching the Allied ships return victorious and nearly unscathed from their strikes on Kerch and Taganrog. Best of all, the ships were laden with bags of oats, wheat, corn, flour, rice, and potatoes, all taken from Russian military storehouses in that city.

Ansaldi's reserve corps had charge of the distribution of the foodstuff on Italian ships. On the third day of that herculean task, the old man did not appear at breakfast. Luigi thought the General was just having a lie-in, but when the old fellow did not make an appearance at lunch either he went looking for him. Luigi knocked on the General's door. There was no answer. He turned the knob and opened the door. The fetid smell of a man who'd lost control of his body hit him like a charging horse. Throwing his arm up against his nose Luigi stepped up to the General's bed. The old man lay in a pool of filth, sunken eyed and pale as death. At first Luigi thought the General was dead, but closer inspection revealed he was still breathing. Luigi looked around the room in a near panic. He took a deep breath and settled himself. He needed to get the medical corps, but first he had to clean the General. The old man would hate it if he knew anyone had seen him this way.

He tried to lift Ansaldi, but the old man was too heavy. Worse, he mumbled and waved his arms around like he was repelling an imaginary enemy. Luigi decided there was no way he was keeping the General's illness entirely to himself so he went looking for help. He found two privates outside the general's quarters. A half hour later they had the General cleaned up enough to preserve his dignity. Luigi then sent one of the privates to the hospital for reinforcements.

While he waited he watched the General. His breathing was labored and his lips were cracked and tinged a grey blue. So was the rest of his skin, as if his body had already given up. The General waved one of his hands feebly and then lurched sideways in his bed. Luigi lifted the General's shaving basin and held it beneath the old man's chin. With a dry, gagging sound, Ansaldi retched, but nothing came out of him except a thin string of spittle. The old man's gums were shrunken and as grey as his skin. Luigi's heart sank. He'd seen this before but he hoped he was wrong.

Two corporals from the medical corps arrived just then, a stretcher between them. They shifted Ansaldi from his bed to the stretcher, which they'd laid upon the ground. Luigi watched them.

The older of the two men caught Luigi's eye. "Cholera," he said, shaking his head slowly. He spat on the General's immaculate floor and then they were gone, leaving Luigi standing alone amidst the stink and mess of the disease that had become the scourge of the Crimea.

A week later, the General was still alive, but just barely.

"It's the dehydration," the doctor said, wiping his hands on his filthy apron. "Every bit of fluid we put into these men comes right back out, one end or the other." He waved his hand around the large ward room. "It's the same for all of them and most of them are half your general's age. It's a miracle he's lasted this long."

Luigi didn't know what to do. Ansaldi had been like a father to him these last few years. Better than a father because he'd never hit him or insulted him. Instead, he'd taken Luigi under his wing and tried, as best he could, to take care of him. He'd done a better job than his real father, that was for sure.

While Ansaldi fought for his life, the work of organizing and feeding the Sardinian Expedition continued. General Marmora, their supreme commander, gave General Di Cavero command of the Reserve Corps. Di Cavero was the polar opposite of Ansaldi. He was no more than ten years older than Luigi, tall, slim, clean shaven and spoke only when absolutely necessary. He was never amused. *Ever.*

One day Luigi found his new general standing outside the tent that had once been Ansaldi's. "Lieutenant, I've heard some gossip that I am loath to pass on, on general principle, but I wonder if it might help." He paused, hands clasped behind his back, rocking on his heels.

Luigi waited. He and Di Cavero didn't have the sort of relationship where he spoke without being asked a direct question first.

Di Cavero blew out a deep breath and spoke again. "I had breakfast with some British officers this morning. They told tales of a woman, a woman of color if they are to be believed, who's set up a hospital. Apparently she's having some success treating cholera patients. Like that Nightingale woman."

"Sir, Miss Nightingale is in Turkey, at Scutari. The journey would kill General Ansaldi."

"Yes, yes, I know," Di Cavero said curtly. "This woman's name is Seacole and she's set up just outside the city. Calls her place the British Hotel. I'd like you to reconnoiter the place and report back. This morning, if you please."

Luigi grinned at Di Cavero, then remembered to salute him before he hurried off with unseemly haste. The new general wasn't so bad after all.

Baree and he made their way down a dusty road that ultimately led to Sevastopol. Baree wanted to stop and munch on the spring grass at the side of the road, but Luigi hurried her along. As in all things, Baree took the disappointment in stride.

About three miles outside Balaclava they came upon a ramshackle building. A hand-printed sign outside read "British Hotel." Luigi came closer to laughing than he'd come in days. The place was cobbled together from dismantled packing cases, drift wood, mismatched pieces of scrap iron, and anything else that could be nailed down. None of the doors and windows matched and it looked like a strong wind could knock the whole structure back into the junk pile from which it came. Oddly, in spite of its mishmash of parts, or perhaps because of them, the place exuded a kind of cheerful harmony that lifted Luigi's heart.

He tied Baree near the front door, or at least the door he guessed was the front door, and went inside. The building's interior was just as eclectic as the outside, though it was clearly clean and orderly. There was a large central room filled with rough wooden tables and benches. The walls were lined with shelves, all of which were stocked with jar and tins of food. The top shelf, near the ceiling and out of reach, was lined with bottles. Given this was a British establishment Luigi guessed the bottles held either gin or rum. He'd tried both back when he was in school and found each beverage equally revolting.

He asked a fellow in a British uniform if he could speak to Mrs. Seacole and was directed to a door at the back of the room. The door led to another room, just as large and lined with beds. An older, thick-bodied woman stood in the middle of the room directing dark-skinned men who seemed to be changing sheets. She noticed him and put her hands on her wide hips. "Need something, boy?"

Her voice had that soft lilt Luigi identified as Caribbean. "I'm looking for Mrs. Seacole."

"I'm her," she said merrily. "Watchoo want, son?"

She smiled at him in a kindly manner, but Luigi could tell she was impatient to get back to her morning's tasks. She had a good smile, one that crinkled the little lines around her eyes and lit up her face. Di Cavour called her a colored lady, but this woman wasn't much darker than the women he'd met in Sicily. Only her wiry hair marked her as someone with African in her family tree.

"It's my general, ma'am. He's very sick. With cholera, ma'am. He's been sick for ten days and he can't seem to get better. I heard you might be able to help."

She waved her hand at Luigi to follow her. She turned and walked across the room and out the back of the room. He followed her outside. She stopped on a bare bit of ground between her hotel and two outbuildings, each as much a patchwork of parts as the hotel. She waved her hand at the two buildings. "I've got men in both those buildings and in the room you just saw. All of them with cholera. Lots of them dying. And you want me to leave them all to take care of one man. 'Cause he be a general? What do I care what he be? You think Jesus cares?'"

Luigi looked down at his muddy boots, thinking carefully about his answer. "It's not he's a general, ma'am. It's that he's a good man. A kind man."

She appraised Luigi thoughtfully. "Is he now?"

Luigi nodded. He wanted to wail and beg. Or throw himself to his knees and beg her to help. But he didn't. He stood quietly, hoping against hope.

"All right then. I'll go take a look at him. He's in Balaclava, is he?"

Luigi nodded, his relief making him speechless.

She stepped up to him and laid a soft hand on him. "If he's been sick that long there's likely nothing I can do for him, son."

Luigi nodded again. It was better than nothing.

They rode back to Balaclava, through the mud and the spring flies, he on Baree, Mrs. Seacole on an army mule. When they arrived at the Allied hospital they learned they were too late. General Georgio Ansaldi had died from the complications of cholera. They'd been in the Crimea less than six weeks and the now the old man was gone. Luigi was all alone. Again.

Chapter Six

SABER AND SIEGE

Sevastopol, Russia—August–September 1855

Luigi laid his kit out on the camp bed, one piece at a time, examining each piece for faults or flaws. He'd been issued a dun-colored knapsack, a plumed hat that matched his blue-grey tunic coat, three cotton shirts and one cravat, and a pair each of cloth pants and cloth leggings. He also had two pairs of drawers, one sash and tasseled cord, knee guards, gloves, and a knitted cap. He dressed himself, taking deliberate care with his cravat. Then he addressed the dozen bright buttons of his coat. When he'd buttoned the last button he strapped on his saber belt around his waist, stopping to admire his new saber. The Sardinian Army had just the previous year adopted a new, and as far as the cavalry men were concerned, vastly improved saber. It was longer than the old one, with a slightly curved single blade with a one-piece iron guard. The ebony hilt had six grooves in it, an innovation that vastly improved the sword's grip.

He seated the saber in its sheath, comforted by the familiar weight of it on his hip, squared his shoulders, and stepped out of his tent. It was still dark, but around him the camp bustled with movement. He could hear men talking softly to each other. It was a thing to take comfort in, the comradely quiet of an army preparing for battle. Luigi took a deep breath of damp air, smelling the campfire smoke that lingered over every camp he'd ever been in. He sighed. They needed a victory today or this siege would go on forever. That was probably why General Di Cavour had allowed the Reserve Grenadier, Infantry, and Artillery brigades to participate in the battle. More importantly, he allowed his aide-de-camp to fight, loaning him to the Osmanli Irregular Cavalry under Colonel Enrico Fardella.

Fardella. Not long after the poor General died, Luigi attended a meeting of Allied commanders, as was his duty as Di Cavero's aide-de-camp. He'd been standing at the back of the room, as all the aide-de-camps did at every military meeting he'd ever attended, when he'd looked across the room and saw Fardella. At first he hadn't been sure. This Fardella wore the striking green and red uniform of the Osmanli Irregular Cavalry, a ragtag band of Turkish-Muslim enlisted men led by British Army officers. Fardella casually made his way around the room until he stood by Luigi. "You sobered up," Fardella whispered out of the corner of his mouth. "How's Mother?"

Luigi had to stifle a laugh. Madame Fardella must have told her son how his friend had come looking for him in Sicily and spent far too much time wallowing in self-pity and wine.

Afterwards they met in the officer's mess where they shared a bottle of brandy and told stories. Luigi told Fardella about cavalry school and his disgrace, which explained his sojourn in Sicily.

Fardella talked about how he'd fled Sicily six years ago and bought himself a commission in an English cavalry regiment. "Then last year I heard about the Irregulars and thought I'd like to fight again. Though now I wonder why."

Luigi agreed. The war just went on and on. The problem was that the Russians had dug into Sevastopol and somehow kept the city and its fortresses supplied, despite the fact that the combined British, French, Turkish, and Italian forces had the ports sewn up tight. A series of naval bombardments of Sevastopol in the months after Ansaldi's death were meant to weaken the Russians, but in June the combined Allied infantries had failed to take the Malakoff Redoubt. So the siege stumbled on, the Russians stubbornly refusing to admit they'd been beaten, the Allies bombarding the city day and night until the ceaseless booming drove everyone slightly mad. Everyone apparently, but the Russians.

As the siege ground on, Di Cavour's Reserves had had precious little to do. As Luigi had learned in the first war, sieges could be deadly effective, but they were also deadly boring. You just sat there in the mud and flies and waited and waited. And waited some more. They'd gone on some reconnaissance missions in the Russian countryside, but encountered little or no resistance from the peasantry. Luigi sensed the Russian people were as tired of war as the Allied army was.

Finally though, he would see some action. Yesterday General Marmora explained the plan to the officers in his command. Once more Luigi found himself in the back of the room with all the other generals' aides. Marmora said they would break the Russian Army tomorrow and in so doing, they would break their will to fight on and end this damnable war.

More importantly, at least for Luigi, was the fact that the British would not be taking part in the battle. Only the Italians and French, along with a small contingent of the Ottoman Army, were involved. The battle would be an opportunity for the Sardinians to prove themselves worthy allies. Marmora was mesmerizing: tall and dashing as only a member of the Sardinian nobility could be; he strode about the room with his dazzling array of medals and rosettes, set off by tasseled cording and a brilliant saffron yellow sash. He was the man who had liberated the old Sardinian King, Carlos Alberto, when he had been taken prisoner in Milan back in 1848. The king made Marmora his Minister of War for that heroic deed. The Sardinian Supreme Commander also had a marvelously thick, dashingly upturned mustache. Luigi, who had never particularly admired facial hair, made a secret vow to himself to grow a mustache just like the general's.

Fardella's cavalry was one of several cavalries leading the charge to the Chernoya River. The Sardinians had the entirety of the right flank while the French had the left. Turkish and English infantry brigades would be behind them, but success would come with a fierce and rapid attack, and that was where cavalry excel. Ride in, fast and hard, screaming and slashing like the berserkers of old. Luigi slept not a wink thinking about the next day. All his cavalry training came down to this: either he was made for it or he was not.

Luigi rubbed his eyes as he made for Fardella's tent in the quiet, pre-dawn of camp. He fell in with several of men in the Osmanli cavalry and joined in a quiet and meaningless discussion of the weather.

As they readied themselves, almost fifty thousand Russian infantry soldiers and another ten thousand Russian cavalry were on the move, advancing on the Chernaya River. Their numbers were no secret. By this point in the war, the Allies knew almost everything the Russians did, not much longer after they planned to do it. Luigi was far too far low in the chain of command to know where the intelligence came from, but he knew the Russians were leaking information like an old fishing boat leaks water. The Allied cavalry's job was to meet the Russians at the river and attack with such ferocity that they prevented the Russian advance. Luigi hoped it would work that way. Battle plans were easily drawn on paper, but rarely did they go the way they were supposed to.

Luigi mounted Baree and brought her into line with the other cavalry officers. Just as he'd suspected back at school, she stood quietly, a calm island of horse flesh in a sea of nervous hoof stamping and squealing.

By mid-morning, it was over. For reasons passing understanding, the Russians crossed the river without their cavalry or, more problematically, their artillery. The cavalry pushed them back to the river's edge in short order. Luigi and Baree rode back and forth before the river, slashing at anyone, man or beast, that stepped out of the water and fog. Luigi had his saber in one hand, his pistol in another, reins wrapped around the pommel. Baree didn't need him. She knew when to dodge, when to rear, when to jump. His saber grew heavy in his arm, but Baree never lost a step. The hours of training at Pinerolo paid off for both of them.

Fardella rode at Luigi's side, his saber a swirl of light and noise, his big bay stallion a blizzard of slashing hooves. Even in the midst of battle, Luigi noticed that the Russians seemed confused, disorganized, and entirely unprepared. By 8 o'clock, the cavalry made room for the infantry at the river's edge. Their work done, Fardella ordered his unit to retreat. They returned to Marmora's headquarters.

The word was that the Sardinians had pushed the Russians back on the battle's right flank and that the French were enjoying much the same experience on the left flank. Luigi could hardly believe the news.

By 10 o'clock, the Russians on both flanks were in full retreat back over the river. Luigi was both exalted and disappointed. The British could no longer diminish the importance of the Sardinian contribution to the war, not after this decisive victory at Chernaya. It was a great day for the Sardinian Expeditionary Force and the rest of the Allied armies. More importantly, it was an exceedingly bad day for the Russians. But Luigi had only had a taste of the fighting before it was all over. All the years of preparation boiled down to a few hours of armed combat. He wanted to go back and fight it all over again.

Luigi removed his hat and wiped the sweat from his brow. It was damnably hot away from the water, hot and sticky. Luigi hated it. A man could dress for cold but there was nothing to be done about heat. And who had ever thought wool uniforms were a good idea?

This morning he decided to examine Sevastopol harbor's southern fortifications, curious about what the place looked like after the last series of bombardments. After the Russian debacle at the Chernaya River in mid-August, the British and French navies bombarded Sevastopol for three weeks straight. Over three hundred cannons fired for hours at the city each time. Luigi heard that the sixth and last bombardment used more than 150,000 rounds. Then the combined Turkish and English infantry attacked the Malakoff Tower, a massive stone fortification that made up the cornerstone of Sevastopol's defense. They took it on the eighth day of September and the next day the Russians gave up the city. Now they were waiting for the Russians to sue for peace.

Luigi climbed the hill, completely astounded at the wreckage and mayhem he saw. No wall of the harbor fortification stood undamaged. No building stood intact. How had the Russians held out as long as they did? How had they survived?

He was picking his way around a pile of stone rubble near the fortress's west wall when he heard someone speaking English, but not with an English accent. Was it an American? He'd never met one of those. Luigi hurried forward to a knot of men standing near the base of the Malakoff Tower. Two were older gentlemen, while the third looked no older than himself, maybe in his mid-twenties. They were definitely Americans. One of the older men had one of those half beards one only saw on Americans, with whiskers on his jaw and chin, but clean-shaven above the lips. He'd heard it called a "Quaker beard." What was a Quaker? He'd have to find out.

He approached the gentlemen at a leisurely pace, curious about why Americans would be touring the wreck that was Sevastopol. Had there been an American contingent in the war? And if so, why had he not heard of them?

He approached the men and introduced himself. The man with the Quaker beard was Richard Delafield, an engineer with the U.S. Army, while the other older man was Alfred Mordecai, an ordnance specialist. The youngest of the three introduced himself as George McClellan.

Luigi nodded at the younger man's dress uniform. "Am I correct that you are a cavalry man?" he asked.

McClellan nodded proudly. "And you?"

"As well," Luigi said with a small smile.

"Your English is very good, but I detect an accent."

"I am Sardinian. I learned my English at military school. Military men should be linguists, no?"

"Exactly my thinking," McClellan agreed. "I learned French at West Point, and a little German. I've been teaching myself Russian the last few weeks."

Delafield interrupted them. "Excuse please. Captain McClellan, it occurs to me that we might learn something from Captain Cesnola here, but we've got that meeting with the Brits." The man turned to Luigi. "Do you have some time, Captain, to speak with our Captain?"

Luigi said he did. "Perhaps Captain McClellan would care to join me for dinner with the officers of the Sardinian Expeditionary Force."

McClellan looked pleased at this suggestion and agreed to spend the afternoon with Luigi.

Delafield and Mordecai walked away, leaving the two younger men alone. Luigi crooked his eyebrow at the dark-haired American.

The man chuckled. "It is a bit irregular, I suppose. We're on a fact-finding mission of sorts. Observing the war, taking note of tactics and armaments. But we've spent the last few weeks with the Russians. Couldn't get permission to approach from the British side of the war. They act like we were going to steal state secrets and give them to the enemy."

"Ah," Luigi said. "And now here you are, with the Allies at last." Luigi waved his hand around at the devastated fort. "I want you to explain the Russians to me. But before that, what would you like to know?" Luigi motioned back at the harbor, indicating they should walk that way.

They went to the Sardinian officer's mess, where they shared food, drink, and cigars. For the next three hours, they peppered each other with questions. Luigi enjoyed what McClellan had to say about the Russians, about their toughness and ferocity.

McClellan seemed most interested in military details. What sort of saddles did they use? Were their artillery guns smooth bore or rifled? What about the siege artillery?

Luigi tried to answer all McClellan's questions. By the time they called for cigars McClellan had explained that the three of them had been sent overseas by the American Secretary of War. They had been instructed to study British military tactics but the British had been unwilling to cooperate with the Americans.

"So we went around them, to Berlin and then Vienna, and on to Constantinople from there, where we met the Pasha. We thought he'd give us permission to visit the front, but he did not. No doubt told by his British allies to put us off. So we gave up and went to Moscow. Met the Czar, who turned out to be a most accommodating fellow."

The two men talked late into the evening. At midnight, as their talk began to run out, McClellan looked thoughtfully at Luigi. "Your English really is exceptionally good. When you're done here you should think about coming to the United States."

Luigi started to disagree, but stopped.

McClellan saw him thinking. "We've got war coming there. I'm sure of it. We'll need men like you."

"Is it your slavery problem?"

McClellan shrugged. "It boils down to that, but it's as much a struggle over competing visions of America. Slavery creates slaveocracy and slaveocracy creates a ruling class. Either you believe in a natural elite or you don't."

"Do you?" Luigi asked. This was a question he'd been wrestling with since he was fourteen.

McClellan shook his head so hard his hair flopped into his eyes. "A man ought to succeed on his own merits and not because his daddy's a rich slave owner. Don't get me wrong, I don't like slavery, but it's constitutionally legal. Neither myself, nor any other man has the right to end it."

Luigi shook his head. "I think it is wrong. I must be free to make my own destiny. If I must be so, then all men must be so. No? Free to succeed or fail on his own merits, just as you said."

McClellan stubbed out his cigar. "True, all true, but governments and constitutions aren't about morality. They're about order and rule of law. And the law in the United States says men have a right to their property and that some of that property is human. But you misunderstand me. Whether I or any other man objects to slavery is not the point because of the law, as it now stands. The war will be over the issue of minority rule."

"Minority rule? I thought America was a democracy!" Luigi shifted uncomfortably in his chair, worried he'd somehow fundamentally misunderstood his lessons.

"In theory it is. But rich men can gerrymander the system so that *they* control it, not the people."

"Gerrymander? I do not know this term."

McClellan stubbed out his cigar. "Rich men can put their men in Congress and then force votes to go their way. They can put men who think their way in the courts and in state legislatures too. Northerners don't like slavery. Oh, they might not object to the idea of slaves, but they sure as hell don't want to compete with slave labor. There's no way to beat a man who can run his business with people he doesn't have to pay. So a minority of men, slave owners, can run the country in spite of everyone else's wishes."

Luigi thought about that for a second. "Such a system would be tremendously profitable and make for great power."

"Absolutely. And that's the real unfairness of slavery. These pro-slavery men, who are in the minority, can force all kinds of concessions upon the anti-slavery men because of their unfair advantage."

Luigi started to argue, then thought better of it. Buying and selling human beings was just wrong. It didn't matter what the law said. Hadn't the great Italian Mazzei gone to America and said this very thing? He'd written about it in his now-famous letter to his friend Thomas Jefferson. "All men were created by nature equally free and independent." Jefferson had borrowed from Mazzei when he'd written "All men were created equal."

Luigi thought to bring up Mazzei and Jefferson, but a gentleman did not argue such points with a new acquaintance during their first dinner together. Instead he asked, "And this imbalance will make for war?"

McClellan once again nodded vigorously. The hair on his head flopped forward and then back. "I think it will. So too does the man who sent me, Jefferson Davis. He's the Secretary of War and a slavery man himself. He sees it coming. War, I mean. That's why this commission is here."

It was past midnight when McClellan clasped Luigi's hand warmly and again advised Luigi to immigrate to the United States. "It's a booming country. A young man of initiative could make his fortune. And when the war begins, as it most assuredly must do, my country will need men of experience. Men like you."

Later that night, in his bed, Luigi decided the idea had merit. Eventually this war would come to an end and then what would he do? Hope the Sardinian Army would take him back? Go home to his family estate? Find another army to fight for? And if he was going to do that, why fight for the Americans? Hadn't his whole life been a fight against the old ways and for independence? Could a nation that had slavery be truly independent? Could there be any freedom for anyone if there wasn't freedom for everyone?

He knew his mother would laugh at him. Peasants were peasants because they were lesser people than the nobility. That's what she'd say. But his father and his uncle had fought for the right of the people to have a say, fought for the right to be ruled by men chosen by the people, not those born into ruling houses. And General Ansaldi? What would he say? The old man had spent his entire life fighting the Bourbons for Italian independence. And what about Fardella? Hadn't he taken a chance on liberty? Like Uncle Alerino, Fardella had stood up for what he thought was right and he'd been exiled for it.

Maybe it was time Luigi did the same. He should decide what he stood for and then stand for it. He lay on his camp bed until almost dawn considering the New World.

Chapter Seven

BECOMING ITALIAN-AMERICAN

New York City—1860–61

Luigi held the small glass vial in his hand. It was so small for something that would offer him release from his terrible mistakes. He couldn't take anymore. Hungry and unable to pay his rent, he could not go on. The worst part was not being able to sleep. He had nightmares every time he closed his eyes. He'd be back in battle, the booming, the blood, and the smell of death. He didn't know why it haunted him, now, when he was no longer a soldier. It never had before.

He was almost thirty years old and he had no prospects, no family, and no country. He didn't even have a horse. Unemployed soldiers couldn't afford to keep a horse, let alone ship one to America. Fardella bought Baree, though it broke Luigi's heart to part with her. The stack of bills the Sardinian gave him for the mare had paid his way to America. He should have stayed home. He should have kept his horse.

This country doesn't want me. He didn't want it either. He lifted the vial of laudanum to his lips and drank. He gagged, surprised by its bitterness. Like life, he supposed. He would do this right, if he did nothing else right in this horrible city. He forced himself to choke it down.

He waited a moment, surprised that he didn't feel anything. Then he did. He felt calm and peaceful. Everything was going to be all right. His eyelids felt heavy. He lay back on his bed, happy for the first time in over a year.

It had begun well enough, he supposed, this coming to America. His ship docked on the east side of Manhattan Island. Customs officials divided the passengers into three groups, Americans, visitors, and immigrants. The immigrants were let off last and ferried to a small island, just offshore from the docks. The entire island was taken up by a massive brick structure that looked a great deal like a fortress. Locals called the building Castle Clinton, though the only sign he saw read Emigrant Landing Depot. His first experience with America set the tone for the next twelve months. He was confused by all the lines, overwhelmed by the noise, and offended by the noxious smell of sweaty fear. When he reached the head of the line he found himself in front of a rough wooden table. At it sat a man in a cheap brown suit.

"Name!" the man shouted at him.

Luigi, who'd heard not one word of Italian since entering the building, made a quick decision.

He told the man his new name.

"Huh?"

He repeated himself. The man turned his book around and pushed it at him. "Print please."

Luigi wrote "Louis P. di Cesnola." He smiled at the man. 'Lewis' was a good English name. That's how he'd pronounce his new name. No more 'Luigi,' which marked him as an outsider. He was an American now, with an American name.

A short cab ride, straight up Broadway, took him to the heart of the city. The streets teemed with people, carriages, wagons, dogs, pigs, and noise. Louis stared out the cab's window in amazement. He'd never seen anything like New York, not even in Paris after the war. Maybe Rome, but Rome was warm and relaxed. This place felt like everyone was late for something.

The streets were lined with massive buildings, some so tall he could not see the tops of them from his vantage point inside the carriage. Unlike Turin, Milan, or even Palermo, most of the streets were treeless, the cityscape unrelieved by green. People crowded the sidewalks, some of them dressed in high style, others no better than shoeless peasants, everyone all mixed together.

The hansom cab driver took him to a mid-sized boarding house that he assured Louis was both clean and affordable. The harried landlady said she had a room for him. With meals, the price was $2.50 a week. At the time Louis thought this a great bargain, but six months later, with no job and his money running out, the sum might as well have been $100 a day.

At first he offered himself as a translator, placing a small advertisement in the *New York Herald*. In a city this big someone would need a man who could speak and write six languages fairly fluently, but he was wrong. There were too many foreigners in the city who could do the same and too few English speakers who needed translation services.

One day he passed a music store. He went in, thinking he might see if the shop keeper would buy his flute. It was pretty much the only thing of value he had. The shopkeeper offered him $3 for his instrument and, to his shame, he took it. He never saw the flute again.

While he was waiting he noticed the store had a rack of sheet music, which gave him an idea. He could write easily playable music and sell it to stores like this one. However, that venture proved even less fruitful than translating. He wasted valuable coins on blank sheet music, wrote out the music for some Italian folk songs and sold not one thing.

He'd tried. Now his head felt fuzzy. The small bottle rolled out of his slack hand and landed on the floor with a small thump. He drifted off, thinking of his flute and hoping he'd wake up in heaven. Surely God would forgive him his self-murder.

He awoke hours later, his eyes glued shut with something sticky. Blind and confused, he wiped at his face, his hand coming away slick with something unidentifiable. And then his nose woke up. He realized he'd vomited in his sleep and then slept in the mess. His brain, foggy with drugs, took long minutes to remember the laudanum. However much New York City didn't want him, neither did God. He'd been spat out from the jaws of death and returned to this hell on earth. He sighed wearily and reached for the wash basin. At least he hadn't dreamed of war.

Four days later, he was standing on Fifth Avenue staring up at the most remarkable building he'd ever seen. He'd been out looking for work, but he'd had to stop. Workmen were still putting the finishing touches on its decorative stone work, but it was clearly open for business. He'd never seen a hotel this big. Louis craned his neck to look up. Five, no six stories high, the building blotted out the sun, creating a wide band of shade on the sidewalk and street in front of it. A tall man, impeccably dressed in a black suit and coat, stepped through the building's tall double doors. He was about to walk past when he stopped. "Admiring my hotel, are you?"

Louis blinked at the man's voice, startled by the interruption. He'd grown used to being invisible in this city. "Why, yes, sir, I am. It's quite a building."

The man swept his beaver top hat off his head and introduced himself as Hiram Hitchcock, hotel manager.

Louis introduced himself, careful to use his full name and title. He felt bad about it, but a man like this might be able to help him and right now he could not afford pride.

"A count, huh? I've never met one of those."

"Yes, sir," Louis said with a small bow. "I'm from the Piedmont region of Italy. My family is very old."

Mr. Hitchcock's full beard and mustache could not disguise his smile. "I know it's short notice, but I was just on my way to lunch. Perhaps you would like to join me. I have to leave the hotel to do so or I won't get a break from the never-ending questions that attend running this fine establishment." Hitchcock waved a hand desultorily at his hotel.

Lunch with Hiram Hitchcock turned out to be the best thing that ever happened to Louis. Hitchcock proved a fount of ideas, advice, and help to his new Italian friend. Their friendship began with that lunch and progressed to twice-weekly dinners. The hotel manager didn't care that Louis had no prospects or that he was bedeviled by terrible dreams. He didn't care about Louis's family ties, nor his brother's title or any thing else. Instead, the New Yorker seemed charmed by Louis himself.

One evening they were sharing an after-dinner drink in the hotel bar, a room distinguished by dark wood paneling, velvet curtains, and thickly upholstered rosewood chairs. The most powerful men in New York City gathered in the bar, from political bosses to rich industrialists. He and Hiram were sitting with two such men, one of whom complained that his daughter was at loose ends since leaving school. Mr. Pearson said his chief problem was that the girl was husband hunting, but that task by no means took up enough of the girl's day. Pearson's business partner, a Mr. Calvert, said he had the same problem with his daughter. "Sons, why, you can just send them off to college until they've matured out of that awkward phase between childhood and adulthood. But girls? What do you do with them?"

Louis had his first good American idea. With Hiram's help, he opened a language school for young ladies. At first he taught French, German, and Italian, but before long he had enough students to hire a German-born lady who had been working as a governess. Miss Abel gave his school an extra fillip of respectability, though Louis's use of his brother's title was probably the school's main draw. He found that Americans, who had no nobility of their own, were fascinated by foreign titles. Louis justified his lie by the fact that in calling himself Count Cesnola he was not usurping his brother's title. His family name was Palma so his brother was Count Palma. They were the Palmas of the town Cesnola. Americans didn't understand Italian naming and he made no effort to correct them. He was Louis Cesnola now.

One winter afternoon, a small, mild-looking young woman entered the small storefront Louis rented for his school. Louis, who was between classes, looked up at her in surprise. He got most of his students through referrals. She was the first woman to walk in off the street.

She hesitated, then stepped up to Louis's desk. She clasped her reticule in front of her and pushed back her shoulders. "I am Mary Reid and I would like to learn Italian."

Louis smiled at her. She was an older lady, a good ten years older than the girls fresh out of school that came to him to polish their language skills. She wore a black dress, as if she was mourning. It was unadorned, but finely made and carefully tailored to make its wearer appear slimmer. Her nose was unfortunately lumpy and her hair mouse brown, but she had skin like fine-napped white velvet and a clear, direct gaze. Louis found himself wanting to pet her, as one would pet a kitten, but he suspected this lady would not at all approve of or tolerate such familiarity.

Louis set up a schedule of private lessons for Miss Mary Reid. At first they met at his school, but by spring they were meeting in the parlor of her brother's house. Miss Reid lived with her brother since her father's death the previous January, which explained her mourning dress. When he told Hiram about his new student his friend nearly exploded in enthusiasm.

"Her father was an immensely important man. He was in the British Navy during the Revolution. The *American* Revolution," Hiram clarified. "He was captured and switched sides. Then in the war of 1812, his ship kept the British out of New Orleans so that General Jackson could consolidate his hold on that city. He and Jackson were great friends afterwards. He made masses of money as a privateer and I hear he just died. So his daughter is an heiress."

Louis didn't sleep much that night. The next day his newspaper said that the Confederates had fired on Fort Sumter, down south someplace called South Carolina. The United States was at war. The place name gave him an uncomfortable twinge, but in spite of himself he found the news of war exciting. He was a better military man than teacher. His new country would need him. He would join this country's cavalry and he would finally belong. Everyone loved a cavalier. That afternoon he paid a call on Miss Reid.

He went down on one knee and took her soft, pale hand in his. "My dear Mary, you are all things that a woman should be. Your heart is large and your soul beautiful. I would be the most happy man in the world if you would honor me by becoming my wife."

Mary pulled her hand from his and gave her head the smallest of shakes.

She was about to say no. How could she? He reached for her hand again. "I swear I will be a good husband to you."

She left her hand in his. "You don't love me." She shook her head again. "Don't argue. You don't. How could you?"

"Mary!" Shocked, he pulled his hand from hers and stood. "Please do not speak that way. You are the best of women."

She snorted a tiny laugh. "I know what I am. I am an old maid, two years older than you, and I have never been a beauty. Papa left me a small fortune, which is my chief attraction, I am sure. That is not love, Louis. If you think it is, you know nothing of love."

He stepped back. "You wound me, my dear."

"Louis." She sighed. "I think I love you. In fact I know I do. But you do not love me and a life lived like that would be torture. I am not much, but I deserve more than a loveless marriage." She turned her head, picked up her little silver bell, and rang it.

The butler opened the parlor door. "Yes, Madame?"

"Hobson, would you please show Mr. Cesnola out?" She still wouldn't look at Louis. Instead, she turned her eyes to the portrait of her father over the fireplace.

Louis knew defeat when he saw it. He left the house and stopped on the sidewalk outside. He, Luigi Palma di Cesnola, son of a count, refused! How did this happen? He thought for a moment, then pushed back his slumped shoulders and lifted his chin. Men of war did not quit and go home after one unsuccessful sortie. No. They returned to the field of battle until they were victorious. He would rise from this setback, as he always did. He walked back to his tiny room and wrote Mary a letter. And then rewrote it until he had it just right.

Mary fiddled with her tea cup and tried to focus. Mrs. Nesmith babbled happily about the details of her daughter's engagement. Her eighteen-year-old daughter. Of course she was pretty. Empty-headed as a newborn chick, but pretty. And an heiress. It wasn't fair. Mary heard the mantel clock ticking and realized Mrs. Nesmith had stopped talking.

"Well, don't you agree?"

About what? Did it matter? "I do, Mrs. Nesmith. Your judgment in these matters is, as always, impeccable."

The parlor's pocket door slid open. Hobson stepped inside, a silver tray in his hand. There was a letter on the tray. "I am sorry to interrupt, Miss Reid, but I thought you'd like to see this."

Mrs. Nesmith rose to her feet, assuring Mary she had shopping to do and should be on her way. After a flurry of goodbyes and cheek kissing, the lady was gone, ribbons trailing in her wake like kite strings.

Through it all Hobson stood quietly off to the side, tray in hand. "It's from Master Cesnola," he said when they were alone. He held the tray out to her.

Mary considered Hobson and his tray. "Hobson?"

"Yes, Miss Reid?"

"What do you think of Mr. Cesnola?"

He stiffened. "It's not my place to say, Miss."

"Hobson, my parents are gone and you've known me since I was a baby. Who else do you think I can ask? My brother? He wants me to spend my life as his old-maid sister so he'll have a free governess in the house."

The butler blinked slowly and bit his lower lip. She saw him decide. "I think Mr. Cesnola is a gentleman, Miss."

"And?" Mary knew there was more.

"He's a lost soul, Miss. Like a ship that has broken its moorings in a storm and is being tossed this way and that."

Mary smiled at her butler. "Hobson, you're a poet."

He smiled back at her, a dry, wintery kind of smile. "Hardly, Miss. But a butler must take careful note of people to do his job well."

"And you are very good at your job." She was conscious of the tray between them. She still hadn't taken the letter from it.

He nodded. "Thank you, Miss. Your Mr. Cesnola is a good man who needs an anchor. And, if you'll pardon me for saying so, Miss, you need a family. You are too good a lady to live out your life in your brother's house, taking care of another woman's children."

"I'd have you," she said softly.

"Yes. That you would. But I'm not enough." He waggled the tray at her and she sighed as she picked the letter up from it.

"I'll be in the kitchen should you need anything, Miss." Hobson left, sliding the pocket doors behind him closed with a soft thump as he did.

She returned to her chair and sat. Hobson knew. She didn't know how, but he did. He knew Louis had proposed and that she had rejected him. Hobson thought she had made a mistake. She opened the letter and held it up so the light from the window would hit it.

My dear Miss Mary,

Please be kind enough to interpret this note of mine as you can, for I have no dictionary to select my words. Still I beg you to be sure that I do not intend to say anything disagreeable to you.

Last Saturday you told me that I do not know what love is and you are quite at a loss to guess what name must be applied to the feelings I have for you. Well, then I shall endeavor to find its name, not only for me but for you. I won't give you a definition of the word—love—because it has as many meanings as there are human beings on earth to feel it. I shall only draw a faithful picture of what I feel for you.

Suppose a man, from the time he was very young, was petted by a society of friends and relatives in the middle of which he grew up and he grew up the master of his own will, in a land where love has been created expressly for all its inhabitants. What could have been his life? Very nice, I think you will say. A man in such a position must have felt love in several gradations, at fourteen the angel-like love of the young, all illusions and dreams, at twenty the love of passions meant to satisfy. Now, at twenty-five this man finds his heart tired.

Now take this man, born in a privileged class, admired by all as a superior young man (although he has the good sense to know his worth) and give him a strong character and a great inclination to independence and freedom. And then imagine he throws his position away in a moment of madness and puts himself in another hemisphere as an outcast, despised as an outsider, degraded to earning his daily bread.

Do you believe that he may still love as he did at fourteen or twenty? No, certainly not. He may have for the woman he considers superior to all others the greatest affection. He can give up his life for her sake. He can devote himself to rendering happy the woman he selects and he will be the most faithful and kind husband, but he shall never be the kind of lover he was when fourteen or twenty years old.

Now you believe that such a kind of man will never be a good husband, but you are in error. He shall be ten years afterwards what he was the day of wedlock and his wife will be happy, while a marriage begun with love and passion shall in short time be followed by indifference and hate and divorce.

I am a man like the above, unable now to feel anything stronger than affection, but true affection, durable till death. If I cannot find a superior woman who is able to understand me I will die alone. I can endure it. I have more things to say but I have run out of room.

Believe me ever,
Your most affectionate
Louis P. di Cesnola.

Mary stood and looked out the window. She wasn't getting any younger and she'd never be any prettier. Louis was most assuredly her last chance. Could she live without love? Wasn't she already? As long as he didn't break her heart, wasn't that good enough? Mary reached for her little silver bell and rang it. When Hobson opened the doors she stepped toward him. "Hobson, would you think me terribly fast if I told you I wanted to visit Mr. Cesnola in his rooms?"

"No, Miss. I'd think you were a smart woman. Shall I call for your carriage?"

She smiled and nodded.

They were married two weeks later, at the Episcopal church she'd attended since she was a child. Rector Montgomery didn't care that Louis was Catholic. And Italian. But quite a lot of other people did care. Her brother dropped her from his social circle and most of her invitations went unanswered. As a result it was small ceremony, but a happy one.

They were happy at first. Her money, inherited from her dear Papa, allowed them to buy a small house in a good neighborhood. Mr. Lincoln called for troops and men flooded to enlist. Louis thought about doing the same. A Hungarian named D'Utassy organized the 39th New York Regiment among the city's immigrant men. Many of the regiment's volunteers were in America because they'd taken the wrong side in the European revolutions of 1848–49—so many that the Regiment took the nickname "Garibaldi Guard," in honor of Italian revolutionary Giuseppe Garibaldi. But the 39th was an infantry regiment and Louis was a cavalry man.

Fardella appeared in New York just days after the wedding, intent on raising his own regiment, but Fardella was also an infantry man. Louis was overjoyed to have his old friend in New York, to be able to ask him to his house for dinner with Mary, to talk as men do of old times and battles past, but even Fardella could not convince Louis to join an infantry regiment.

However, his cavalry preference was not the only thing that kept him home. It was Mary. She did not want him to go to war and she had made it a condition of their marriage.

"I have just found a husband," she said. "I will not lose him to a war I don't care about."

He had agreed, thinking that she would eventually change her mind. Instead Mary put up some money for Louis to start a cavalry school.

"You've trained at the finest cavalry school in Europe," she explained one evening over dinner. "You can do more good training a hundred cavalry officers than if just you, one man, went off to fight."

Louis thought her logic was irrefutable. And frustrating.

Fardella introduced him to Percy Wyndham, an Englishman who'd fought with Fardella in Rome. Wyndham had a varied military career, from the British cavalry to the French Navy and then a brief stint in the Austrian cavalry before switching sides in the Italian wars to fight with Garibaldi. He'd also briefly served in the Sardinian Army, where he'd done so well that King Victor Emmanuelle knighted him.

He and Wyndham found an old stable, complete with a riding ring, out on the far end of Broadway and opened their cavalry school. They offered classes in topography (Louis's old specialty), fencing, engineering, gymnastics, and riding. Wyndham spoke as many languages as Louis so they offered instruction in Italian, French, German, Spanish, and English.

They struggled along with only a few students for several weeks. Louis advertised in newspapers and had hand bills printed that he distributed about New York by himself. One day a heavyset man with lank, chin-length brown hair strode into their school and introduced himself as Senator Ira Harris.

Harris, it turned out, thought the Union Army's cavalry woefully ill-prepared. "All the real horsemen in the country live south of the Mason-Dixon line, ya' see. And they're with the Confederate Army now, riding in their cavalry. You mark my words, the Union is going to ignore this problem until it cain't no more."

Louis agreed with Harris. Most of their students sat on a horse like they were peasant farmers, not the sons of rich men. With Harris's patronage, the school's student body expanded precipitously.

And still Louis wasn't happy. It felt cowardly to sleep in a soft bed in a nice house while men were fighting and dying in Virginia. Men didn't need lessons in theoretical engineering or mapmaking. They needed to know how to ride a horse while simultaneously wielding a saber with one hand and a gun with the other, managing all three while the enemy tried his best to kill him. A man didn't learn that in school; he learned it in battle.

Why not organize a cavalry regiment? Hadn't D'Utassy and Fardella done that? Right now the Union Army had a handful of Italians in it, though as far as Louis knew, no Italian-trained cavalry men. There were even Italians fighting for the Confederacy, though why any decent man would do that Louis had no idea. Probably the same men who fought with the Austrians to maintain the Bourbon occupation.

Night after night Louis lay awake in bed after Mary was asleep and thought about going to war. He had to fight for this country. He'd be accepted then. The thought of going back to war quickened Louis's heartbeat. He wasn't good at anything else, but he could fight. He damn well could fight. But first he needed to convince Mary. Regiments weren't cheap.

Chapter Eight

OPPRESSED, HE RISES AGAIN

New York and Washington City— March–August 1862

Louis stubbed out his cigar and frowned. He stood on the balcony of the two-story building that served as the 11th New York Cavalry's temporary regimental headquarters on Staten Island. It was a windswept, barren plot of land, devoid of charm and warmth. Luckily, the cold snap had frozen the mud but it was still the worst cavalry training ground in the history of cavalries. In other parts of the world the cavalry had horses. Not in New York apparently.

Two months ago he'd joined James Swain's regiment almost on a whim. He finally convinced Mary to let him join the Army, but she drew the line at funding a regiment. Instead he went down to the recruiting office next to the Astor House and enrolled in the 11th, popularly known as "Scott's 900." Colonel Swain made him a Major and set him to drilling the young recruits. Unfortunately, they had no horses, a lapse that Louis was hard-pressed to understand.

Worse still, it turned out that Swain wasn't a military man. He was a reporter with good connections, which is probably why Swain hired Louis in the first place. It was a prestigious regiment, one whose commanding officer had been appointed directly by the president himself, but no one seemed to know the least little thing about cavalry techniques. Louis tried not to let it bother him. As Mary pointed out, Swain's inexperience created an opportunity. He'd make himself invaluable and rise in the regiment's command.

Every day he drilled his recruits. He taught them to march and wheel in a column, thinking if they could do it on their feet it would be easier to teach them to do it mounted once they got horses. The men also practiced daily with their carbines, pistols, and sabers. Louis was pleased to discover that American men were good with firearms but he wished they were half as good with a sword. They spent twice as much time learning sword fighting than they did in target practice. Still, the men seemed eager to learn and made good progress. Louis spared the frozen parade ground a last glance, then turned to go. It was time for dinner. He reminded himself that with patience it would all turn out fine. He'd make a mark for himself in this new country and in the process make Mary proud. And he was sleeping better.

Two months later, he marched into the headquarters of the 11th in Washington and resigned. Flanking him were Henry Calvert and George Pearson, young men Louis first met when Senator Harris brought them to his school. He slapped his discharge papers on the young lieutenant's desk and left, refusing the lieutenant's offer to make an appointment with Colonel Swain. He'd had all he could stomach from that popinjay Swain. They got their horses when they moved to Washington and the men were learning quite quickly, no thanks to Swain. The journalist hid in his office smoking cigars and reading the New York and Washington papers, remaining as ignorant of his cavalry as any new recruit.

Louis waited outside the building for Calvert and Pearson. When they appeared on the sidewalk, he grinned at them. "Well, boys, we're on our way now."

Both young men shuffled their feet and Pearson looked as if he were about to cry.

"It's no good, Major," Calvert said with a shake of his head. "Swain came out of his office and he's mad as a wet hen. He said he'd be glad to take both our resignations just as soon as we refunded our signing bonuses." Pearson shook his head, his golden hair shifting against the movement of his head. "And we don't have the money."

Of course they didn't. They'd gambled and drunk it away, probably with some whoring thrown in for good measure. He'd left them standing there on the sidewalk, too disappointed to even look at them any longer. He didn't have their problem. A gentleman did not volunteer for military service for pecuniary interests, but for the honor of the post.

Not that this posting had any honor in it. At least in this country's Southern states gentlemen took horses seriously and with that attitude came capable cavalry officers. Why, Jeb Stuart had nearly run the federals ragged in the Shenandoah Valley last summer, and that was after he'd all but defeated the Union Army at Bull Run single handedly. And that Wade Hampton fellow was nearly as good as Stuart, some said better. He had done all right at Bull Run too, holding off a contingent of Union men until Stonewall Jackson could ride in and make sausage of the lot of them. Men like Swain were not going to stop Stuart or Hampton, let alone Jackson. And Louis didn't think he wanted to. Swain said they were protecting the capital, but they didn't patrol, they weren't attached to any of the defensive fortifications, they didn't even have rifles. And all the while, men were fighting and dying in the Shenandoah Valley just to the east: it was shameful.

Worse, after only a few weeks in Washington, it had become clear to him that Senator Harris had been all too correct. The Union Army did not take cavalry forces seriously. Instead, they put their faith in guns and artillery. In machines, not men and horses. The Army recruited poor, unfit men at a prodigious rate to fill up regiment after regiment with men who would be no more than cannon fodder in a real battle. Louis couldn't bear it. One day the Army's high command would wake up and realize they needed a professional cavalry. When they did, he wanted to be there with one of his own.

Louis packed his kit and went home to New York and Mary. She hugged and kissed him, then held him at arm's length. "What's wrong, my dear?"

He looked down at her soft, round face. "Nothing, my darling. You were right. I should teach."

She shook her head. "No, I wasn't right. I was selfish. I was afraid to lose you. But I see now I'll lose you if I don't help you."

He shook his head. "I meant what I wrote, Mary. I'll always be a good husband to you. I'd never leave you."

She put her hands on either side of his face and pulled it down to her own. "I know, dear," she said softly. The next morning, he found a bank draft for $2,000 next to his breakfast plate.

Hobson, who'd come with Mary when she set up housekeeping, just smiled down at Louis and bid him good day. Louis wished Hobson was young enough to go to war with him. The phlegmatic butler would have made a good cavalry officer.

He set up a recruiting office on Sixth Avenue, behind Hiram's hotel and hired a likely lad who had just graduated from Harvard to act as his recruiting agent. Then he opened another office in the Bowery, hiring a tough old Irishman to be his recruiting officer. A cavalry could not function with officers alone and Louis learned to respect the Irish while he was in the Crimea. They were resilient and not afraid to spit into the abyss that was war.

Then he walked over to the Calverts' house and had a talk with the young man's father. The senior Calvert had been only too glad to front his son the money to resign his commission, particularly after Louis explained just how much danger his eldest would be in should he stay in a regiment as ill-prepared for war as the 11th was. Mr. Calvert promised to speak to Mr. Pearson about the matter as well and then made Louis a donation of $1,000 to recruit his own regiment, with the stipulation that he accept his son into the regiment and keep him as safe as possible for the duration of the war. It was deal Louis was only too glad to make.

Louis returned to Washington and set up yet another office, this one two blocks from the massive white stone building that was the War Department. By the end of the month, he had the beginnings of a fine regiment. He'd recruited almost a hundred men and purchased almost as many horses when disaster struck. He was writing letters in his office the morning of June 20 when two burly enlisted men burst into his office. The larger of the two slapped a piece of paper on Louis's desk.

"Yer unner arrest, sir."

Louis reared back his head and peered down his nose at the man and his companion. Both were dressed in the navy blue of the Union Army, though each man managed to make their uniforms look slovenly. The larger man's dubious dental work, or lack thereof, did little to enhance his appearance, while the smaller man, who was still easily as large as any heavy-weight pugilist, didn't appear at all familiar with soap. His greasy hair hung down under his cap in shiny hanks that swung sullenly to and fro as the man rocked on his heels in what appeared to be happy anticipation.

"Now none of your sass, Mister High and Mighty," the greasy fellow said. "You coming with us one way or the other so ya' might as well come quiet like."

Louis looked at the larger gentleman. The behemoth grinned at Louis, revealing several rotten teeth. "It's like Pete says."

Louis held up his index finger in reply and picked up the paper. It did indeed order his arrest. For inciting mutiny, no less.

He read a paragraph further down the paper. Colonel Swain charged that Louis was encouraging the men of the 11th to get out of that regiment and into his own. Swain further charged Louis with doing so both for financial gain and to assume his own command position in direct odds with Swain's.

"These charges are nonsense," he told the two men, aware as he spoke that he was wasting his time. These men had one job to do and it was not to hear his case.

Which is how he ended up in a cell in the dank Old Capitol Prison.

Louis grasped the black Mariah's bars, his handcuffs rattling against iron and sighed. Mary would have a—what was the word she used? A conniption. He tried to imagine her visiting him in this jail. It was a huge, square brick building sitting on a barren lot, as if grass refused to grow so close to the misery that must surely be inside. The windows were barred and men patrolled the building's perimeter. Louis tried to convince himself he had nothing to worry about.

Once inside, two men took him to an office near the front door and shackled him to a bench that had closed metal loops conveniently screwed into it. The place smelled like misery and old brick. The clerk didn't seem to understand Louis's name. Thank goodness he hadn't said Luigi. It would have been even worse. Still, it would be a miracle if Mary found him under whatever nonsense the fellow wrote in his big book of prisoners.

A scrawny sergeant with a smiling sort of face and a pronounced limp escorted him to his cell. Louis took a chance and spoke to him. "What sort of men do you keep here?"

"There be all manner o' men in the Old Cap. We got Confederates in the basement, bounty jumpers on the second floor and, well, look here." He stopped and pointed at a door with a small window. Louis peered through the grimy glass. Inside was a matronly dark-haired woman and a girl no older than ten. The two of them were sitting on the room's narrow bed looking at a book. It appeared to Louis that the older woman was reading aloud. *A woman in prison!* It was true what they said: in America all things were possible.

The guard, who'd revealed himself Irish by his accent, clapped Louis on the shoulder. "That be the notorious Rose Greenhow. And her little un. She looks real nice, don't she? But you gotta watch her like a hawk. She's wily. And she's got a sharp tongue, the like of which I'd not tolerate in a wife."

Of course Louis had heard of Mrs. Greenhow. Everyone had. She was a Confederate spy, caught by the Pinkertons last summer. They'd kept her under house arrest until public opinion forced them to move her to the prison this past winter. But Louis had forgotten all about her; he supposed they all had.

The guard tapped him on the shoulder to tell him to move along. He walked Louis two doors down from Mrs. Greenhow's room and stopped. "This is where we keep officers that have got themselves in trouble. Luck would have it you're our only one right now."

He took a ring of small keys from his belt, unlocked the door and held it open. "In ya' go," he said merrily. They stepped inside and the sergeant unlocked his handcuffs. Despite the warm spring air outside it was cold inside and smelled faintly of urine. The room was big enough to house a dozen prisoners, with narrow beds lining the wall, interspersed with chipped wooden chairs. "Breakfast is at 7 and supper at 4. You're allowed one visitor a day. Visitors can bring ya' provisions just as long as they pass inspection." He turned to go.

"Wait," Louis said, fully aware of the anxiety his voice betrayed. "How will my wife know I'm here? I was alone when I was arrested, you see...." His voice trailed off. She'd have no way of knowing what had become of him. He'd just disappear in this horrible place and Mary would find someone else. "Please. Could you get word to her? I'd be most grateful." His words rushed out of him before he could stop himself. A gentleman did not beg.

The sergeant threw back his head and laughed heartily. "Most grateful. You toffs are something, ain't ya'?" He pulled his cap from his head and wiped at his eyes with it. "Gimme her name and address. And I'll be perusing the basket she brings for items meant jess for me. You take my meaning? Tell her to ask for Sargent O'Hannon."

Louis nodded, the lump in his throat too big to allow for words.

Mary visited the next day. The door opened with a rattle and there she was, glorious in a lavender dress trimmed with white flouncing. She stood uncertainly in the doorway until O'Hannon gently pushed her forward and locked the door behind her. Louis stood. She burst into tears. He strode across the room and took her in his arms, never so glad to see anyone in his entire life. When he kissed her he meant it.

Afterwards they sat on the edge of one of the beds and talked. Louis explained his predicament and together they made a list of things she could bring to him. When O'Hannon returned for her, Louis kissed her again. As he did, he discovered, much to his surprise and delight, that he had fallen in love with his wife.

He pulled one of the chairs up to his bed to use as a table. This morning Mary brought him a blanket, a change of undergarments, and a small letter-writing kit she usually kept in her desk. She'd also brought O'Hannon a bottle of whiskey and large jar of honey. The quirky Irishman refused the whiskey, but took the honey. Louis had met Irish men who didn't drink, but only rarely. Mary promised to bring O'Hannon some apricot preserves the next time she visited.

Louis had been thinking about a number of men he could write to, prominent New Yorkers who might intercede for him. Mr. Calvert, for example. He bit his lip and thought about it. He'd go straight to the top. To General George McClellan, Commander of the Army of the Potomac. McClellan should remember him, even if they'd only met once, seven years before. One did not forget men met in circumstances like the siege of

Sevastopol. Louis nodded to himself. He'd appeal to the general, not as a supplicant, but as an equal, gentleman to gentleman.

To General George McClellan,

I write to you as a fellow man of the world and one with an appreciation of continental military techniques of strategy and leadership. I fondly remember our discussion of such in Sevastopol, where we first met. You will recall you were with the Delafield Commission and I aide-de-camp to General Di Cavour.

I am under arrest and presently locked in the Old Capitol Prison for encouraging mutiny for both personal and monetary gain. I have done nothing of the sort. I endeavored to raise my own cavalry regiment in order to serve this country. I previously served under Col. Swain of the 11th NY Cav. My observations of him led me to believe that Colonel Swain is as ignorant as a new recruit. He is a danger to the men who serve under him and a danger to any command structure that depends upon him. I shared my concerns with General James Wadsworth, should you care to consult with him on this matter.

It is Swain, not myself, who robs the U.S. Government and yet no justice is done against him. Only myself, a newcomer to this land sits in jail, accused of heinous crimes against this glorious country. Swain withholds his men's pay, purchases inadequate horses for his regiment and in all ways uses the regiment to personally enrich himself. I, on the other hand, seek only to further the Union cause by raising a well-trained, well-horsed cavalry regiment of men such as those in the enemy army who do such damage to the cause of American freedom.

Yr. Obt. Servant,
Louis Palma di Cesnola

Louis read over his letter. Was it too enthusiastic? Too fervent? Mary said he was too Italian in his temperament for the restrained Anglophiles who ran this country. How could he be too Italian? He simply was Italian and there was nothing to be done about that. But Mary had taught him that Americans, like the British, preferred quiet restraint to emotional exuberance. He would have Mary look over the letter tomorrow before he sent it. Her sense of American style was better than his. He closed with a post script saying that, when freed from this prison, he would prefer to serve directly under McClellan himself, or failing that, under General Sigel, a German trained in European-style warfare. He folded the letter and set it aside.

He was released from prison ten days later.

O'Hannon unlocked his cell after breakfast and handed him a sheaf of papers. The top sheet ordered his release from prison and reinstatement in the U.S. Army on the grounds that he had done nothing improper. The paperwork underneath ordered Colonel Louis Cesnola to join his recruiting efforts with the 4th New York Volunteer Cavalry under the command of Colonel Dickel, part of the Army of the Potomac, General George McClellan commanding. His division commander would be Major General Franz Sigel. The 4th was currently stationed in the Shenandoah Valley.

Louis fought the urge to throw the papers in the air and leap for joy. Instead he grinned broadly at Sergeant O' Hannon. "I'm going where there's fighting. Real fighting. In command of a cavalry regiment. How about that?"

O'Hannon smiled broadly and clasped Louis on the shoulder. "Go and may God keep you safe, Boy-o."

Chapter Nine

THIS WAR WILL NEVER END

Shenandoah Valley, Virginia—January–March 1863

Two more dead horses. Louis stood in the clearing where the 4th had its horses staked out. The ground was stomped into frozen mud, made worse by the last few days' freezing rain, but it was the trees that were the most notable. Every tree in sight had been chewed down to only the branches too large for a horse to eat. The bark had been stripped from the trunks as well.

Parnell gestured around the clearing. "The good news is there are fewer horses to feed."

Louis snorted. "And fewer mounts for the men. We're never going to catch the blasted Grey Ghost with our horses in this shape."

"I'll take a party west tomorrow. See what we can find."

"Take the wagons. If you can't find grain, bring hay of any kind. I'll file another report. For whatever good that will do."

Louis walked back to his tent. He made an effort to keep his shoulders squared and his chin up. It wouldn't do to have the men see him look despondent. This was as bad as that winter outside Sevastopol. All it did was snow. The men were cold and hungry, the horses starved for lack of forage. And that damn Mosby and his Rangers conducted raid after raid, making fools of the federal cavalry.

Once inside his tent, his shoulders slumped. Last summer and fall his star had risen in the Union Army so much that he'd begun to think he'd at long last found the place he was meant to be. His 4th became the shining regiment in Sigel's Corps, his men and horses outperforming every other cavalry regiment. And whatever men they lost were quickly replaced by recruits from their Staten Island induction camp. Everyone wanted to join the 4th, or so it seemed in the halcyon days of the war.

General Sigel, recognizing his Italian colonel's worth, put Louis in charge of the 1st Maryland, 6th Ohio, 17th Pennsylvania, and 9th New York, as well as his beloved 4th. Along with Brigade command came promotions to Brigadier General, at least in theory. So far his promotion hadn't come. It wasn't fair, but Louis decided to see the snub as an opportunity. He'd outperform these provincial American military men and they would see his worth and have to promote him.

At least that's what he'd thought last summer. Now that winter was upon them there was quite a bit less enthusiasm for the war, and not only in the Shenandoah Valley where they'd been stationed since last summer. Back on Staten Island, Major Pruyn reported that desertions were at an all-time high. Men joined up in a lather of loyalty, then, faced with the discipline and hardship of army camp life, sneaked away in the dark and went home. Other men were no more than professional bounty jumpers, men who used false names to join a regiment, collect the induction bounty, and then defect at the first opportunity, only to do it all over again somewhere else. In his last report, Pruyn wrote that he didn't even have enough weapons to arm camp guards.

Well, that problem would soon be solved. On Louis's orders, Major Parnell had boxed up six revolvers and sent them to Mary. Louis included a letter in the package directing her to deliver the revolvers to Pruyn on Staten Island.

It was too bad he couldn't trust the men at his own regiment's induction camp, but a Colt revolver was worth good money these days and men who would desert would also steal. Mary would see they got to Pruyn. He smiled at the thought of Mary. In her last letter she wrote that she was expecting their first child, conceived on his last leave. She hadn't couched the news in any of that vague talk of delicacy or French. No, not his Mary. She was a straightforward lady who said what she meant and wrote it too. "I am with child, dear Louis," she wrote, "and expect the baby by late summer."

He put away his thoughts of Mary and wrote yet another report on the condition of the regiment's horses. Parnell joined him about an hour later. He entered Louis's tent chuckling and shaking his head.

"What?" Louis set down his pen and pushed back his chair. He kept Parnell around for a good number of reasons, not the least of which was his story-telling ability.

"It's terrible and funny at the same time," Parnell said with a laugh.

Louis rolled his hand, signaling he had time to hear the story.

"Well, it was raining last night so old Mosby decided to take his men for a ride. They rode right through a gap outside Centreville and right into Fairfax, past many federal pickets. They rode right up to the house General Stoughton's been using as headquarters and disarmed his sentries. Apparently the fools let Mosby's raiders walk right up to them. They went right in and upstairs to the General's bed chamber, pulled down his bed clothes, and spanked his naked nether regions."

Louis guffawed in spite of himself. He'd met young Stoughton and not cared for him one tiny bit. Typical spoiled young man given a post above his ability because his daddy had money. "And then what happened?"

"Well, here's the best part. Mosby told Stoughton he was surrounded on all sides by Jeb Stuart, but seeing as how they'd known each other at West Point and were old friends and all, Mosby would get Stoughton out before the town was overrun. So Stoughton got dressed and rode off with Mosby's men. Took him back to Culpepper from what I hear. The poor devil will no doubt be in Libby Prison by the end of the week."

"Egad!" Louis half shouted. "Stoughton will never live it down."

Parnell slapped his knee and agreed. Then his face grew serious. "But how much would you give for a regiment of men like Mosby and his raiders?"

"We'll get there," Louis said. He pulled a pair of cigars from a box Mary sent him last week and handed one to Parnell. "Mosby's horses aren't starving because his army takes cavalry seriously. He succeeds on grain, which gets him more grain. All we need is one big success and the army will take note. The men are ready for it. You watch and see."

Before Parnell could reply, a knock came at the tent door. Parnell stood and pushed open the wood-framed, canvas-covered door.

It was Billy, one of the drummer boys. "Urgent dispatch, sir. The courier said I was to bring it straight to you." Billy shuffled his feet and bit his lower lip.

"That's fine, son. Hand it over then," Louis said patiently. The drummer boys made him feel a hundred years old, though he hadn't been much older than young Billy when he'd first gone to war. Louis rummaged in his kit and came up with a peppermint stick candy for the boy. After a suitable amount of shuffling and saluting, Billy backed out of his colonel's tent, leaving Parnell and Louis alone again.

Louis unwrapped the twine that held the dispatch case closed and pulled out two sheets of paper. He started to read.

Parnell watched his friend and commanding officer go white. "What?"

Louis wordlessly offered Parnell the papers.

They crinkled in Parnell's hand as he took them, but otherwise they seemed entirely harmless.

Whereas the shameless plunder of public property can only be suppressed by prompt and summary punishment of offenders, Col. Cesnola is dismissed from service in the United States Army, Cavalry Corps, 4th New York. He is found to be the receiver and dealer in public property, marked as such as his own, stolen or fraudulently disposed of and is unhesitatingly expelled from service as the primary offender in such dealings.

Signed
Judge Advocate General Joseph Holt
Office of the Provost Marshall, Washington D. C.
Lafayette Baker, Investigator-in-Chief

The second and third page contained a fuller accounting of the so-called crime. In January a clerk at the Adams Express Company in Washington City opened a box addressed to Mary R. Cesnola, 37th Street West, New York. The clerk did so on orders from the Judge Advocate General to open all packages over one square foot in size coming from any military personnel. Inside the box the clerk found a summer-weight officer's uniform and six brand new Remington revolvers stamped U.S. Cavalry on their stocks. The clerk brought this to the notice of his superior, who contacted the city's new Provost Marshall, one Lafayette Baker. Baker turned the guns and case over to Joseph Holt, the army's chief lawyer, who sent a report to Secretary of War Edwin M. Stanton. Stanton himself ordered Cesnola's dismissal.

Parnell read through the pages and handed them back to Louis. Louis's cigar sat forgotten on his camp desk, smoldering and dropping ash on the wooden surface.

"No one even questioned me. I could have explained." Louis dropped the papers into his lap. "I could have explained," he repeated.

Parnell shrugged. Both of them knew that some men got the benefit of the doubt and some men did not. In a war to free the slaves and ensure American liberty, few saw the irony of treating immigrants as anything but inferior. "Muster out and go home to Italy. To hell with this country. You've tried. They already put you in jail once. Mary would go with you and from what you tell me of your mother, she'd welcome you back with open arms as long as your wife is making babies."

Louis felt a white-hot fire spread through him. He shook his head. "No." He shook his head again, then rose to pack. "I will not run. I will fight. I will fight and I will win." Louis felt his conviction grow as he spoke. He stubbed out the smoldering cigar and reached for his kit bag. "I'll be back. It's you and I, Parnell. We will finish this war together and we will show them who we are. Whether they like it or not."

∽

He was in Washington two days later, primed to do battle. He took a room at the Willard Hotel, a hostelry so grand and so large it outshone even the 5th Avenue Hotel, and set out to make his case. He tried the JAG office, but had no luck. No one there would talk to him. Next he tried Baker at the Marshall's service, which proved to be a huge mistake. Baker saw him, but told Louis he was lucky he hadn't been arrested for treason and jailed. *Again.* Baker accused him of the most heinous crimes, dredging up the old mutiny charge and calling Louis a thief. Louis tried to explain but the man would hardly let him get a word in, so self-satisfied was he in his anger and outrage. He next went to the Secretary of War's office in the Old Executive building but Stanton wouldn't or couldn't see him. His assistant did make Louis an appointment to see one of Stanton's assistants. Asst. Secretary Watson seemed inclined to hear Louis's case but told him to write it all down and get corroborating witnesses for everything he said.

Back in his room at the Willard, Louis began making lists. He needed a letter from Major Pruyn attesting to the problems at the Staten Island induction camp, another from Mary asking her to send him the letter he'd included in the box of pistols. In that letter he'd been explicit about what she was to do with the pistols after they arrived in Manhattan. He also needed a letter from General Sigel about the general difficulties of being a cavalry commander. Oh, and Mary could get some of her rich friends to write letters attesting to his good character. Louis wrote and re-wrote letters over the course of the next three days, availing himself of the hotel's dictionary over and over. His letters needed to be perfect, with not one whiff of foreigner about them. If Mary hadn't been in the family way he'd have asked her to come.

She was so much better at this business of using the right English words and striking the correct American tone.

On his second day at the Willard, he received his formal discharge papers from the Army. *Dishonorably discharged, February 2, 1863.* He could hardly believe it. A son of a count and a man who'd fought honorably in two wars before this one. Dishonorably discharged. He almost took to his bed with a large bottle of American whiskey, but then thought better of it. First, whiskey tasted terrible. If only he could find a bottle of grappa somewhere. Second, getting drunk would be an admission of failure. Of giving in. He wouldn't do it. Instead, he wrote to several of his commanders in the Crimea and Italy, asking them for letters of character.

And then he waited. First a package from Mary came, one that included a bank draft for his hotel bill. Then other letters began to pour in, from Pruyn in Staten Island, from General Sigel, his commanding officer in the Shenandoah. Telegrams from Europe came, messages of letters arriving by diplomatic courier before the end of the month. By the third week in February he'd gathered his letters and re-written his explanation for the last time. He bundled the papers together in a leather pouch and delivered them to the Secretary of War's office. And waited some more.

During the days, he waited and took walks. Washington City was warmer than the Shenandoah, Louis supposed, because it was closer to the ocean. It was a city of black people too, some of them slaves, some of them free, which was new for him. Oh, there were blacks in New York, but not in the part he lived in. Here they sold produce on the streets, ran the omnibus cars and blacksmith shops, and were in all ways everywhere. He'd never really seen anything like it. In New York, the blacks lived in their own neighborhoods, but here they lived mixed among the whites, in shacks that fronted the alleys behind white people's houses.

He walked and watched, trying to figure out what the fuss was. They looked different from the Anglo-Americans, that was for sure, but so did he, with his olive skin and black hair and eyes. They worked hard, kept to themselves, and sang whenever they had an opportunity. In fact, they reminded Louis of the Italian peasantry, people never too poor for a song or a quick word of jest.

Finally, at the end of the month he could take the waiting no longer. He wrote Secretary Stanton a personal letter.

I am Col. di Cesnola, 4th NY Cav., who has these three weeks suffered the effect of a gross mistake; my name, heretofore one of the purest in the U.S. Army, is disgraced, my family in desolation, my reputation soiled. And yet no redress comes to me. If you look into my case you shall see I am an innocent man.

I have no friends here. I am a foreigner and I am an innocent man. I have had trouble of this sort before, with Col. Swain. I was helped then by kind men who wished to do right. I am an excellent cavalry officer. I have captured more Rebel prisoners, arms, and horses than any other colonel. If the officers who are fighting for their country have to be treated this way this war will never end.

I most respectfully request you to see that full justice is done to me and my good name returned so that I might return to my regiment.

He sat his pen down and re-read the letter. He picked up his pen and added one more word.

Please.

Then on the first Tuesday in March, he awoke to find an envelope pushed under his hotel door. He picked it up, noticing it was from the JAG office. He carefully laid it on the small table he used as a writing desk and dining table. He ordered his breakfast and a pot of the disgusting beverage Americans passed off as coffee. He dressed himself for the day in a plain brown suit. He ate his toast and drank his coffee, all while pretending not to see the envelope.

When he was done he picked up the envelope and tucked it into his jacket pocket. He left his room, carefully locking the door behind him and took the stairs to the Willard's lobby. He greeted the dark-skinned doorman and asked after his wife, who had been ailing the previous week. Assured that she was better, Louis walked down Pennsylvania Avenue to the park in front of the president's house. He took a seat on a bench. He looked up at the sun, took a deep breath, and removed the envelope from his pocket.

March 3, 1863

Judge Advocate General's Office
General Order #50

Colonel Cesnola's dishonorable discharge is hereby revoked. Colonel Cesnola is ordered reinstated to his command provided the vacancy has not been filled, he having shown the property was not stolen by himself or any other person in his command and that in improperly forwarding said property to a civilian no wrong was intended.

Louis looked back up at the sun, squinting into the glare. Water leaked from the corners of his eyes. The sun was very bright for March.

Chapter Ten

COLD LIKE A STONE

Virginia—June 8–9, 1863

Parnell scrabbled ahead of Louis, through bushes thick with spiky branches and thorns. The Irishman paused, looked over his shoulder, and grinned broadly. Louis looked over his own shoulder and waved up the men behind him. They crawled nearly soundlessly through the underbrush that lay on the banks of the Orange and Alexandria Railroad line. Louis crawled forward until his shoulder brushed against Parnell. Off to the side ranged Major Stedman from the Ohio 6th and two captains from the 1st Rhode Island and a Lieutenant Colonel Curtis from the 1st Massachusetts.

Parnell handed Louis his field glasses. "You won't believe it till you see it," he whispered.

Louis held the binocular field glasses up to his eyes. He fiddled with the focus and then gasped as the sight before him swam into view. "What are they doing?"

Stedman chuckled. "Looks like old Jeb Stuart is showin' off. Again."

Louis put the glasses back up to his eyes. It looked like a full field review. Hundreds of mounted cavalry men were amassed at one end of the field. Maybe thousands. Artillery units hauling field pieces with heavy-limbed draft horses were parading down the field. Behind them were more mounted soldiers. Louis had never seen so many men on horseback in one place in his whole life. He laid the glasses on the ground and wiped the sweat from his eyes.

Parnell nodded. "It's too hot for a parade. Isn't it?"

Stedman laughed softly again. "Seems just right to me. They're going to be mighty tired out tonight."

The men watched the parade from the undercover along the railroad line. From this distance it was hard to tell who they were parading for, but it was most certainly Jeb Stuart's cavalry corps. Louis thought it probable that a show of this magnitude was for General Lee. He lifted the field glasses to his eyes again and looked for Lee's white horse. He saw several white horses so that was no help.

Birds twittered, mosquitoes droned, and the day heated up. Louis felt sweat run off his back and down his sides. His uniform front would be soaked when he got off his belly. Just as he was about to suggest they crawl back to their horses, the artillery started moving again. Gradually the mass of men and horses divided itself into two sides.

"What are they doing?" Curtis asked, disbelief in every word he said.

Louis knew because he had seen enough of them in the Crimea; the British had loved them. "It's a simulated battle."

The cannon boomed. They crawled back to their horses, using the noise as cover.

They made haste back to camp. Stuart's pride would be his undoing this time. First they went to General Gregg's tent, then with him to General Pleasanton's headquarters. By dinner time they had a plan. By midnight they were on the move.

Louis and his brigade, consisting of the 1st Massachusetts, 6th Ohio, 1st Rhode Island, and the 4th New York, took the left wing of the attack, under General Gregg's Second and Third Cavalry Divisions, while General Buford took the smaller right wing attack with his First Cavalry Division. General Pleasanton accompanied Buford and three thousand infantry north, across the Rappahannock at Beverly's Ford, where the water was low and slow. Just as the sun rose they would attack from the east.

In the meantime, Gregg's divisions would come at Stuart's camp from the south, crossing the railroad at dawn. The idea was to catch Stuart's much-vaunted cavalry forces sleeping off the rigors of the previous day's grand troop parade and practice battle. They would squeeze them between the two arms of Union Cavalry until they popped like an infected boil.

Louis publicly agreed with General Pleasanton that this was a chance to knock the stuffing out of Stuart and prove once and for all that the Union Cavalry was not a second-class operation. Privately Louis thought this chance at cavalry glory would provide him with much-needed redemption. He had no doubt that his recent troubles were an artifact of Pleasanton's dislike of foreigners, but his problems were compounded by the low esteem in which the Union Army and federal government held their cavalry.

Louis surveyed his men, who waited behind him in the dark. A low ground fog obscured his view, but he knew it would also keep the Confederates from seeing them until it was too late. He pulled out his pocket watch and held it up to his nose to check the time. Then he snapped it shut and nudged his horse, called Red, up alongside General Gregg. Gregg nodded at him.

Louis pulled his saber and held it aloft. Behind him he heard hundreds of sabers do the same. He lowered his arm, slashing the saber down at his side. At the same time he spurred Red forward. They were off, charging across the railroad tracks toward Jeb Stuart's headquarters.

Time slowed down and sped up after that, stretching out and back, as it always did in battle. Off to the north he could hear artillery boom. It was the Confederates firing on Pleasanton and Buford's forces.

They swept between Stuart's artillery, off to the west near the small town of Brandy Station and his main camp at the base of Fleetwood Hill, essentially crippling the enemy artillery, who dared not fire for fear of hitting their own men. It was a gloriously fast sortie. In nearly every cavalry charge he'd ever been in, the action would slow down, horses would be injured, and they'd dismount and fight hand to hand. Not this time. It never slowed down. He rode from rebel to rebel, slashing and shooting. His carbine grew hot under his hand, his sword arm got heavier and heavier. And still he fought, putting into it every bit of his rage at his mistreatment, at being an outsider, at his adopted country's refusal to treat him like a man, equal in all ways to other men. Red sensed his rage and ran heedless into other horses, knocking men right off their mounts.

Louis spared a moment's thought for Baree and then a thought for the man who had owned Red before him. Whoever the man was, he'd done Louis a favor, training this horse the way he had. Doubtless among the glorious dead now, his chestnut horse passed to the next fighting fool.

By noon, they'd routed Stuart from his headquarters, driving him and his men north into the arms of Buford and Pleasanton. Off to his left he saw his friend Judd Kilpatrick leading his men up the hill. Louis saw a break in the action and spurred Red through it, hollering for his men to follow. They crested the hill at the same time as Kilpatrick's men. He and Judd grinned madly at each other.

Before there was time to say anything, Parnell called, "To your right!" Louis wheeled Red, felt Kilpatrick behind him. A phalanx of Rebel cavalry charged up the back of the hill, up and over, crashing into them with a wave of flashing sabers and barking carbines.

"It's Hampton's Brigade," Kilpatrick shouted. "I'll have his head!"

Louis laughed in spite of himself. The patrician Wade Hampton, third of his name, was a cavalry legend second only to Stuart. If anyone could take Hampton's head it would be Kilpatrick, so rash and full of himself he might as well be Italian.

They battled back and forth for the rest of the afternoon. Sometimes they had the crest of the hill, sometimes the Rebels did. At one point one of Gregg's regiments hauled up a howitzer, but the gun did little good. Howitzers were fine when fighting in a straight line with the enemy ranged neatly out in front of the gun, but this fight was anything but that. Finally, as the sun sat low in the sky, the Rebels took the hill and the howitzer, but by then the gun's supply of balls was gone and the captured artillery piece did them no good.

Louis tried not to let the loss of the hill upset him much. They had without a doubt surprised the Rebels and done quite a bit of damage. Still, the Rebs fought back like men who knew what they were doing. The field of battle was littered with dead men and horses, as many in blue as in grey.

It was almost dusk when they made it back to camp. Louis dismounted and handed Red over to one of the reserve infantry, but not before patting the horse on the neck and telling him he'd find him later with a treat. The animal reeked of sweat and blood, but otherwise was entirely unharmed. It was ever so. Louis would ride off to battle, lose friends and brothers-in-arms and return to camp unharmed. He longed for a wash and some dinner, but instead made his way to Pleasanton's tent for final reports. As he walked across camp he heard the sound of voices raised in song: it was the men gathered around campfires, singing to each other. He stopped here and there, congratulating his men for their valor and survival. There was little more both jubilant and sad than an army in camp after battle. Louis heaved a sigh, missing the days when he was just one of the men.

It was two days before the newspapers got ahold of the news from Brandy Station. The *Washington Evening Star* called it the greatest Union Cavalry victory of the war. The *Times* spoke specifically about Louis, saying he "dashed upon the enemies with his usual impetuosity, scattering them and pursuing them." Louis smiled when he read that. No doubt Mary would see it and know he was alive and well.

They'd lost more men than the Confederates, but they'd scattered Stuart's cavalry and proved they could fight. No one could argue that now, not even the shopkeeper colonels and generals who had no business being in charge of an army. Even Pleasanton, who thought the war should only be fought by "real Americans" had to commend Louis on his brigade's performance.

Louis's men reveled in the redemption. Even better, with the Army of the Potomac on the move to Pennsylvania for a show-down with General Lee's army, the cavalry corps would be used the way they ought to be. They would have to be. No one, not even the Union high command, could miss the lessons of their latest cavalry battle.

Five days after Brandy Station, Louis had his orders. He was to move the 4th up the valley to Aldie Gap. Lee had his army aimed at a small town in Pennsylvania called Gettysburg. Louis's brigade would do what it could to stop the Confederates be-fore they got there. They would see what happened when they gave command to someone other than Americans and his heart, which had grown cold as a stone since his discharge, would at last thaw. They would see that no one was more enthusiastic for the fight than he. His heart felt less cold.

Part II

Chapter Eleven

LIBBY-LICE-SEE-UM

Winchester and Richmond, Virginia—July–September 1863

A light interrupted the darkness. Louis felt it shining on him. Was this heaven? His eyes tried to open.

"Got one here," a voice over him yelled. "Wooeeee! A colonel by the looks of it."

Louis knew a Rebel Yell when he heard one. He needed to wake up. To get away. He turned his head toward the voice. A fractured lightning bolt of pain ripped through his head and he was gone again, back into the dark.

He came to again, sometime later, his cheek still pressed against the cool of the ground. Something or someone was tugging at his leg. He tipped one eyelid open, careful not to move his head as he did. It was dark still, but there was a lantern light just over him.

"Hold on, Yankee man," someone said. "We gonna drag this here off ya'."

Louis became suddenly conscious of his leg, trapped beneath something dreadfully heavy. Then he remembered. Red.

Poor Red. And then it felt like someone was trying to pull his leg off. He screamed.

"Steady on, Yankee man," came the voice again.

The pain stopped, the pressure on his leg suddenly gone. His foot must have been still in the stirrup when they pulled Red off him.

"Yer gonna have ta' get up, Mister."

Louis recognized the accent of a poor Southern man, though which state or region he could not tell. It was hard enough to tell the Northerners from the Southerners, though he could tell a German from a Swede in a heartbeat. He carefully turned his head up to the light. It hurt. He tried to push himself upright and discovered a new pain when his right arm screeched in protest. Clutching his arm to his torso he pushed himself into a sitting position with his left hand. The world swirled and then lurched. His stomach lurched with it. He gagged, trying not to vomit. Nothing came up so maybe he succeeded.

A head appeared in the halo of lantern light. "You gonna get up? Cause I'd hate to have ta' shoot ya." The voice sounded apologetic, even kindly, for someone threatening his life. Louis tried to stand. His left leg, the one that had been under Red, refused to cooperate. He tried again. His head spun and then the world with it.

When he next came to he was in the back of a farm wagon, crowded between two other men, his head bumping on the bare boards of the wagon's bed. Thumpety, thump, thump, thump. He groaned and lifted his head. The man on his left was either unconscious or dead. Did it matter? Louis scrunched down and shifted sideways so he could lay his poor abused head upon the man's chest. The man's wool uniform was warm and scratchy, but underneath it the man felt hard as a paving stone. Dead then. Louis mentally shrugged. If the man was dead he wouldn't care if Louis used him as a pillow.

They bumped along like that for much of the day. Louis gradually became aware that he felt thirsty. Then warm. Then hot and desperately thirsty. His tongue felt large and wooden in his mouth, sweat poured off his forehead into his eyes, and the dead man started to smell. Finally, after what felt like seven hundred hours the wagon stopped. A large man in the butternut-colored uniform of a Rebel enlisted man pulled his pillow out of the wagon. He heard the man's body land hard on the ground. Then the same man grabbed his boots and before Louis could speak, yanked him out of the wagon. Louis head thumped onto the ground. Louis wrenched up his head and grunted at the man.

"Arghhh," the fellow yelled and dropped Louis's feet. "I thought this were a dead wagon." The man turned and hollered again. Two men appeared, dressed in the same butternut cloth, though they were considerably younger and smaller than the first man. Together they carried Louis over to a nearby tree and laid him on the ground. Then they forgot all about him. He lay there the rest of the day, shifting in and out of consciousness. Twice he tried to ask for water but he could not find his voice. Near dusk someone poked his shoulder.

"Is that you, Captain Cesnola? I mean Colonel. What in heaven's name are you doing *here?*"

Louis opened his eyes to find a familiar face. "Sergeant Morley?" His voice came out a whisper.

Morley smiled broadly. "I'm a Captain now, if you can believe that blarney. We've both come up in the world."

"Water?" Louis croaked.

An hour later Louis was sitting up against the tree feeling considerably better. Morley fetched a small bucket of water from the creek, half of which Louis drank and promptly threw up. His second attempt stayed down and revived him somewhat. Morley dumped a second bucket over Louis's head and arm in attempt to clean his wounds. While the Captain examined him and dabbed at his wounds with a piece of his shirt tail, Louis peppered him with questions.

"Where are we?"

"Just outside Staunton."

"Where General Jackson had his headquarters?"

Morley nodded. "That be the place. Of course old Stonewall's gone to meet his Maker and good riddance to bad rubbish if you ask me." Morley's Irish accent became more pronounced as he spoke. "You've got yourself quite a gash here on your head, but your skull's intact. It's true what they say, Italian heads are as thick as fence posts."

Louis grunted a small laugh. "Much like an Irishman's. And thank the Blessed Mother for that." He held out his arm so Morley could tug off his jacket. "So you say Stonewall's dead?"

"Yep. Got himself an injury and took sick, I hear. 'Course I best not gloat. Cause we're prisoners, Colonel."

Louis looked up at Morley. The last time he'd seen the man he'd been a crusty sergeant in the British Army in Crimea. "What are you doing here? In America?"

"Same as you I 'spect. Making a new life and doing a poor job of it."

Louis sighed. That did about sum it up. "After what we saw in the Crimea I wanted a new start." He shook his head, then regretted it. Grimacing, he added, "I see my mistake now. There's only one world and it's full of war and killing."

Morley stopped probing Louis and looked steadily at his old comrade-in-arms. "It never ends, does it?" Then he sighed and returned to his task.

Two weeks later they were lined up, along with two dozen enlisted men, by a tall Confederate Captain who did not look old enough to shave. He told them they would walk or die. Louis felt his heart speed up at the announcement. He'd never make it, not in the shape he was in. He was dizzy all the time and his crushed leg would hardly bear his weight.

"Permission to speak, sir," Morley barked.

The Captain walked down the line to Morley and stopped in front of him. "Yes, vermin?"

"I'm sorry sir, but there's men among us who cannot walk more than a few steps." Morley nodded at Louis. "The Colonel here is a good man and, begging your pardon for impertinence, but the rules of war say you have to treat officers with honor."

"Honor, is it?" The Captain spoke in a soft, reasonable voice that nonetheless managed to sound menacing. "What do you think about that, Sergeant?"

A grizzled older man standing just behind his captain spit out a stream of tobacco juice and snorted. "Didn't know Yankees had any honor, Captain."

"Hm." The captain rubbed his clean-shaven jaw. "I am forced to agree. I do have a few extra horses." He stepped over to Louis. "Turn out your pockets."

Louis blinked at the order, but otherwise remained motionless and wordless.

"Turn out your damned pockets before I put a bullet in your damned head."

Louis turned out his coat and trouser pockets, removing from them his watch, pipe, keys, money clip, and a small bundle of matches.

The captain plucked out the money clip and watch and put them in his own pocket. He nodded at Louis to keep the rest. He turned and walked away, the sergeant following in his wake. Louis felt a sick sense of panic. He'd always thought he'd die in battle, leading some charge up some hill somewhere. But to die like this, shot on the side of a road as a prisoner of war … Well, what would Mary say?

The sergeant returned, leading a sway-backed horse of uncertain breeding and parentage. Morley grinned broadly as he helped Louis mount the poor beast.

Tears sprung to Louis's eyes at his reprieve and Morley's kindness.

"Now none of that," Morley said gruffly. "You Italians need to learn a little English stiff upper lip, you do."

Louis smiled weakly at Morley, seeing the man had his own set of wet eyes. "You're no Brit. You're Irish."

Morley wiped at his eyes and took the horse's reins. "And the angels wept," he said.

They began walking. It took days to walk all the way to Richmond, but the weather stayed cool and there was plenty of water so it wasn't entirely awful. Contrary to the unnamed captain's claims, no one was shot along the way. Men who couldn't walk were loaded into wagons or slung across riderless horses. All the horses looked spavined and worn out, though the spring grass was lush upon the roadside. Louis knew that war used up horses worse than men. It was a fact of life, but it was sad nonetheless.

Like poor Red, moldering in a field somewhere, crows and buzzards picking at his carcass as if he hadn't been one of the finest cavalry horses Louis had ever had the privilege to ride.

They rode until they came to the outskirts of Richmond late in the day as the sky was turning from pale blue to grey-purple. In spite of the hour the city streets teemed with people, wagons, carriages, and more people. They were marched down Broad to Twentieth Street, where they turned south. Louis could see a river at the end of the street. He briefly wished for a better grasp of American geography, then reconsidered. It didn't matter much what the river's name was. It's not like he'd be sailing on it or even walking on its banks anytime soon. They were most certainly headed for one of the Confederate capital's many military prisons. They turned again onto Carey Street, which appeared to be a warren of brick warehouses. One block down, the soldiers stopped them.

Morley, who'd walked beside him for days, sighed and shook his head. "I was afraid this is where we were going."

Louis looked down at the Irishman, cocking an eyebrow in question.

"It's Libby Prison."

Louis drew in a deep breath. He looked at the massive three-story brick building, its many windows barred and closed. He'd heard that Libby had started its life as a warehouse, but after the war began Confederate officials converted it and other warehouses into prisons. Almost from the start Libby had been notoriously overcrowded, or so said the Union military men who had spent time there before being paroled out. According to them, Libby had no beds, no furniture of any kind, only large open rooms full of inadequately fed and clothed men. Floggings were administered daily for the tiniest of infractions and no man was exempt from the threat of the lash.

Inmates were divided into two groups. The enlisted men were led around to the back of the building, while Morley and Louis were taken in through the front door, along with two other officers Louis did not know. They were herded through the door to a small waiting room lined with benches. As the ranking Union officer, Louis found himself at the head of their tiny line. A door at the far end of the room opened and one of the guards pushed Louis through it. Inside the room, behind a neatly ordered desk, sat a small, clean-shaven, dark-haired man. A name plate read Major T. Turner.

Louis took one look at the man and felt bedraggled and dirty by comparison. Turner was perfectly coifed and turned out, hair oiled into place, buttons shining like a man who'd never been in the field, let alone in a battle.

Turner let Louis stand there for what felt like a long time but was probably only a few minutes. Louis, who'd seen other commanding officers play this game before, stood stock still and waited. The quiet scratching of Turner's pen was the room's only sound. Finally Turner put his pen down and looked up. "Name and rank," he barked.

Louis had played this game before too. He gave the man his particulars, keeping his tone even and respectful.

"Turn out your pockets," Turner said, jutting his chin at the table that stood on a sidewall of the room. Louis walked over to the table and emptied all his pockets. He had only his pipe, keys, matches, and a small pen knife.

"Money too," the captain ordered.

Louis shook his head. "I don't have any."

"Don't lie, prisoner. You Yankee officers always have green-backs." The captain abruptly pushed back his chair and rose. He walked to the door, opened it, and called out. "Private, could you come in here, please?"

A young man, no older than seventeen, entered the room behind Captain Turner.

Turner motioned to Louis. "Search the prisoner. He's hiding his money."

Louis sighed in frustration. "I am not hiding anything, sir. My money and my watch were taken from me by the captain who brought us here."

"Are you accusing a Confederate officer of theft, sir?"

Louis looked steadily at Captain Turner. He'd about had it with this fellow. "Are you questioning the word of a superior officer, Captain? I remind you, I am a colonel."

"Not in my Army, you're not. You're a traitor and a Northern aggressor and a foreigner to boot. Filthy dago, we wouldn't have the likes of you in the Confederate Army, no, we wouldn't. Real Americans, that's what we are." Turner ignored the young enlisted man he'd called into the room and began patting Louis down himself. "I'll find your money and know you for the filthy, rotten liar you foreign types always are."

"His boots sir," the private said as Turner finished his search. "They keep all manner of things in their boots."

"Remove your boots," Turner half-screamed at Louis.

Louis shook his head. "No."

"NO?" Turner's face turned bright red. He looked a little less dapper now.

Louis shook his head again. "I am the son of a count. I do not remove my own boots. I have servants for that." This wasn't at all true, but Louis would be damned if he was going to pull his boots off for this wretched excuse for a man.

Turner balled his hands into fists and struck the top of his desk. Then he sighed and seemed to catch himself. "Private, remove the prisoner's boots."

Louis managed to "accidentally" kick the private in the face during the boot imbroglio, which turned out to be a waste of time. Gentlemen did not keep their effects in their footwear. Captain Turner wouldn't have known that, not being a gentleman himself. It was a helpful point of etiquette that Louis was glad to point out to the Captain. Turner failed to be suitably grateful. He refused to return Louis's frock coat and boots to him. Louis lost his pipe and keys too.

A half hour later Louis found himself in a large, first-floor room of the prison, one reserved for Army officers. He bitterly regretted the loss of his pipe. He rarely smoked it and certainly wouldn't have tobacco for it in here, but it had been his father's and he carried it for good luck. Looking around, he was forced to concede that perhaps the pipe's store of luck had run out.

Morley entered the room a few minutes behind Louis. "What did you do?" the Irishman asked, looking down at Louis's sock-clad feet.

"Refused to take my boots off."

Morley chuckled, then looked around the room. A dark-haired, dark-eyed man in a ragged shirt and pants approached them and in a Spanish-accented voice said, "Welcome to hell!"

Life in Libby Prison quickly settled into a routine. The man who'd first introduced himself turned out to be Federico Cavada, a Sicilian and lieutenant colonel in Professor Lowe's Hot Air

Balloon Corps. He'd been aloft sketching enemy positions when his balloon had been shot down and he was captured. Cavada introduced them to a number of the other officers in the room, most of whom were lieutenants and captains, though a few majors and colonels dotted the room, as well as one brigadier general. Their quarters consisted of one large room, 103 feet long and 42 feet wide. Louis was sure because he had measured it one day with careful heel-to-toe steps. The room had five barred windows along the long outside wall, but prisoners were encouraged to stay away from them. Guards on the outside of the building took delight in shooting at any face that appeared in a window.

The necessary facilities consisted of half a dozen buckets placed behind a sheet strung on a rope in the corner of the room. These buckets served the needs of over a hundred men; the number varied on a daily basis depending upon who'd been newly admitted and who'd died. Some days no one died. Some days several men died, usually from scurvy or the bloody flux. They ate only bread and beans. Sometimes the beans had stringy meat in them, sometimes not. Louis heard that the enlisted men were fed only wormy corn bread. Occasionally the officers were served corn bread as well, or something bread-like in shape. The loaves were so hard and dry that the men jokingly called them iron-clads after the armored ships of the same name.

There were no beds and only a few tables and benches. Men sat against walls and squatted in the middle of the floor during the day. At night they slept cheek by jowl on damp plank floors. The lucky men had ragged blankets or coats, but the Confederates took a lot of their coats and tunics. Louis shivered in his shirtsleeves night after night, with only the man next to him to keep him warm. Louis thought it boded poorly for the Confederacy that they needed to steal clothes from their prisoners. A nation that could not clothe its army could not hope to win a war against a nation that could.

The men tried to keep busy, as best they could. Some of them created an organization jokingly called the *Richmond Prison Association*. One of the men drew a sign for the organization on the wall in one of the room's corners, near one of the tables and some rough benches. The letters *RPA* was printed in the middle of a circle of lice, under which was written, "Bite or Be Damned." They met there in the afternoons and volunteers gave lectures on their individual fields of expertise. Louis gave several talks. The one on Italian Independence had been particularly well-received, though not as popular as Cavada's talk on hot-air ballooning. They called the lecture series the *Libby-Lice-See-Um*, a play on the Greek word for a temple dedicated to education. It made Louis smile every time someone said it out loud.

In the midst of Louis's second week in Libby, the cell block's door opened and a dozen new men were pushed through. Louis gazed across the room idly at the men, more from boredom than from any real interest. Then he looked again. He pushed himself to his feet from his place on the wall and strode across the room. He grabbed one of the men and pulled him into a hard embrace. "Parnell, what are you doing here?"

Parnell held Louis out at arm's length. "About the same as what you're doing here, I'd imagine."

Louis smiled. Parnell had an Irish lilt not unlike Morley's, but unlike Morley, his was an upper-class accent that was considerably softer and more British than Morley's.

"They got me at Upperville, not even a week after Aldie. Right after Kilpatrick made me Lieutenant Colonel and put me in charge of the 4th." Parnell ducked his chin and blushed. "Just until you get back, you understand, Colonel."

Louis shook his head and clasped Parnell again. "Of course I do, you ninny. You were the best man for the job."

"The next best man, you mean."

Louis wasn't so sure, but he was awfully glad to have Parnell think so. A man could do worse than have a fellow like this at his side. Morley joined them, making their meeting a small version of the Crimean War reunion. Parnell explained how he'd come to be taken prisoner, a long, typically Irish tale that Louis suspected was only about half true. Which was fine. In Libby, a good story was worth rubies.

Some days there were visited by Confederate ladies. Mostly the ladies came to gawk and laugh at the men, but a few of the kinder ones brought books, jellies, and other treats. Louis soon found out that the best days were the days Miss Van Lew visited. One day he, Cavala, and Morley were sitting against the wall, talking desultorily about their favorite meals, when a commotion erupted by the room's one door. "It's Miss Van Lew," Cavala said, and pushed himself to his feet. He hurried off with no explanation. Morley shrugged, stood, and held his hand out to Louis. Pulling him to his feet he said, "Might as well go see what the fuss is about."

They pushed through the crowd to find a small older woman surrounded by smiling men. She had sharp, pointy features like a diminutive elf and was well past the age where a woman could be considered attractive. Still, there was something lovely about her. Her eyes took in everything and everyone, missing nothing. She reminded Louis of his mother, a lady of immense capability and who looked at life as a challenge to be won. A young, dark-skinned woman accompanied Miss Van Lew. She held an immense basket from which she was distributing soft rolls stuffed with pieces of ham. Louis took two, handed one to Morley and bit into his with more gusto than was gentlemanly. It was, quite simply, the best thing he'd ever tasted. Soft, sweet roll, salty, smoky ham, and a smear of something sticky. Louis peeked in his roll. It looked like jam, in between the ham and the bread. He gobbled the rest of it in one bite. He was licking his fingers when someone passed a magazine to him. It was a *Harpers Magazine*, full of articles and pictures. His heart sang at the simple pleasure of having something to read. After that he looked forward to Miss Van Lew's visits more than would have been, in different circumstances, proper for a married man. Some days Miss Van Lew brought food and books, other days she brought clothing. As the days grew shorter and colder she began bringing blankets and items that might serve as blankets. Louis ended up with half of what he suspected had once been a velvet curtain.

Best of all, Miss Van Lew carried notes and letters in and out of the prison. She and the ladies she brought with her, sometimes her mother, who looked just like her but was older and even smaller, sometimes the young black woman, had hiding places all over themselves, in concealed dress pockets, bonnets, muffs, and even in their hair. One day she took a letter to Mary out for Louis. He used a scrap of paper from the back of one of the magazines and a pencil he borrowed from one of the men. Whether or not she got it or not he did not know, but the writing of it helped to ease his loneliness. After that he would lie on his patch of floor at night and write Mary letters in his head, letters that would never see paper let alone postage.

It was enough because it had to be.

Chapter Twelve

Richmond, Virginia—October 1863–February 1864

By October, conditions at the prison had deteriorated to such an extent that not even Miss Van Lew could bring succor to the suffering prisoners. Food rations were reduced, then reduced again. The meat disappeared from the beans, and the wheat bread was replaced with hard corn bread. And for some reason the beans were always undercooked and hard to chew. Captain Turner became increasingly irritable, roaming the prison looking for infractions that he could use to punish the men in his charge. He took increasing delight in beating the men. One day Turner saw Colonel Rose spit at their spittoon box and miss. He sent the poor man to the cellars, to solitary confinement for forty-eight hours. That was the bad news. The good news was that Colonel Rose came back from the basement with an escape idea.

Rose's plan was a simple one. During the day the men were allowed to roam the building, though the officers generally confined themselves to their space and the enlisted men to theirs. When the guards let Rose out of the solitary cell they just unlocked and opened the door, leaving him to find his own way back. Instead Rose explored the building's basement. At the far end of the building he found a room with dirt floors and walls made from crumbling stone. He thought they could tunnel out from there.

For the next four months men took turns making their way to the basement and digging. They used spare toilet buckets and bean spoons and whatever else they could find. Some men dug a hatful of dirt and removed it, dropping it out one of the windows at night. Some of the men managed to get word to Miss Van Lew about their plan. She organized a crew of people to remove the dirt from under the windows before dawn each morning, thereby preventing their plan from being discovered. The men also spread some of the dirt around the basement floor, tamping it down so that it blended in with the existing floor.

Louis took his turn digging at their tunnel. They removed a large rock from the wall and worked their way west. The idea was to pass underneath the prison yard and exit inside a small storage shed at the far end of the property. They only worked an hour or two each day, both so not too many men went missing at one time and because the narrow tunnel could not accommodate a large number of diggers. Louis found tunnel digging invigorating. The work was easy and every inch of progress they made created hope.

The other bit of good news came in late October. Captain Turner announced that he would allow packages from the United States Sanitary Commission, a private relief agency that had the support of the Union government. Turner put Brigadier General Dow in charge of distributing the items, mostly clothing and blankets, but also some canned and dried food. The Sanitary Commission sent crates and crates of stuff to Libby and another prison camp on Belle Island. In his new role, Dow was in the enviable position of being able to leave Libby several times a week to distribute goods at Belle Isle, in the midst of the river, just outside Richmond.

One cold morning in mid-November a boot nudged Louis's shoulder. He peered up to find one of the guards staring down at him.

"Captain Turner wants to see you. *Now.*"

Louis's mind spun. Had they found out about the tunnel? He sat up and looked around the room. Everyone else was sleeping. No. The discovery of an escape tunnel would have caused a bigger response.

He pushed himself to his feet and followed the guard. Captain Turner sat behind his desk again, as dandified as ever.

Turner gestured for Louis to sit. "Colonel Cesnola." Turner abruptly stopped speaking and shuffled some papers. "Ah, here it is. I've terminated General Dow's appointment as Commissioner of Distribution for the relief goods. As the next ranking Union officer, the job is now yours. Do you understand?"

Louis nodded, his mind awhirl at the idea of leaving this place, even for only a few hours a week. "Thank you, Captain. When do I start?"

"First thing tomorrow. There's quite a lot to do. You will be escorted to Belle Isle by two guards. You will not start by distributing goods. You will take down the names of prisoners and catalogue their needs. My men will distribute the goods, per your written instructions. The Sanitary Commission has provided these forms." Turner held a sheaf of papers to Louis and continued. "You will not speak to the prisoners other than to collect their names and record their requirements. You will not have conversations with the prisoners, nor carry communication for them. If you do you will be terminated. As I did with General Dow."

Ah! Dow was a good man, Louis thought, and he had no doubt that Dow had tried to help the Belle Isle prisoners and been caught. Louis bit his lip and thought. "Am I to accomplish this task alone?"

"You may choose two men, but I must approve them. You will leave Libby each morning at 10, starting tomorrow, and be back before dinner roll call at 4 until you've worked your way through all the prisoners at Belle Isle. Do we have an accord?"

Louis agreed that they did.

After that Libby Prison life got both better and worse. The good news was that he got to leave the prison each day. The bad news was that he had to go to Belle Island to do it. And Belle Island turned out to be the worst place Louis had ever been.

That morning Louis chose Colonels Boyd and Von Schrader, both infantry men, to be his assistants. By afternoon he had Turner's approval for the two men. He'd have liked to have taken Parnell and Morley, but both men were sick with the flu and in no shape for anything more strenuous than hourly visits to the necessary buckets.

The next morning they were escorted to the prison doors, handcuffed, and put on a wagon. The guards assured the three men that they'd be uncuffed when they were safely across the river to the island, then re-cuffed for the trip home. Louis was so glad to be out of the prison that he didn't care if they'd stripped him naked and paraded him through Richmond.

It was a cold day, but clear and calm. The ride to the river took only minutes. They were ordered out of the wagon and onto a small barge for the short trip across the water to the island. As they crossed, Louis peered ahead. The island was small, with a short hill in the center. A few bare trees studded the landscape, but the overwhelming impression was of barren ground, covered with so many men that it looked like an angry anthill. Most worrisome of all was the dearth of buildings or even tents. He could see just one building, which probably housed the men in charge of this place. Louis feared that while he was feeling put out about sleeping on a floor with an old curtain for a blanket these men had been sleeping outside, exposed to the Virginia winter.

They were met by the man in charge of the island prison facility, a small, fastidiously groomed man reminiscent of Captain Turner but the two men's resemblance ended at their appearance. Lieutenant Bossieux was polite, well-spoken, and in all ways gentlemanly. He ordered Louis, Boyd, and Von Schrader unshackled and afterwards treated them as if they were equals, not prisoners.

"A leetle tour is in order, then, eh," he said in a heavy French accent. He gestured them to follow him across the empty parade ground that stood in front of his headquarters. "I have over six thousand Union prisoners under my care and I regret to say that they are not as well taken care of as I'd like. I have repeatedly requested tents and been refused. I designed a series of barracks that would have housed the men out of the weather for very little cost, but was also refused. There is little I can do, I'm afraid."

Louis gazed around him. Men in faded blue pants and ragged shirts stood everywhere, as thick on the ground as lice in a Libby Prison inmate's head. All the men looked gaunt and hollow-eyed. Most had neither coats nor hats. They shivered in the cold, half-naked and exposed to the chilly November air.

Louis was horrified to note that none of them had boots. He knew why. The Confederate Army had its own problems, chief among them an inability to provide soldiers with adequate footwear, clothing, and food. The Union prisoners' boots went to Confederate soldiers, leaving the prisoners to wrap their feet in such rags as they could find. They huddled around small, smoking fires, but, unlike every military camp Louis had ever been in, this one released no cooking smells into the air. Nor coffee smells. And it was quiet, as if the men were too tired and down-hearted to behave as men in camp did, singing songs, telling tall tales in loud voices, and in a hundred other ways acting like men without female supervision.

The first day, Louis, Boyd, and Von Schrader enrolled one company of a hundred men. Louis thought he'd never seen a more wretched group of men, emaciated, dirty, and hollow-eyed like wild men from the pages of a fantasy novel. They split the men into three lines and each of them took a group, interviewing the prisoners one at a time. Theoretically the men were supposed to only volunteer their names and their needs, but each man had a story to tell, a special request, some terrible and unfillable need. Louis began to dread each man who stepped up to him, unable to hear more heart-rending tales of need. By the end of the week, Louis and his two assistants had begun to envy General Dow. The entire delight of leaving the prison each day was consumed by the mental toll their job exacted. Part of the problem was the sheer scale of the job. They had six thousand men to get through and until they did, no man got a single blanket or coat. And each day the weather shifted more toward winter. Louis felt an almost hysterical need to work faster and longer.

At the end of the first week, the three of them decided to apply for permission to stay at Belle Isle, rather than returning to Libby each afternoon. As bad as the island prison was, there was just too much to do and not enough time to do it before the snow fell. Louis carefully composed his letter and gave it to Turner to send up the chain of prison command. The answer came in three curt words: *No, certainly not.*

At the end of November, food rations at Belle Isle were again reduced. Each company of men got one bucket of boiled potatoes or corn bread to be shared amongst all one hundred of them. Of course there wasn't enough to go around. Pneumonia, brought on by starvation and the cold, spread like wildfire through the camp. By the time the blankets, boots, and coats were distributed it was too late for too many of the poor buggers. Louis tried talking to Lieutenant Bossieux about the conditions, but the lieutenant was powerless to do anything about it, or so he claimed. Louis wanted to believe him but as the days grew colder and the death tolls mounted it was hard to believe anything that came out of the mouth of a man clad in Confederate grey.

Plundering compounded their problems at Belle Isle. The Sanitary Commission stores were kept at a warehouse next to Libby and were, at least theoretically, under guard. But each morning when Louis, Boyd, and Von Schrader visited the warehouse to pack up the day's supplies, they found boxes missing. Some mornings they found ragged Rebel uniforms stuffed in corners, clearly left their by men who broke in and re-outfitted themselves in donated clothing. Louis complained to Captain Turner about the thefts, but Turner wouldn't even admit there was a problem, let alone act to fix it.

Each day the three of them returned from Belle Isle entirely down-hearted and exhausted. Though food was becoming as scarce at Libby as on the island, Morley and Parnell managed to save Louis a morsel or two most days. They also kept him updated on the prisoners' basement project, which was making good progress.

Miss Van Lew continued to visit, though she too was having a harder time finding enough food to share. Apparently everyone in Richmond was suffering that winter, not just the Union prisoners. Christmas was a grim day, made only slightly better by the prisoners' attempts to cheer themselves up with carols and tales of home. Mostly they told stories of dinners they'd eaten, or talked about favorite foods cooked by beloved mothers and wives.

Louis missed these meager festivities. Instead he spent the day on a little makeshift bed Morley rigged for him. Christmas morning he woke up with the fever sweats and by evening he was having trouble breathing. Morley thought that Louis had caught a cold from the men at Belle Isle. Or maybe pneumonia. Scurvy, the scourge of all the prisoners, exacerbated his illness. He'd been weak and achy all through December, like most of the men who'd been kept for months on a diet of corn and beans. Louis's scurvy was compounded by the fact that he never ate lunch at Belle Isle and often got back to Libby after dinner and so missed that meal too. Both Morley and Parnell did what they could to save him food, but it was never enough. Louis was not surprised that he had finally fallen really sick. Instead he wondered how any of them, in either prison, were still alive at all.

It took Louis two weeks to recover from whatever ailed him. Or at least to recover enough to go back to work. He coughed up great gobs of green goo every day, but he kept to his feet and that was good enough. When Louis returned to Belle Isle after his enforced sick leave he found that someone in charge had decided that he, Boyd, and Von Schrader could do more than make lists: they could distribute supplies. This made their job somewhat less awful. There was little more gratifying than giving a freezing man a blanket or a scrap to eat. And in spite of the pilfering back at Libby, there seemed to be a near-inexhaustible supply of crates from the Sanitary Commission.

One cold and miserable day, a group of five Confederate officers—one colonel, one major, and three lieutenants—showed up in the yard with a pile of handbills. The lieutenants handed them out while the other two stood around consulting with Lieutenant Bossieux. Louis took one of the bills and read it. They were offering four hundred soldiers the chance to be paroled from Belle Isle. All they had to do was work in a shoe factory making boots for Confederate soldiers for six months. Louis waited until the Confederate men and Bossieux were done, then called all the men in the yard together.

"Listen, this sounds like a good deal, but it's treason. Every boot you make, you put a soldier in the field. That soldier kills one of us. Or more. Every boot will cost Union soldiers' lives. And if that doesn't convince you, you can bet the Army will court martial anyone who works for the Rebs. You'll be paroled, free for a few days, then arrested and thrown in a Union prison. Spread the word. Tell the men that no one volunteers."

"But we'll die in here, sir."

Louis looked at the ragged, emaciated man who'd spoken. "There are worse things than an honorable death."

The men nodded in agreement.

Louis turned away to find Lieutenant Bossieux standing behind him. The Frenchman was red in the face with fury. "I have to report this, you know. You'll lose this position and die in Libby."

Louis summoned up a fat gob of phlegm and spat it at the Lieutenant's feet. "There are worse things than an honorable death."

He did lose his Belle Isle job the next day, but he heard through the prison grapevine that when Confederate officials returned to Belle Isle they could find not one Union volunteer for their Shoes for Amnesty deal.

When the tunnel was finally finished Louis couldn't stand. Weakened by his Belle Isle work and even smaller food portions at Libby, his pneumonia came raging back. He burned white hot, then freezing cold, reminding him of the time he'd had typhoid in the Crimea. His chest felt like it had an anvil on it and his exhalations sounded like he had a tiny steam train in his chest.

They came to him in the middle of the night, both Morley and Parnell.

"It's time, Louis," Morley whispered.

Louis had already made up his mind. He'd thought about it hard and he couldn't do it. He couldn't endanger the rest of the men. Or, if he was honest, to hell with all the men. It was Morley and Parnell he couldn't endanger. They were the ones he cared about. If he let them, they'd sacrifice themselves for him, but he couldn't let them. He shook his head slowly, back and forth, his hair rubbing against his boots, which he'd taken to using as a pillow.

"Yes," Parnell hissed back. "There's two of us and one of you. We can get you out."

"Can't crawl that far," Louis whispered back. He wasn't giving up this chance for freedom lightly. There was no way Louis would make it down the tunnel. The men reported it was a good sixty feet long and just barely big enough for one man. He'd collapse and plug up the tunnel like a cork in a bottle.

"You can do this, Colonel!"

Louis could hear the desperation in Parnell's voice.

Morley, the more practical of the two, spoke up. "He's right and you know it, Parnell."

Parnell spoke into the silence. "Then we'll stay. If we leave him, he'll die."

Louis shook his head again. "Go. Tell." Louis looked hard at his men. He could see it in their faces. They wanted to go, but felt guilty about the wanting. He mustered his strength. "I'm ordering you to go."

After they left Louis lay there in the dark, tears running down his face, soaking into his boots. And then he remembered to pray.

The guards discovered the missing men at dawn roll call. It took a little longer to discover the tunnel. At first the guards thought the missing men were simply evading roll call. Soon enough they figured out it was no trick and went looking for the escape hole. It took them a few days to find it. The last escaped prisoner had rolled the rock back into the foundation wall, effectively disguising the tunnel.

After the escape, Miss Van Lew visited. Secreted in her basket of corn dodgers was a *Richmond Examiner*. Louis waited his turn and, when the newspaper made its way around to where he lay, he read the article. The headline read:

119 Prisoners Escape Libby!
Guards Arrested &
Placed in Castle Thunder

The article said that Richmond authorities believed the guards let the Union prisoners out of the prison after being bribed or paid off. Louis chuckled at the thought.

In the end forty-eight men were recaptured in the woods outside Richmond and two unlucky fellows drowned in the James River when the boat they had stolen capsized. The rest of the men, fifty-nine in all, made it out of Confederate-held territory. Both Parnell and Morley were among that fifty-nine, a fact for which Louis thanked the blessed Madonna in his prayers each morning for weeks afterwards.

In spite of the fact that less than one in ten men had escaped the prison, the mood among the men left behind was ebullient. The guards lost their self-confidence and counted roll call several times a day and sometimes in the middle of the night, but even that couldn't dampen the prisoners' spirits.

Cavada took over Louis's care and feeding. The Sanitary Commission sent cases and cases of canned German cabbage to the prison, a pickled delicacy called sauerkraut that Louis had eaten long ago in Italy. The briny juice stung the sores in his mouth, but within two weeks of daily doses of the stuff Louis began to feel better. So too did a number of other prisoners.

When Cavada asked him if he missed being the Commissioner Louis admitted to having mixed feelings. "It was nice, leaving the prison. And seeing the way the sun sparkled off the river, that was good too. But," Louis shook his head, "I do not miss the island."

Cavada cocked his dark head at him. "Why not? You were doing good there, weren't you?"

Louis shrugged. "I suppose. But it was too much. Like trying to hold back the tide, you know?"

Cavada shook his head uncomprehendingly.

Louis thought about how to explain. "It wasn't right, that camp. I've been a soldier by profession my whole life. Since I was a boy. I've been to war in Europe and in the Crimea. I've seen death, in all its different aspects. All soldiers have."

"True," Cavada said, "though I admit I do not have your experience. I have only ever been in this war and then I've seen my battles from the air, high above the blood misery. It is little like being God."

Louis laughed a humorless laugh. "Most soldiers see death, not like gods, but like men. Up close, where it's dirty and terrifying. But nowhere have I seen anything like Belle Isle. Those poor men, their feet frozen, their long, pale, hungry faces; a kind of perpetual motion given to their bodies by the millions of vermin that devour their flesh. They fight, month after month, a weary fight against scurvy, fever, diarrhea, lung congestion, and despair. They would cry out to me, in life and in my dreams, 'Oh Colonel! Give me something to eat.' I think it was my heart that made me sick and the scurvy and pneumonia are only words for the nameless horror that comes of seeing men like that."

"It sounds terrible," Cavada said quietly.

Louis shook his head. "Terrible is not the word. There is no word for what it was. And is still now, I'm sure."

Ten months after he first entered Libby, Captain Turner called Louis to his office. This time he did not offer Louis a seat. "If it were up to me none of you damned Yankees would be paroled, but it seems that Jeff Davis has a friend recently captured who he wants back. You're to be traded for some colonel named Brown."

Louis stood stock still, afraid he'd heard wrong.

Turner held out a piece of paper. Louis took it and read. It was indeed his parole paper. There was a short note from Senator Harris, telling Louis he could thank his wife for his release. It was Mary who had engineered the trade for Colonel Brown, a man who was a personal friend of the Confederate president.

Louis smiled as he read the note. Leave it to Mary to find one of Jeff Davis's friends among the thousands and thousands of men in Union prisons.

Forty-eight hours later, he was back in Washington City and twenty-four after that he arrived in New York. Mary met him at the station. He was nervous about seeing her. When he'd last seen her he'd been fit as a fiddle. Now he was skin and bones, had missing teeth, and his hair was patchy. And he was pretty sure he still had lice.

She didn't seem to notice. She was wearing a broad smile and holding a small bundle. She held the bundle out to him. He shook his head, mindful of the lice, then he leaned over it and looked into the blankets. It was tiny, dark-haired, dark-eyed baby, born while he'd been locked in Libby.

Mary pulled back the soft, ivory-colored blanket so he could see his daughter. "I named her Gabrielle, after your mother."

It was happiest day of his life.

Chapter Thirteen

UNTIL THE BITTER END

New York and Virginia—March–September 1864

He'd had enough of war. He'd done his part and he was tired all the way down to his bones. He ate as much as he could and slept when he could, but his body felt like it belonged to someone else. And the dreams were awful. And then there were Mary and Gabrielle. His girls needed him.

Then Parnell came to visit.

Hobson showed him in. Mary took one look at Parnell in his cavalry uniform, put down her knitting, and wordlessly left the room. Later Louis realized she'd known exactly why Parnell was there.

The Irishman didn't mince any words. "The 4th needs you, Colonel. The men, they believe in you." Parnell was perched on the edge of one of Mary's delicate French chairs, looking as out of place as a horse in a kitchen. "And after last summer, the Army's convinced of the cavalry's importance. The 4th could make the difference. And if the Union Army has another great victory like Gettysburg the country will re-elect Mr. Lincoln, but if we lose, they'll elect a peace candidate as sure as I'm sitting here."

Louis sighed. "Peace sounds like a good idea to me. And I've liked McClellan." George McClellan had pretty much declared himself the peace candidate, even though the election was still months away. "I'd think you'd be for peace too. After Libby." He left the rest unspoken.

Parnell stood and paced up and down the parlor. "I'm a soldier. It's all I know. And I don't want peace if it's not an honorable peace. Nor do you. We've given too much for it to be wasted. This war is like your Italian war, it's for real freedom."

Louis snorted. "Parnell, your people are not exactly fond of the coloreds."

"My people have been abused by the English for centuries. No one knows poverty and inequality like the Irish Catholics. 'My people,' as you call them, hate the blacks because they've got no one else below them. They've got to blame their misery on someone, you see. But they're wrong. As long as there's one slave in this country none of us will be free. Louis, you've said as much yourself." He shook his head, then crossed the room to stand in front of Louis. "I'm a soldier. You're my commanding officer. We need to finish this thing so it's done right."

Louis sent Parnell away without an answer.

Mary cried when Louis told her he was thinking about going back. When she was done crying, she argued. "We need you too, you know."

Louis decided she was right. That night in bed he promised her he'd stay home. And after the way he'd been treated by the army he wasn't too sure his new country needed him. They still had not recognized his status as a brigade commander with a generalship.

Then the next day the newspaper said that General Halleck had been relieved, at his own request, of command of the Army of the Potomac. Mr. Lincoln put General Ulysses Grant in Halleck's place and gave General Sherman the western army.

Louis thought about it all day. Mr. Lincoln might just win the war with that combination. Everyone said Grant and Sherman knew how to fight. But he'd made a promise to Mary and a man didn't go back on his word, not to anyone, but particularly not to his wife.

Parnell wrote him from Virginia, where the 4th was once more running reconnaissance missions. Louis put the letters away and played family man for the first time in his life. He and Mary went shopping together, ate together, and slept together. In the mornings over breakfast he scanned the *New York Times* for word of cavalry corps. He helped little Gabrielle build castles of blocks on the floor of the nursery. She was really too small for blocks, but she seemed to like lying on the carpet with him.

One afternoon, Mary caught him using blocks and tin horses to show the baby some cavalry maneuvers. "Did you see the newspaper this morning, dear?"

He put down the horse he'd been holding and looked over to where she was standing in the doorway. "I did."

"General Grant put Sheridan in charge of the cavalry corps."

Louis noticed that while his wife looked relaxed, her hand, which gripped the door frame, was white with tension. "And about time too. Sheridan's the real thing," he said.

"You admire General Sheridan."

He nodded. "He knows how to fight. And he respects his officers."

It was her turn to nod.

They looked at each other for a moment.

Finally Mary spoke. "I'm sorry, Louis." She let go of the doorway and started to cry.

He scrambled to his feet so fast he startled the baby. Gabrielle wailed so he picked her up and carried her to where Mary was standing. "Sh. Shush now, baby." Mary held out her hands for the baby. As he handed Gabrielle to her mother he asked the question. "What are you sorry for?"

She wiped her eyes with her sleeve. "I tried to keep you here. It was wrong of me. I knew what you were when I married you. I promised myself I would honor who you are and here I've kept you away from what you were meant to do."

"Oh, darling." He put his arms around his wife and daughter. They smelled like rose water and baby powder. For just a second he wondered about the men on Belle Isle. How long had it been since any of them had smelled anything half as sweet? "We married as a business deal. But then I fell in love with you. I didn't mean to but I did. That changes everything."

She wiped at her eyes with the back of her hand and shook her head. "It doesn't. Your Parnell was right. I was listening at the door. He said your men needed you. What he didn't say is that you need your men."

He felt a hot flood of shame at the realization that she should see into him so clearly. He owed her. They had a child now. A man didn't belong to himself once he had a family. "I don't," he protested.

"You do," she insisted. "I want you to go and I want you to win this damn war. And then I want you to come home. We can be together until we die. After the war." She looked at him, her eyes squinted in fierce determination. "You must. It's who you are. And that's the man I've come to love."

He left them a week later. It was the hardest thing he'd ever done, but part of him was relieved to be going, which only made it harder.

~

He rejoined the 4th just in time to march on Lee's armies in the Virginia wilderness. Louis was glad to be out of the Shenandoah Valley, where the Union armies had never had much luck against the Rebs. And now, with General P. T. Beauregard back in charge in the Shenandoah, it was a good place to avoid. Grant sent General Butler to sortie with Beauregard, but kept most of his cavalry corps for his own attack on Lee.

One morning in early May, General Sheridan called all his regimental commanders to a meeting at his headquarters. There were too many of them to meet in the General's tent, so they sat outside in a conglomeration of camp chairs and tree stumps. Louis couldn't have been more surprised when he first saw Sheridan. Based on the reports of Sheridan's prowess in the western theater he'd been expecting an overwhelming bear of a man, someone larger than life and twice as hard. Sheridan had gained fame not only for his battlefield successes but for his absolute intolerance of theft and privateering. Every army Louis had ever been in had problems with theft, from soldiers stealing food and horses to civilians commandeering military goods and selling them on the black market. In Missouri two years ago, cavalry officers had been applying for reimbursement for horses they stole from civilians. Sheridan found out about it and put an end to the practice, declaring that no force on nature could compel him to steal. The officers' corps had a fit, but General Halleck backed him up and Sheridan prevailed. A man who could stop military corruption would be a giant of a man.

So when a small, brown-haired chap stepped out of the commander's tent Louis took little notice. Then he noticed that all the colonels and majors stood and saluted. He did the same and looked harder at the fellow. He wore the pale blue trousers with a yellow stripe down the side that were the hallmark of a cavalry officer and his shoulder straps carried two stars. Was this the great Philip Sheridan? It wasn't just that he was not a bit over five and a half feet tall, he was funny looking, with the short, bandy legs of an Irishman and disproportionately long arms. Louis couldn't believe it. But then the man began to speak and Louis did believe it.

"Men, this Army has long failed to believe in the cavalry. We've been used for scouting, defensive maneuvers, and the like. Previous commanders of the Army of the Potomac failed to understand the uses to which a cavalry corps might be put, and in so doing made grave tactical errors. General Grant will not make those mistakes. I fought with him in the west and I'm here to tell you, he knows how to use the cavalry."

A rousing round of "huzzahs" came from the cavalry officer corps, made all the more impressive by the fact that officers did not generally engage in that sort of enthusiastic outburst. Louis joined in. It was good to be back in camp with men who understood the art of war.

Sheridan waited for the men to quiet before continuing. "General Grant commands that we take this war to Lee. No more reacting to Lee, waiting for Lee, chasing Lee. We're going to put ourselves between his army and Richmond. He'll have no choice but to attack. And we'll keep at him until we've exhausted his men, his horses, and his supplies. Grant says we'll hammer them into submission." Sheridan swung his Hardee hat up onto his head and ordered them dismissed.

After that, each regimental commander, most of them colonels, reported to their division commanders. After the second division's successes at Gettysburg, the 4th New York's star had risen. Though the regiment had lost a number of officers on the road to Gettysburg, on the last day of the three-day battle they'd managed to repulse Jeb Stuart's raid on the Union flank.

In spite of Sheridan's brave words, in the early days of the Overland Campaign General Meade relegated the cavalry to its same old tired tricks: reconnaissance and protecting the army's rear. It was exhausting and disheartening work, with no chances of glory and plenty of chances for death and mayhem. At the end of the three-day Battle of the Wilderness, Louis sat exhausted in the doorway of his tent. They'd accomplished little in the battle. The scrub brush had been too thick for anything but infantry fighting. They'd had their chance on the third day. At one point Grant realized Lee was moving his men around to the crossroads and sent Gregg's cavalry division on a swift mission to stop them, but they'd been too late.

Louis eased off his boots and sighed. His arm ached, as did his head. The only thing this damnable part of Virginia had going for it was a bunch of creeks, making water plenteous, which was good for men and horses. He was thinking about turning in for the night when Parnell came striding across the camp toward his tent.

"Wait till you hear this, Colonel," he said. He took his hat off, sketched a quick salute, and then slapped his hat against his thigh. "We've got new orders."

Louis shook his head. "What is it? Tending supply wagons? Baby-sitting the rear flank? And have you replaced me as the regimental commander?"

Parnell shook his head and grinned. "No. Gregg sent me to Sheridan's tent with a parcel of papers. I was standing there waiting when General Meade came along, mad as a wet hen. So I stepped back and made myself kind of inconspicuous like. Meade was yelling at Sheridan about how the cavalry had failed in reconnaissance and let Lee get through. So Sheridan, he goes all calm-like and he says, 'What say we go see Grant about this?'"

Louis perked up. Suddenly the gathering gloom seemed less dark. "Really?"

"Uh-huh. So I tagged along. Grant's just a few tents down from Sheridan. When we get there, Meade's ranting and raving about how Sheridan made a mess of things. Then Sheridan says, 'If my men had a chance to fight, like you said we would, we'd whip Stuart tomorrow.'"

Louis smiled. "What did Grant say about that?"

"Well, that's the best part." Parnell chuckled. "Meade started blustering like he does, then Grant says, 'Well, I reckon he knows what he's talking about. Let him start right out and do it.'"

Louis leapt to his feet. "You're not making this up?"

Parnell shook his head, grinning from ear to ear. "We're off after ole Jeb Stuart tomorrow."

In celebration, Louis broke out a bottle of brandy from a case he'd hauled down from New York and the two of them got mildly tipsy. Then they went bed early.

The U.S. Cavalry mustered before dawn. As the spring sun crested the horizon, turning the sky from purple-blue to light blue, Louis gathered his men, hurling orders over his shoulder every few seconds. An hour later, the most powerful cavalry force ever assembled in North America rode out of camp. They had over ten thousand mounted men and thirty-two artillery pieces, mostly 12-pound Napoleons. The Napoleon was, in Louis's estimation, the finest light field cannon ever made, notable for its reliability and deadliness. The gun was also extremely suitable for lightning raids, being maneuverable and light enough to be pulled by a single healthy horse. Their goals were simple: engage and defeat Jeb Stuart's cavalry and in the process distract Lee from Grant's larger force.

The first day, they button-hooked north, then east, around Lee's army. When they hit the turnpike they headed south, making good time for a force of their size. They bivouacked just north of the Anna River. Gregg sent out scouts who found the Confederate Army not five miles to the west, seemingly unaware that a huge cavalry contingent was circling behind them.

The next day, they crossed the river and took Beaver Dam Station on the Virginia Central Railroad line. The best part about taking the station, at least as far as Louis was concerned, was the Confederate train they took while they were there. The rail cars were stuffed with captured Union soldiers on their way to Belle Isle prison. They loaded the men down with food and medical supplies and sent them back to Grant's army with a small cavalry escort. Louis's heart rejoiced at the sight of the blue-clad men marching away. They had no idea of the hell that had awaited them in Richmond and now they never would.

The main cavalry body continued south, using a rough mountain road. Every hour Louis expected Stuart's cavalry to burst from the trees and attack but it didn't happen. They rode along unmolested for the entirety of the second day. When they made camp that night all the men could talk about was their luck and the hope that it would hold. According to scouts they were one day's ride from Richmond, the capital of the Confederacy. Louis was not the only man in Sheridan's force who went to bed that night dreaming of marching into Richmond the next day, unopposed and victorious. It was unlikely, given that rear scouts reported Stuart was on the move and across the Anna River, but it was hard not to dream.

The third day, just outside a tiny town called Yellow Tavern, Stuart's cavalry finally caught up with them. From the river he must have swung east and used Telegraph Road, which was wider and smoother than the road they were on. The Confederates fired from a low ridge line that ran along the road, but Sheridan wheeled the cavalry and they took their positions, outshooting the Rebels with their new, rapid-firing Spencer carbines. After three hours of skirmishing, cannon fire, and general mayhem Louis's 4th was in the brigade that charged the hilltop.

Slashing and screaming as he rode, Louis could see Jeb Stuart at the top of the hill. The man waved his sword and hollered encouragement to his troops. Louis watched as the 5th Michigan Cavalry crested the hill. They overran Stuart's position, but before Louis could blink, Stuart's men pushed them back. Louis watched astounded and in disbelief. It was no wonder Stuart was widely considered the finest cavalry man the United States had ever produced. Before he could turn his horse and join the retreat, one of the men from the 5th Michigan stopped his horse halfway down the hill and dismounted no more than ten yards from where Louis was. The man calmly pulled his pistol from his belt, leveled it, and fired at Stuart.

Stuart jerked like he'd been swatted with an invisible hand. His saber arm flew backwards and the rest of his body followed. He leaned and fell off his horse. Louis watched the man's plumed hat tumble off his head and roll upon the ground. It stopped, a good six feet from the man who used to wear it. The men around Stuart froze for what seemed like an hour, but was probably no longer than two or three seconds.

That night in camp they took stock. The battle at Yellow Tavern had been, by any measure, an immense success. True, they lost six hundred men and nearly as many horses, but they also freed thousands of Union prisoners and captured three hundred prisoners of their own. Most importantly, Jeb Stuart was dead. The great bugaboo of the Union Cavalry, long thought nearly invincible, had been killed in Sheridan's raid. Louis thought about Parnell saying that Sheridan had claimed he could whip Stuart if Grant let him go. He had. *They had.* If they could do that, what else could they do?

They found out over the course of the next month. The day after Yellow Tavern they circled east in the driving rain, skirmishing at Meadow's Bridge to force a crossing. General Custer led the charge across the bridge. Though Custer was five years younger than Louis, who was two months shy of his thirty-second birthday, he was already a General. Louis marked it down to the man's unquestionable bravery and brash American style.

The Confederate Cavalry still stood between them and Richmond so they made for Petersburg. Each morning before dawn, the regimental commanders met at Sheridan's headquarters. These meetings were often the best part of Louis's day, in part because Sheridan usually had updates on the main body of the Army of the Potomac. Sheridan described how General Grant harried, poked, and engaged Lee at every turn. At Spotsylvania, North Anna River, and Totopotomoy Creek, Grant fought Lee's army like a man who didn't know better. They were not always victorious, but Louis and the others understood that victory wasn't the point: wearing out the enemy was. The Confederate Army was smaller, less well provisioned, and, if the news was accurate, each casualty-laden battle cost Lee men he could no longer replace and made Southerners less eager to continue the war. Louis also enjoyed the meeting because they provided him occasion to see and hear General Sheridan. The more he knew of the man the more he respected him. Here was a man who knew how to fight and he surrounded himself with men who would fight. Every day the war went on Louis faced death and he was glad to do it. It was far better to die in the saddle fighting for men who understood how cavalries and armies worked than to die by inches in a place like Libby Prison. Or at home.

In early June, Sheridan gave orders to attack Charlottesville, Virginia, just to the northwest of their current position. Their objectives were twofold: draw the Confederate Cavalry north with them and destroy a section of the Virginia Central Railroad.

Sheridan's words that morning were blunt. "Make no mistake, men, many of us won't be coming back from this venture. We'll get a jump on them, but they'll catch up while we're tearing up tracks and blowing bridges and they'll hit us hard. It's what I'd do because if they lose that railroad they will lose Richmond. Not right away, but losing the Virginia Central will be the beginning of the end."

After the meeting Louis walked up to Sheridan and held out his hand. "Whatever happens, sir, it was an honor to serve under you."

Sheridan brusquely nodded his head. "You're that Italian fellow, aren't you?"

Louis clicked his heels and offered his general a salute. "Louis Palma di Cesnola, sir."

"I hear this is your third war. Ever think about quitting?" Sheridan took a seat at his camp desk and gestured Louis to join him.

"Never, sir." Louis paused. "And every day, sir."

The two men shared a grim smile. Around them the camp bustled, men moving to and fro, packing horses, mules, and wagons. In front of Philip Sheridan's tent the two battle-hardened warriors had a quiet talk, creating an island of calm in a sea of hustle and bustle. Sheridan asked him about the siege of Sevastopol, clearly thinking about the possibility of besieging Richmond. Louis asked the General about the American west, where he'd spent years fighting the Indians. Sheridan said a man couldn't believe how big the west was, how large the sky or the mountains, until he saw it for himself. Louis thought maybe he'd go some day, when this wretched war was finally over. They parted after an hour, each to prepare for the next battle.

Later, Louis heard that the battle for Trevelyan Station was the largest cavalry battle of the Civil War. It was hard to tell from the inside of it. It was certainly the bloodiest battle Louis had ever been in.

They left their camp outside Cold Harbor at dawn and struck north, back up and around Richmond. Sheridan kept their pace deliberately slow. There was no purpose in playing the stalking horse if they didn't make themselves an enticing target. Nonetheless, scouts didn't report Confederate movement in their direction until their third day's march. Happily for the Confederates, Sheridan's Army was making its way north over the countryside on small, poorly maintained roads, leaving the wide turnpike for the enemy's use. General Hampton's cavalry caught up with them on the road between Richmond and Charlottesville.

They fought for two long, hot days. Louis's New York 4th, as part of General Gregg's division, took the Confederates' right flank, while Sheridan sent General Custer's unit wide around the Confederate rear guard. They pushed the Rebs back all that day, but at tremendous cost. It wasn't the sort of thing a man liked to think about later.

That night at roll call Louis discovered that over thirty of his men had been killed or captured. It could have been worse, he reflected. General Custer's 5th Michigan lost nearly half its men. The next morning, Louis ordered his men to destroy the train station. Other regiments destroyed several miles of track on either side of the station, effectively cutting off rail service to Richmond. In the afternoon, Gregg sent the 4th on a reconnaissance mission up the road toward Charlottesville. Almost immediately they ran into the entire Confederate Cavalry set up behind hastily constructed wooden breastworks. They attacked and counter-attacked all day and into the night, sustaining heavy losses. Louis rallied his men countless times, but the Confederates proved impossible to dislodge. Night fell and still they fought, cannons booming and flashing in the dark. When the night finally fell quiet the road and surrounding fields lay strewn with dead and injured men and horses. Louis gathered his men and took roll call. Another forty men were missing, among them Parnell. They made rough camp that night, just bed rolls on the ground, not daring to light fires for fear they would create a target for the Rebs. He lay there on the cool ground, too tired and heart-sick to properly mourn. He'd fought alongside Parnell for years, on two continents, and he'd come to depend on the man.

At dawn he walked the field of battle, surveying the carnage and looking for Parnell. He found him trapped under his dead horse, just as Louis himself had been trapped last year. He was covered in saber cuts, the worst of which had nearly slashed his nose off, but once the men dragged the horse off him Parnell got to his feet, refused medical attention, and walked away under his own power. Louis tried not to smile too broadly. Too many men had died, but he was happy nonetheless. Parnell was alive.

The war improved for the U.S. Cavalry Corps after Trevelyan Station. Though they'd lost too many men to declare victory, their feint north had given the main body of the Army of the Potomac the time and space to attack Petersburg. In August, Sheridan's cavalry, including the 4th, skirmished at Front Royal, driving the enemy farther and farther back. Louis watched as the Confederate retreat turned into a rout. He gathered his men and they charged the fleeing Rebels. That day they captured two enemy battle flags and hundreds of prisoners.

General Merritt saw Louis's charge and afterwards gave him command of the Second Brigade of the First Cavalry Division. Louis was back in his element, commanding not only his 4th, but three additional regiments of cavalry. Five days after Front Royal they pushed the Rebs back again, this time at Kearnysville. His brigade held the right flank and when the Rebels turned to run he once again led the charge after them. They drove the enemy a mile back, skirmishing and killing as they went. That night, Louis walked the camp congratulating the men. He'd served in so many iterations of the Union Army that he had lost count, but he'd never been prouder of a fighting unit than he was of his Second Brigade.

His pride though, was bittersweet. Kearnyville was the 4th's last engagement. The men were due to muster out in late August, their three-year stint in the army having come to an end. Louis briefly considered asking his men to re-enlist and fight with him to the bitter end, but he couldn't do it. The 4th had taken heavy casualties in too many battles. He'd lost too many men to death or capture. Worse, they'd not earned enough respect from the Union Army for their bravery. There were still complaints that the 4th didn't speak English, weren't American, or were otherwise misfits. They'd fought anyway and for that they deserved to go home. This war wasn't over, but it was over for the men of the 4th New York.

Louis's three years were up too. He thought long and hard. Then he decided.

On August 30, 1864, Louis received his orders. He was to proceed to Harper's Ferry and accept an honorable discharge. Louis stared at the paper. The United States government thanked him for his service. He snorted a little when he read that. Three years, multiple brigade commands, and he was still a colonel. Was it because he was Italian? Because Pleasanton and others disapproved of foreigners in the army? Or was it him? Had he somehow failed his adoptive country? He didn't know and he decided he didn't need to know.

And what would become of this nation in the aftermath of such horror as he'd seen and caused? How did they bind up the wounds caused by the deaths of over half a million men? Louis had no idea. He shook his head, knowing that it wasn't his problem to solve. He was a soldier. Soldiers fought the wars, they didn't make the peace. Louis knew only one thing. He was done. Done with war, done with fighting, done with death. *Done.*

He wanted to turn his horse and ride home to Mary and Gabrielle right then, but he had orders. He'd go to Harper's Ferry and from there he'd go home.

Chapter Fourteen

A SOLDIER'S HEART

New York—1865

Mary had her hand on his arm, shaking him. Louis jolted awake. The dreams again, always the dreams.

She was out of bed and standing beside him. "You were moaning. Was it the one at the camp?" His wife pulled up the hem of her cotton nightgown and wiped at his brow as she spoke.

He pushed himself up into a sitting position and shook his head. "The funeral one."

"Oh, Louis," she whispered softly. "I wish you wouldn't."

He'd described it for her once, months ago when he'd first come home. It started out harmlessly enough. He was coming home, walking up the street, eager to go inside and see his wife and daughter. Soldiers had "going home" dreams all the time. Dreams of seeing their families and being wrapped in comfort, food, and love. This dream was different.

He walked up the stairs and opened the door. A crowd of people stood inside, the men and women wearing black. They held small glasses of punch and ignored him. He pushed his way through the melee, dread filling him with every step. And then he was in the parlor and it was full of coffins. Sometimes two, sometimes three, sometimes dozens. He'd walk up to the closest one, a dour box of black and brass and look inside. Mary lay in the first coffin, always Mary. Her face serene and blank and dead. The second coffin usually held his daughter, sometimes his mother or Abrielle or Carolina. Once Ansaldi. In his dream he'd look up and everyone would be looking at him. Always a scarecrow of a man would step forward and raise his hand. He'd point a bony finger at Louis and intone, "You left them and now you are alone."

"You know you're safe here, don't you, dear?" Mary's face scrunched up in worry.

He shrugged. "I think I do." He squeezed his eyes closed, then opened them again. "While I was at war I never had a bad dream about you or the baby. Never one. You were always safe in my dreams. I'd kiss you and hold you." He hadn't had any bad dreams while at Libby either. Instead, like all the men, he'd dreamed of food, night after night. He had a recurring dream of roast beef that was so vivid he'd wake up tasting it. It had been oddly pleasant.

Now his dreams were quite the opposite. Sometimes he dreamed he was covered in lice. They were biting and biting and biting him. He could feel it, the pain and the itch, while he slept. He'd wake up scratching, convinced he was covered in invisible vermin. Worse, sometimes he'd dream he was back at Belle Island trying to distribute food and blankets. He'd be surrounded by walking cadavers, grey-skinned, hollow-eyed dead men, starving and freezing cold. And no matter how hard he worked, no matter how hard he tried, he couldn't get them the food nor the blankets they needed. The goods wouldn't come out of the wagon, or he'd lift out a pile of blankets, turn to give them out and they'd disappear in his arms.

Mary smiled gently down at him. "Maybe now you can be afraid. You couldn't then. It's this Soldier's Heart they're talking about. Or "nostalgia," which I think is a perfectly terrible name for it. You men couldn't dream about the horror while you were in it, so now you all do." She held up her hand to forestall an argument. "I'm sure it's all of you. No one talks about it, but you must all suffer. You'll never talk about it, none of you." She grimaced. "Men. And you'll all suffer. Probably for the rest of your lives."

He wondered if she was right. She was no beauty, his little wife, but she knew what was what. He'd take her over a dozen beautiful women any day. Then he looked at her, really looked at her for the first time that night. "You're going catch your death, Mary. Hop back in bed and let me warm you up."

She smiled her wicked little smile. "Oh, you're my handsome devil, aren't you? No, not right now." She turned and pushed her toes into a pair of bedroom slippers and pulled on her rose-colored wool robe. She turned, tying the belt about her thick waist, then flipping her brown braid over her shoulder. "You're going to be awake for a while and Gabrielle will be awake too. I'll go make tea and we'll have a little snuggle until the baby cries. Then we'll bring her into bed with us and we'll all curl up together and everything will be all right." She kissed his forehead and left the room.

While she was gone he sat there in bed, covers pulled up to his armpits, thinking. At their last dinner, Hiram said the insane asylums were full of men who'd gone mad from the war. Louis knew people thought those men were malingering or just weak, but no one who wasn't there knew what it was like. They read about the battles and talked about glory, but they didn't see all the dead men and dead horses. Or smell it. The smell of bowels unlocked in fear. They'd never been caught in a prison camp without enough to eat, covered in fleas and lice. They'd never had to shoot a favorite horse in the head to put it out of its misery. And he'd been an officer, with a tent and a camp bed and food and drink aplenty. He couldn't even begin to imagine how much those poor enlisted men had suffered. Were *still* suffering.

He had tried to do something about Belle Island. He sent letters to all the powerful men he knew, trying to get someone to care about the conditions in Confederate prison camps. He gathered photographs of men in camps, one photo a group of three human scarecrows at Belle Isle. He'd known all three men. They were dead now, except for the fact that they lived on in a picture taken two years ago in the last weeks of their desperate captivity. But no one cared, not enough to do anything about it. The nation wanted men to fight the war and they wanted to talk about glory, even the glorious dead, of all the ridiculous things. Glorious dead! As if there was such a thing. No one wanted to help them once they were of no more use to their country.

Thank goodness the war looked to be over any day now. Grant just about had that old fox Lee sewn up in Virginia. Louis figured by summer Lee would have nowhere to go. Petersburg had just fallen to the Union after an almost year-long siege. Richmond couldn't be far behind it. He smiled grimly to himself. He was glad he hadn't had anything to do with the siege of Petersburg. He'd had his fill of sieges. Boring, deadly things, sieges.

He hadn't told Mary about his nervous attacks. He'd be somewhere, feeling fine one minute, and then his throat would close up and his heart would gallop and he'd feel like he was going to die. It was like nothing he'd ever felt. He never knew what would set one off. The other day he'd been walking past a blacksmith's shop and a man had dropped something heavy. It made a loud sound and for a second he was back on the battlefield, artillery shells exploding all around. It was ridiculous really. There he was, perfectly safe in New York City, not even in uniform and miles away from any battlefield and yet, one loud noise and he was back in it, but terrified and frozen. He'd never been frozen while he was in it. Never once. But now? Walking past a blacksmith? He felt a depth of shame he could not talk about with anyone, especially not Mary.

But maybe Mary knew anyway. She was a woman of few words and she'd just said something about Soldier's Heart. Maybe she knew. Without him ever telling her.

He thought his problem wasn't just the war. It was being back with nothing to do. He'd been a military man, in one form or another, since just after his fourteenth birthday. The only time he'd had no meaningful employment had been his sojourn on Sicily, after Carolina and his dismissal. Maybe that had been some kind of breakdown too. He'd never done that before, just ridden off and checked out of life. Sicily made him think of Baree. Baree reminded him of Red. After Red he'd refused to get too close to his horses, refused to name them. Cavalry horses didn't live long. He supposed he thought about horses the way he thought about women. He'd had two heartbreaks and gave up. Then there'd been Mary. Maybe it was time to get a horse of his own. Or a new job. A new life.

He heard a sound in the doorway and looked up. Mary stood there, beaming, the baby snuggled into her arms. She came toward the bed and laid Gabrielle down. "You watch her and I'll fetch the tea."

He scooped up his daughter, now almost two years old, not really a baby anymore. She was the spitting image of his mother, the Countess, with her dark hair and eyes. It was too early to tell about her nose. He loved Mary, but he wouldn't wish her nose on any daughter of his. Gabrielle yawned hugely, exposing pink gums with tiny pearls of baby teeth, then she frowned at him and fell back asleep. Mary came back with a tray, upon it a tea pot, two cups, and a small dish of lemons. She knew that ever since the scurvy at Libby he craved citrus. She made sure he had lemons in something at every meal. She poured two cups, slipped a slice of lemon into one and handed it to him. He laid the baby on the bed between them and carefully, oh, so carefully, took the cup. She held her cup out to him. He took that too. She climbed into bed next to him and took the second cup from him.

"There," she said. "Isn't this nice?"

He had to agree that it was.

He thought that maybe his problem was that he didn't have anything meaningful to do. When he'd first returned to New York last fall, he'd thrown himself into politics, championing his old friend George McClellan for the presidency. He liked Mr. Lincoln well enough, but Lincoln wasn't a military man, not really, and he'd as much as said he'd continue the war until the Confederates surrendered unconditionally. Liberty and freedom were one thing, but the wholesale slaughter out there, the prison camps and everything else was inhumane. The nation cried out for peace. And McClellan promised that peace, a peace with honor, a peace for men who'd fought, whose friends had died. In November, Mr. Lincoln decisively won re-election, putting an end to the hope of immediate peace. A tiny part of Louis's heart felt relief. Peace wasn't the same as victory.

Then Louis read an article in *Harper's Weekly* that advised men suffering from "Soldier's Heart" to re-enlist. A return to combat was said to shock the system out of its morbid state and return a man to health. Louis didn't know if he believed that, but all he knew was the military, so he tried to re-enlist. He applied for the Invalid Corp, which took injured and crippled men and used them for light duty. The idea was to free up able-bodied men for combat. He thought that surely his adopted country could use him in some capacity, but the answer was no. The letter they sent said that the Invalid Corp was at the present time for men who had not yet served out their term of enlistment. Since he had served out his term he was not eligible.

He next offered to teach military and cavalry tactics at any school in the U.S. Army. Once again the Army turned him down. So he tried another tactic: he wrote to Secretary of War Stanton and Secretary of State Seward suggesting that each state have its own military college. The college at West Point was clearly inadequate for the nation's needs. He offered to organize such a college in New York if federal funds could be found to provide some support. Both secretaries rejected that idea as well, citing budgetary constraints and the imminent end of the war.

Louis had to wonder if his problem wasn't the same old American anti-Catholic, anti-immigrant, anti-Italian sentiment that had plagued his service. Even the Republican Party, which was firmly anti-slavery, tolerated the xenophobes and hysterical nativists. He might be from an old and noble family, but no one in America cared about that. No, Mammon and nativism held sway here. A man with money was a king and a king without money was no better than a peasant. An Italian Catholic like himself had little chance in a country that burned convents like they'd done in Massachusetts. The nation's much-vaunted talk of religious freedom boiled down to the freedom to join any one of a half dozen socially approved Protestant sects. Everyone else, from the Mormons to Catholics, had to fight for the right to be considered an American.

In mid-March, he received a letter from the War Department notifying him that he'd been nominated for appointment to brigadier general because he had, on several occasions, commanded brigades. Louis took the letter as a hopeful sign. If the army would give him the rank he'd already earned maybe it would change its mind about the Invalid Corps.

Then in April two things happened, one great and one terrible. First, Grant finally forced Lee's surrender. The Army of the Potomac took Richmond, the Confederate capitol, then they took a supply train at Appomattox, leaving Lee with nowhere to go and nothing to feed his army. Lee had no choice but to surrender his Army of Virginia. On April 12, the two men met and signed a peace accord at Appomattox.

Louis read the newspaper accounts from his comfortable study in New York and fervently wished he could have been there. He and Mary celebrated with a bottle of champagne at dinner that night. Then, two days later a mad man shot the president while he sat at the theater, watching the great Mrs. Keene perform *Our American Cousin*. Newspaper accounts contained grisly descriptions of the president's wounds and the way he had lingered through the night. Louis hadn't voted for the man, but he'd admired him nonetheless. That the poor fellow would die only two days after the war ended seemed immensely unfair. It was too much death. Too much loss.

After Lincoln's death, Louis looked up his old friend Percy Wyndham, who'd also been mustered out of the army. Together they re-opened their old cavalry school, using recommendations from Generals Sigel and Hooker to promote the venture. There wasn't nearly as much interest in the school as there'd been at the beginning of the war, but there were enough interested young men to keep the school afloat. Their promotional material emphasized the need for cavalry in following the nation's "manifest destiny." Pushing west and subduing the natives would require an army that was agile on horseback. That argument convinced more than a few young fellows, each more eager for glory and adventure than the one before. Working with them made Louis felt older than his thirty-three years.

Midsummer Louis had another idea. The *New York Times* reported that the current United States consul to Cyprus was a Virginian. Virginia had seceded from the union and joined the Confederacy, engaging in what could only be called an act of treason and war. Thus the *Times* wondered how a citizen of an enemy nation could represent the United States. More scandalously, the newspaper found out about the man when he asked to be transferred from Cyprus to Alexandria, Egypt, a post with a larger salary and more prestige. The newspaper editorial was understandably piqued that a man whose state was in insurrection had been collecting a federal paycheck for the past four years.

Louis seized his chance. Cyprus was close to Italy, so he could visit home more often. And maybe he'd feel better if he got away. Cyprus would be like Sicily: rural, Mediterranean, and without the pressure of high-society New York. First he wrote the Adjutant General's office for a certificate of service. It arrived one month later, attesting that he had loyally served the Union for three years. He then penned a letter to Secretary of State Seward asking for the

Cyprus consulship, enclosing his certificate to buttress his case. He also visited Senator Harris and Hiram Hitchcock and asked them to write Seward letters of support.

His letters sent, he waited. He held out little hope. Every letter he'd ever sent to anyone in the federal government had been answered in the negative. When no letter came answering his request, Louis decided to travel to Washington and see Secretary Seward in person; it was worth a try.

Chapter Fifteen

STARTING OVER

Cyprus—December 1865–1868

Mary smiled at him from her place on the rail. He found himself grinning back at her, despite himself. The sky was ominously grey, the harbor choppy, and the weather cool enough to require a jacket, though it was considerably warmer than Rivarola, not to mention snowy New York. It was also Christmas Eve.

"This is the best Christmas present I've ever got," Mary yelled into the wind.

Louis had to laugh. The town ahead of them was singularly unimpressive. The buildings were low and dingy white, the palm trees looked dry and worn out, and no one seemed to be around. Perhaps they'd see people when they got closer. Someone nudged his shoulder. Louis looked over to find Alessandro standing on the other side of him. He was every bit as excited as Mary. Louis was suddenly glad he'd followed his impulse and invited his younger brother to come with them to Cyprus. There had really been nothing for him in Rivarola, not as the third son of a none-too-prosperous noble family. Alerico tried to keep him busy, but the estate wasn't really big enough to require more than one manager.

In August, Mr. Seward officially appointed Louis the Consul at Cyprus. There'd been a delay when the State Department found out he wasn't a citizen. After the brouhaha with the Virginian they weren't going to allow an Italian national to take the post. He applied in July and on August 16th he became a citizen of the United States. Louis had always thought citizenship unnecessary given that he'd fought in the Union Army, but he'd been unaccountably touched when the Superior Court judge handed him the papers. Days later, Mr. Seward made his appointment official.

Mary, Gabrielle, and Louis left New York in September on an iron-hulled, screw-propelled steam ship that made far greater speed than the old sailing ships. Ten days later they docked in Liverpool. From there they boarded a three-masted clipper ship for Genoa. That passage had been significantly more difficult than the trans-Atlantic trip, the clipper being smaller and the seas rougher.

Louis had always sailed well, but he'd greatly feared for Mary. Though she was carrying their second child she insisted on coming with him. They'd fought about it, but only briefly. A strong woman had raised Louis and if he knew anything it was that arguing with a lady who had her mind made up was a waste of time. In Genoa they rented a carriage and headed for Rivarola. They arrived to much adulation and excitement. His mother took Gabrielle straight from Mary's arms and declared the baby hers for the duration of their stay. Alerico looked just like what he was, a prosperous, slightly bookish local lord. He was fat, balding, and overjoyed to see his younger brother.

Abrielle was there too, older, stouter, but still beautiful in spite of the fact that she'd had four children, three of them sons. Louis was surprised to find that seeing her didn't hurt at all. They stayed in Rivarola for almost two months, eating fresh cheeses and pasta, drinking the local wine, and talking almost non-stop to the family and neighbors who stopped by. Alerico took him on a tour of the estate, explaining his new system for grape growing and showing him his new pig barn. Best of all, Louis got to know his younger brother Alessandro. Alessandro had been only six years old when Louis left Rivarola. Now twenty-four years old and taller than Louis, Alessandro bubbled over with admiration for his brother's travels and adventures. Louis came to the conclusion that his brother needed more from life than grape vines and pigs and invited him to come to Cyprus.

On the first day of December they took a coach to Milan, where they caught a train to Ancona, on the east coast of Italy. From there they took a paddle-wheel steam ship to Cyprus. It would have been considerably more convenient to leave from Genoa, but the only Italian shipping service that ran a regular line to Cyprus sailed from Ancona. Fifteen days later, they steamed into Larnaca, on the Southern coast of Cyprus.

The ship slowed as it approached the docks. Louis could see the flags of France, Russia, and the Ottoman Empire flying from a row of buildings on the east side of the port. Reassured by the presence of other foreign legations, he took Mary's arm and walked her toward the ship's stern, from which they'd disembark. Alessandro followed along with Gabrielle, both of them as enthusiastic as puppies. They watched as a low-slung, long craft crowded with red-fez-wearing men approached the ship. The captain, a portly older fellow who'd been terribly nice to them during the trip, hailed the group and waved them aboard.

On deck the men crowded around Louis, studiously ignoring Mary as they did. Each of them carried a weapon, from rusty pistols to polished knives. Happily one of them stepped forward and greeted Louis in perfect Italian. Louis offered his hand to the man, who took it in his fingertips and kissed it. The fez-wearing men sprang into action after the hand-kissing, lugging first the trunks and then the bags onto their small boat. Then the men ushered the Cesnolas aboard. Mary took a seat on a plank in the center of the small boat, clutching Gabrielle tightly to keep her away from the water. "She'll have to learn to swim," Mary said, doing her best to pretend unconcern.

Louis agreed, nervously watching the squirming three-year-old try to get her fingers into the waves. The men rowed the boat toward shore. They were nearly there when the boat suddenly stopped. A brief investigation determined that the boat was so heavily laden it was stuck in the sand. One of the larger men sprung out of the boat, landing in chest deep water. He gestured at Louis, then at his shoulders. Louis looked askance at the man, but the fellow seemed serious. The local man who spoke Italian waved Louis forward. Guessing that it would be insulting to refuse and not wanting to begin his consulship on the wrong side of the locals, Louis complied. And thus, in this undignified and undiplomatic style did Louis Palma di Cesnola arrive on the shores of Cyprus, sitting astride another man's shoulders, boots dangling in the waves.

The large man waded ashore and bent so Louis could dismount. He handed Louis his disreputable red fez and returned to the boat. Soon a half-dozen men were moving boxes and people from the boat, through the breakwater, to the sandy beach in front of town. Allesandro joined Louis on land, wet nearly to the neck because he'd leapt in and waded to shore without help. A crowd gathered on the quay, laughing and pointing. The whole thing turned into a farce. Louis wondered: did all consuls and ambassadors arrive in Larnaca in such an undignified manner, or only his party?

Through it all Mary sat in calm splendor in the center of the boat, holding little Gabrielle. When all the luggage was ashore she handed the baby to the man who'd first jumped out of the boat. Louis could see his daughter's little arms waving in delight as the man carried her across the water. The man handed Gabrielle to Louis, who smiled as he took her in his arms. The family had another adventurer on its hands. Or, more accurately, an adventuress.

Finally it was only Mary in the boat. Louis watched her, worried. He knew as surely as he knew anything that she would not consent to ride a strange man's shoulders, pregnant or not. She would return to New York before she submitted to anything half so improper. Happily, once the people and luggage were out of the boat it floated loose from whatever sand bar that had been holding it. The men tugged the boat to within six feet of the beach.

Mary stood, swayed slightly with the motion of the boat, and sprang into the water.

Louis gave a great guffaw of delight. She waved at him as she strode through the shallow waves to shore, her skirts soaking wet, but on her face an amused happiness. He met her at the water's edge and pulled her into a one-armed hug, feeling her swollen belly against his hip. Gabrielle crowed in delight, clearly happy to see her Mama play in the water. Alessandro clapped in delight. They were all adventurers, all four of them. Feeling the unborn baby kick, Louis corrected himself. *All five of them.*

❧

It took a few months to get settled, but once they did, life in Cyprus settled into a pleasing rhythm of domestic happiness. They'd left almost everything they owned back in New York, having been told that the consul's house was fully outfitted and ready to live in. Nothing could have been further from the truth. Louis toured the American Consul's house the day after they arrived, finding it humble in appearance and delightfully large and airy, but nearly empty of furnishings, linens, and kitchenware. Apparently the Virginian who'd previously had the consul post took most everything with him when he left. Larnaca had no hotels, no guesthouses, nor any stores in which to buy household furnishings. One of the Italian families in town took them in while their own house was readied for occupation. Mary kept herself busy scouring the island for pots and pans, towels, sheets, and the like. The English Consul, a jovial man named Lang and the Belgian Consul, Mr. Wilkinson, donated furniture from their households to fill in the gaps Mary couldn't fill. After only a month they moved into the residence meant for the American Consul, and except for summer sojourns in their home up in the hills, they lived there for the next eleven years.

While Mary furnished the house, Louis spent his first weeks in Larnaca receiving or returning calls: From the British Consul's sister, who served a high tea the like of which Louis had never seen, to the local Imam, an intensely polite Muslim who spoke not one word of any language other than Turkish. To his delight, Louis discovered that while many Cypriots spoke Turkish, about half of them spoke Greek. He'd learned Greek over twenty years before and was still fairly proficient in it, which relieved him a good deal. Louis made a note to hire an interpreter or two for the Turkish speakers. When they weren't interpreting they could teach him the language.

Mary had the baby in the spring, another little girl. Louis had hoped for a boy, but it was not to be. They named the baby Louise because she was born with a scratching of dark red hair atop her head that matched her father's.

Louis spent the first year of his consulship traveling from town to town, getting to know the island and its people. The island, which stood at a shipping crossroads in the east Mediterranean, had been conquered and occupied by various countries for centuries. Currently the Ottoman Empire, or the Turks, controlled Cyprus. Louis enjoyed the Turkish people quite a bit, finding them hospitable and easy-going, but he also found that he did not enjoy the island's Governor or Caimakam one bit. The man was arrogant, temperamental, and often cruel. One day Louis discovered that the man required all Cyprian prisoners to pay for their own food. Anyone who could not afford food starved and since the Caimakam locked up people for the most petty of offenses, his jails were pits of hell on par with Belle Island. Louis tried to talk to the Caimakam, a corpulent man with greasy black hair and bad English, about the how the prisoners were treated. The man waved his swollen, ring-encrusted fingers at Louis and declared it none of his affair.

One of these poor prisoners, recently released from jail, made his way to the consular offices and begged Louis to hire him. "The Genab Effendi wishes me dead. If you would swear me into your service he could no longer hurt me or my family."

Noticing the scrawny man looked like the island's Muslim people, though he spoke Greek, Louis asked him if he spoke Turkish as well. When the man said he did, Louis hired Mustafa Fefsi as his interpreter and body guard for his trips around Cyprus. Not long afterwards he received a summons to the Caimakam's office. The governor offered Louis other men as interpreters, saying that Mustafa was a bad man who should not be employed by anyone as important as the American Consul. Louis was having none of it. He'd spent enough time with Mustafa to know he was perfectly trustworthy. He boldly told the Caimakam that it was none of his business who the Americans hired. The Caimakam greeted this declaration with the sort of excessive politeness that suggested he was furious. Four months went by. One day Louis sent Mustafa to deliver and pick up the mail from the port's shipping office. When Mustafa did not return, Louis went looking for him, only to find that the Caimakam had arrested Louis's interpreter for deserting from the Turkish Army.

"What will you do?" Mary asked. She and Louis were having lunch and watching the girls play. Gabrielle, at four years old, was helping Louise, who had just learned to sit up unassisted, build a house of wooden blocks that Mustafa made for them the week before.

"I'll have to go over the Caimakam's head. I want Mustafa back, but just as importantly, I can't let that swollen leech of a governor run over me like this. If he gets away with it, he'll never give me a moment's peace." Louis paused. He pushed back his cake plate. "I'll have to go to Constantinople. Will you be all right here without me?"

She narrowed her eyes at him. "Alessandro's here. We'll be fine. Go. And hurry back."

Louis sent a telegram to the American Ambassador in the Turkish capital and packed a small bag. It took a week to sail around the Turkish Peninsula to the empire's capital on the Bosporus Strait, between the Mediterranean and the Black Sea. He'd been to Constantinople ten years before, after the war in the Crimea. The city teemed with trade, making it all too obvious why the Ottoman Empire hadn't wanted Russia in the Black Sea and at Istanbul's back gate.

Louis enlisted Edward Morris, the American Ambassador, to help him with the Turkish officials. The first men Louis saw put him off with the usual administrative nonsense, but he persisted. Eventually he and Morris went to see the Turkish Minister of Foreign Affairs, Vizier Ali Pasha. Morris reminded the Pasha that arresting a consular employee was a violation of diplomatic immunity and that the United States did not appreciate such violations. He blustered and resisted, but in the end he had his clerk pen a document that ordered Caimakam's dismissal, Mustafa's release, and a payment of ten thousand piasters to Mustafa for his illegal arrest. The Pasha also ordered the Governor General of Cyprus to write Louis a letter of apology for the mistake his subordinate had made.

Louis left Constantinople more than satisfied with the outcome of his case. Then, as if the gods were smiling on him, his ship steamed into the Larnaca harbor right behind two American naval ships, the Ticonderoga and the Canandaigua. It was entirely accidental, but he didn't tell the Caimakam that. He almost felt sorry for the poor man, but not sorry enough to allow him to keep his job. And so Mustafa came home and Louis had no more trouble with the local authorities.

Louise, who had just turned two, was having a tantrum about her lunch. Cook was trying to get her to eat something besides pasta and cheese, but the girl stubbornly refused to eat anything not white or beige. Louis was smart enough to stay out of it, but he didn't blame Louise. Cheese did taste better than most green things.

Mustafa appeared at the kitchen door and shouted over Louise's cries of woe. "Mr. Lang is here. I put him in your study. Here," he said, reaching for the spoon in Cook's hand, "let me try." He held the spoon of wilted spinach out to the little girl, who took a bite without further demur. Louis looked gratefully at his right-hand man. Mustafa had filled out in the last two years and now looked like a young man who got regular meals and had the money to buy decent robes. In his spare time, he made the girls wooden toys and they adored him for it.

He entered his study to find the British Consul about to pull a book from Louis's bookshelf, a heavy and deadly dull tome on the history of the Ottoman Empire.

"Robert," Louis called out rather more sharply than he'd intended. "Put that back immediately."

The British Consul startled and nearly dropped the book. "I'm sorry. I didn't know you minded."

Louis laughed. "It's not that. It's a terrible book." Louis reached up to the top shelf and plucked a thinner volume down, this one bound in maroon leather. "Here. If you want Ottoman history this one is far better."

They sat in a pair of comfortable wing-back chairs that Louis kept in the corner of his office.

Lang held the maroon volume in his hand, stroking it with his thumb. Louis couldn't help but like a man who liked books. He'd met a number of British upper-class men over the years and a lot of them could only talk about hunting and riding. Not Lang though.

"How can I help you, Robert?"

"It's more a matter of me helping you, I'm pleased to say."

Louis sat forward. "Really?"

Lang nodded and smiled. "I've got a visitor right now. An English lady of means. I want you to meet her."

"On tour, is she?"

"That she is. With a companion."

"Ha!" Louis guffawed at the joke. "I've met the type. They're all tweedy respectability and dry scones, if you take my meaning."

Lang smiled again. "Normally I'd agree, but this one is different. Trust me. Come to dinner tomorrow evening, eight o'clock. Bring Mary of course. You know how my sister adores her."

And that was how Louis met Octavia Thompson, the woman who would change his life without meaning to.

Chapter Sixteen

DIGGING FOR TREASURE

Cyprus—1868–1877

"You really must read Mr. Schliemann's thesis," Octavia Townsend pronounced, waving her pudding-laden fork for emphasis. "I know he's immensely controversial, but I think he's quite brilliant. Just what the field needs."

They were seated around the long dining table at the British Consul's house. Robert sat at the head of the table and his sister, a widow of quiet beauty, sat at the other. On the table's long sides, surrounded by ivory china and sparkling crystal goblets, sat Louis, Mary, Mr. and Mrs. Wilkins of the Belgium delegation, and Lang's visitors, Miss Octavia Townsend and her companion Miss Harriet Pentwhistle. Alessandro sat next to Miss Pentwhistle. Louis was sure Miss Lang had put the voluble Allesandro next to the mousy Miss Pentwhistle on purpose, but all of his brother's considerable charms seemed to have no effect on the lady.

"Which is?" Louis tried not to stare at the stout lady seated across from him. She really was a most vexing combination of ridiculous and fascinating. At first glance she appeared almost a stereotype of that species that vexed Europe, the well to do, intellectually inclined Spinster on an Adventure. Such ladies populated the streets of Budapest, Cairo, Istanbul, and Rome. They were always stout, firmly corseted, loud in their opinions, and believed that they were infallible. In short, they bent the world to their will, but were as blithely ignorant of it as any infant. This lady had all those characteristics, but somehow managed to elude the stereotype.

"You are unfamiliar with his ideas? Oh, my, I really must rectify that lapse. Particularly given you are here, on this gloriously historic island." She put down her fork and leaned forward to lecture. "Mr. Schliemann proposes that the places named in the works of ancient writers like Homer and Virgil are not fictional, but rather were real places. Thus, he posits that these places are still out there, buried quite literally in the sands of time, and that a combined study of both archaeology and the classics will yield these locations."

Louis leaned forward. "So Troy, for example, might really exist."

"Exactly," the lady cried. She slapped the table with her gloved hand for emphasis. "And think of Egypt! The places we must go looking for. I'm getting together my own dig for the upper Nile."

Miss Pentwhistle patted Miss Thompson's upper arm and murmured something too low for Louis to hear.

"Ah, Harriet thinks I forget myself. But really," the lady looked around the table, "How could one not be excited by these ideas? And Schliemann is excavating for the French, so we English simply must put some people in the field to outpace him."

"Here, here," Consul Lang said lightly, raising his claret glass. "To the British Empire."

Miss Thompson turned her head back to Louis. "You, sir, you could do invaluable work on this island. Think of it. While the rest of the digging hordes head for Egypt and Syria, you could have Cyprus all to yourself. I shall send you some of my books. You'll have to return them of course, but I'll send along a list of booksellers and other titles you should have. It is a surprisingly difficult field of study, requiring some facility with language, culture, and organization, but from what Mr. Lang tells me you're a man of many talents."

Mary laughed at that. "You have no idea, Miss Townsend. He's a lifelong military man and he's been everywhere. Now he's retired from that life and he's not even forty."

"Then he needs an occupation, wouldn't you say?" Miss Thompson smiled conspiratorially at Mary who smiled back.

Louis had to admit that the idea had some merit, even if the ladies appeared to have organized it with little or no input from him.

That night, after they'd arrived home and climbed into bed, Mary turned to him. "Cyprus has a long history, doesn't it? As a kind of crossroads of every powerful nation in any particular time?"

He chuckled. His wife was indeed a perceptive woman. "Yes, dear. It is a place rife with history, ancient and recent. Perhaps more so than some other places."

"And the consulship does not require all of your time, does it?"

He shook his head. "Not like when I first got here two years ago."

They were both quiet for a while. Then Mary spoke again. "It's something to think about." He didn't have to ask her what she meant.

~

Over the next year he toured the island again, this time paying less attention to town officials and economies and more attention to the local landscape. He talked to farmers and sheepherders whenever he could, on the principle that men who made their living from the land would know things city folk would not. As he talked his way around the island he drew a map of sites, both contemporary and ancient, that might make interesting excavations.

The island was the third largest of the Mediterranean islands, behind Sicily and Sardinia. A long chain of rugged mountains divided the island, the highest of which was 6,500 feet high. Most of the year the island was dry, but in winter, when it rained, small rivers sprung up and ran to the sea, making it hard to get around the island. Louis knew the island would be difficult to map and excavate, brutally hot in the summer, wet and impassable in winter.

Mrs. Thompson sent him a crate of books, among them Heinrich Schliemann's dissertation, William Cunnington's books on excavation techniques, and James Hutton's books on recording strata of soil in a dig. He read those and ordered every book on her list, as well as several books by Pliny, Ptolemy, and Strabo, all of whom had written about Cyprus.

That winter, Louis looked at his handmade map and decided to begin his archaeology career close to home. Just outside Larnaca, at Paphos, he found ancient ruins that looked promising. He applied for a firman from the new Caimakam and soon after began to dig. He made Mustafa his right-hand man, or dragoman, in charge of hiring all the diggers and put Alessandro in charge of the accounts and payroll. The two of them also dug most days, and later, as the site began yielding artifacts, cleaning and sorting their finds. They worked all winter, when the men had less work to do in their fields and it was not too hot.

What they found astounded Louis more than he thought possible. At first they dug and dug, exposing piles of stones that seemed like no more than a mishmash of ancient walls, but eventually a pattern began to emerge. The site was a lost village, complete with houses and several tombs. In fact, the cemetery seemed quite a bit larger than the village, causing Louis to wonder if there hadn't been a larger city nearby. The tomb inscriptions were clearly ancient Greek and, with a little study, he determined that the Phoenicians had once lived in the village. They found a variety of small statuettes of female figures, countless pots and urns and, in the most exciting find of that season, a large tomb blocked by a massive rock. It took them a week to dig the tomb and rock free and a day to move the stone with block and tackle, but once inside they found it had been worth the effort.

Louis set a guard on the tomb overnight and entered it the day after they'd opened it, having read that only a fool rushed into a funerary site closed for millennia. The tomb was shaped like a giant baker's oven, and like a baker's oven, was made of clay bricks. Inside they found an ornate stone sarcophagus, terra-cotta vases of every size, from three feet high to small cups. Many of them were decorated with animals or groups of female figures—goddesses, Louis thought. Some of the urns contained jewelry, gold necklaces, earrings, and pectorals as shiny as the day they had been made, along with silver, black with age, and heavy bronze items that looked like tools or weapons. More astounding than the gold, they found glass bottles, saucers, and tiny figurines. Louis had no idea that the Phoenicians could make glass. Later he discovered that his finds at Paphos were not particularly unique or historically significant, but no dig site ever gave him the thrill of discovery like Paphos.

The summer after their first dig, the family moved up to the mountains to escape the heat. The summer house was high on the southern slope of the nearby mountains. The house was considerably smaller than the spacious house in town, but the days were cool and the nights cooler. Mary and the girls took to wearing soft cotton shifts, emulating the local women's sensible garments. Louis spent his days re-writing his field records and cataloging his archaeological collection. And he read. He read everything he could get his hands on, everything about Cyprus, everything about the ancient Greeks and Romans, everything about archaeology principles. He started a record of tomb, vase, and statue inscriptions, categorizing them by age and type, separating those that were in Greek from those in ancient Cypriote. Mary helped him with drawings of the more significant pieces, creating a visual catalog of the collection. She also suggested they buy a camera and learn how to use it. Louis thought they should hire a photographer, but Mary expressed an interest in the photographic arts so he ordered photography books from London and a Le Phoebus box camera from France for her.

The next digging season, Mr. Lang joined him in the field, working an adjoining site. Louis, Mary, and Mustafa worked the south and west side of an ancient site called Dali, while Mr. Lang's crew took the northeast. Back in 1862, Count de Vogue excavated the site and declared there was little of note to be found there, but Louis thought otherwise. He read his Aeneid and found mention of a temple at Dali. By the end of the summer, Lang had uncovered the temple and Louis had found more than fifteen thousand tombs. They began at the spot where the French count found a bronze tablet, but instead of digging a few exploratory holes and giving up, as de Vogue did, they marked the field off in a grid and chose several squares to dig systematically.

It had gone well at first. They found ceramics too numerable to count and quite a few more statuettes. In fact, from Louis's experience in Paphos, it seemed as if they were finding too many things. Then one day he re-examined the strata and realized he'd been making an amateur's mistake. What they had was two cemeteries, one on top of the other. In digging down to the older one he and his men destroyed the newer necropolis. The older one was purely Greek, the newer one Greco-Roman. Louis reminded himself that artifacts lay in the ground like a layer cake, and that each layer had something to tell the careful archaeologist. It was a mistake he never made again. The discovery of a purely Phoenician layer made the site of particular importance because so many Cyprian sites were the newer, Roman-influenced towns and cemeteries. To find one so old it pre-dated Rome was the sort of thing that made a man's reputation. Also, ancient Greek items fetched a higher price at auction.

Louis discovered so many artifacts at Dali that he had to divide them up by category. In the end he had thirty-three pages of descriptions of glass items, twenty-nine pages of terra-cotta, thirty pages of "ancient style" jewelry, nineteen of stone heads, and almost eighty pages of vases, which he classified further by varnish and paint color.

In 1871, Louis offered some of his collection at auction in London. As much as he hated to let go of any of it, the gargantuan number of items he'd accumulated started to overwhelm him. He realized that it was a lot more fun to discover the stuff than it was to manage it once it had been dug up. Also, the excavating expeditions were expensive and his consular pay only $1,000 a year. He could fund larger, more professional digs if he sold some of his collection.

He sent Mary and the girls to Rivarola for Christmas that year and he went to London along with sixty-six boxes of antiquities. Alessandro took thirty boxes to Paris, to antiquities agents who would sell the goods to either the Louvre or to the general public. In London, Louis handed over his prizes to Sotheby's, who printed a catalog of the collection. He left London after the January sale, but authorized Sotheby's to mount another auction in the spring to sell everything left over from the first London sale and the remains of the Paris sale. He would have vastly preferred to sell at least part of the collection to the Smithsonian or the new museum in New York, but neither institution seemed particularly interested. The Smithsonian's letter suggested it was concentrating on American art and antiquities, while the museum in New York simply didn't have the authority to buy anything yet. This didn't surprise Louis one bit. The museum had just been incorporated only weeks before his first Sotheby's auction and its managers hadn't yet figured the museum's goals, let alone its budget.

After his second season, Louis's Cyprian excavations became larger and his finds more exciting. He found he had a knack for handling the Turkish authorities that no other consul could claim, not even Mr. Lang. Louis credited his eighteen months in the Crimea, both for the respect his war experience earned him from the Turkish authorities and the experience he had dealing with the byzantine nature of Ottoman bureaucracy. Also, unlike a good number of other European archaeologists, he had little trouble with his local diggers. It helped a great deal that he spoke their language or languages and also that, as an ex-military officer, he had a knack for getting enlisted men to follow orders. Alessandro also learned Turkish, and had a better grasp of the local vernacular than Louis did.

They often took the girls out to the dig. Gabrielle, who was three years older than Louise, went digging with her father and uncle during their second season and learned to dig through screened dirt for worthwhile objects when she was only seven years old. When Louise was old enough, Mary insisted the whole family go on digs. She purchased a mammoth, two-room tent that she kitted out quite comfortably. And because the weather was generally pleasant, they mostly lived outside. They had a dining room under an awning and several hammocks tied from tree to tree. One of life's little pleasures was to dig all morning in the cool, stop midday and have lunch, then take a hammock nap in the afternoon.

Louise often followed Louis around the dig, peppering him with questions.

"Papa, why is it fine for you to get dirty, but not me?" She gestured down at her spotless, white pinafore.

Louis wondered the same thing, but Mary did insist upon certain standards even on a dig, one of which was that the girls were not allowed to get dirty. He shook his head at the question, saying, "Because Mama says so." It was the best he could do.

"What's that?" She'd ask whenever she saw anything new. Louis always explained, except the time she'd asked about a funerary jar with drawings of what could politely be called "fertility rites." That time he'd taken the vase from Louise's hands and sent her back to her mother to fetch a canteen. By the time she'd returned she'd forgotten all about the tangled limbs and unmentionable body parts featured on the red-glazed vase.

Gabrielle rarely asked questions, preferring to figure things out herself. She would watch the workmen carefully and do what they did. When she was old enough, she began to read Louis's books. He'd watch her sitting in a camp chair, some enormous tome in her lap and think it was too bad she'd been born a girl. If she'd been a son she could have gone to college and become a professionally trained archaeologist. There were some ladies working in archaeology: Miss Thompson and Miss Edwards were both quite famous. Miss Edwards had a dig in Egypt now, and Mr. Schliemann's second wife Sofia took an active part in his excavations in Greece. Louis kept an active correspondence with Schliemann and no one was happier than Louis when he discovered the site for Troy. Why, he'd even heard there was a French woman excavating in Egypt who wore men's clothing. It seemed a sensible thing to Louis, though he was glad his own wife preferred skirts.

At the end of Louis's third season of excavation he received a letter from the New York Metropolitan Museum of Art. His old friend Hiram Hitchcock, who had made enough money speculating in the stock market to buy the 5th Avenue Hotel and a few other New York buildings, succeeded in talking the new museum into purchasing everything Louis excavated that year. He'd made a mammoth excavation at Golgotha and come away with thousands of artifacts. The thought of keeping them all together in one collection in his adopted city made him very happy, but not so happy as the thought of the collection going to New York where he might visit it when his consulship ran its course. Even better, he would finally be independent of the Reid money. Not that Mary ever begrudged him a penny, but a man did like to make his own fortune.

He took the family home that winter, leaving Alessandro to supervise their latest excavation. He and Mary wanted to introduce the girls to New York, and Louis needed to supervise the installation of his collection at the Metropolitan Museum of Art. The number of artifacts overwhelmed the museum's temporary quarters on Fifth Avenue, just down from Hiram's hotel. Mr. Johnston, the railroad magnate who was the museum's first president, told Louis that he was negotiating with the city for a piece of land in Central Park. The trustees hoped to build a grand museum there, one on the scale of the Louvre or the British Museum. Louis agreed with Johnston that until New York had a world-class museum it would never be considered one of the great cultural centers of the western world. But in the meantime, museum employees crammed crates of vases, jewelry, and statues into the building's basement and an outlying warehouse.

After a six-week visit, Louis took Mary and the girls back to Larnaca. He and Mary were sad to go, but the girls were anxious to get back to Cyprus. It occurred to Louis that as much as Mary and he thought of themselves as Americans and New Yorkers, the girls were Cypriots. That thought worried him a great deal. It was all right as long as they were both still children, but as they matured into young ladies he'd have to take them back to New York. Either that or be prepared to have them marry some young fellow in the diplomatic corps of a foreign nation and lose them to that gypsy style of life.

Louis kept excavating. It never grew old. Always there was something new to find, something new to learn. It was a little bit like being in the military too, with a clear hierarchy of men, each strata important and dependent on the men above and below. That's what people misunderstood about military life. It wasn't generals lording it over everyone, or officers pushing around enlisted men. The beauty of military life was all the men, regardless of rank, working together toward some common goal.

By the time Louis and his family left Cyprus in the summer of 1877, he'd excavated sixteen ancient cities, fifteen temples, sixty-five necropolises, collecting over 35,000 objects in the process, from huge stone sarcophagi to strings of tiny glass beads. But it was time to go. Gabrielle was fourteen years old and looked like a young lady. Mary wanted to send her to a finishing school where she could make the right kind of friends. Little Louise was only eleven and she'd never known anything but Cyprus, but even Louis noticed she was running wild in the relaxed atmosphere of camp life. But most importantly, Louis had a job offer. The New York Metropolitan Museum offered to buy his entire collection and pay its shipping costs. In return for a price somewhat less than what he could have gotten if he'd split the collection between the major European museums, the New York museum offered to also make Louis a trustee. Louis took the deal. It was time to go home to his adopted country and begin a new adventure.

Chapter Seventeen

MAKING A MUSEUM

New York City—1880

Louis looked over Central Park from his seat on the dais. Though it was a damp, grey day in March, they had a crowd for the museum's opening. As well they should. The Met, as they were calling it, would one day be the greatest museum in the United States. He would make it so. Carriages lined Fifth Avenue, most of them belonging to the best of New York society. Men in gleaming black suits and ladies in gloriously large hats of all colors filled the audience at the Long Branch entrance. Louis could make out the Morgans, Belmonts, Vanderbilts, and Roosevelts. The president's wife sat on Louis's left, his own wife on his right. He was a long way from his squalid East Side tenement room. To think he'd once thought this city didn't want him. No one could say that now.

The 7th New York's regimental band played *Hail Columbia*. Louis looked over at the gray-bearded older man now at the podium. They'd gotten Rutherford B. Hayes, the nineteenth president of the United States, to give the opening address.

"This museum belongs to the people," Hayes declared, "Gifted to you from the great and powerful of New York City." The crowd responded with wild clapping and cheers. Hayes paused until the noise died down. "I officially declare the Metropolitan Museum of Art open to the public." He swept his arm out, gesturing at the massive building behind him.

Louis couldn't help himself. As the band began to play the overture from *Carmen* he turned to stare at the building. It was a massive thing, made of red brick and sturdy grey stone. Critics said the building was out of date before it was completed, its high Victorian style incompatible with the modern 1880s. Louis disagreed. The facade spoke of wealth and solidity, as it should. His museum would be the finest in the country, perhaps the finest in the world.

And it *was* his museum. He'd acted as trustee for two years, but the museum's growing collections quickly outpaced the first building on Fifth Avenue and then the museum's second building on Fourteenth Street. It became clear to the trustees that they needed not only a much larger and more permanent building to house their ever-expanding holdings, but a director who could organize and manage the massive enterprise that was the museum. And since the Cesnola collection of Cyprian antiquities made up almost half of the museum's holdings and because he had experience organizing large numbers of persons in the Army and on digs, Louis got the job.

It helped that he'd written a book about his Cyprian excavations, published at the end of their first year back in New York. He'd used his field notes and drawings, making his *Cyprus, Its Ancient Cities, Tombs and Temples* as specific as possible. Now he was working on a much larger project, a three-volume catalog of his antiquities collection. He was halfway through the first volume now and expected the massive project to be ready for press in three or four years.

The band finished up and the President stepped to the side of the podium. Louis gestured Mr. Hayes into the building. They stepped through the massive front doors and into the great hall. The room was an architectural splendor, all Romanesque arches, gilt, and gold-veined marble. It was every bit as magnificent as anything the Louvre had to offer, though without the patina of age. Louis beamed at his museum. He liked the glamour and shine of America. It was a brash and confident country, ready to lead a new age, with new ideals. This museum would be not just a temple of art and artifacts for the idle rich, but a place that welcomed the regular people, from the respectable middle-classes to the working poor. The museum would lift up their spirits and educate the masses, inspiring children and adults alike. He thought of Ansaldi and Fardella and Garibaldi, men who'd fought for Italian freedom, freedom from the Austrians, yes, but also freedom from the crushing yoke of the ruling classes. He was sure they would approve of his museum.

By midwinter he was no longer so sure of his museum. There were more problems to solve each day than there were hours to solve them. His first problem was the people. They touched everything. The tops of his Cyprian stone sarcophagi were grubby with greasy dirt and the jewelry display cases smeared with oily fingerprints by midday, every day. Louis hired two assistants and then two more to manage the herculean task of keeping the artifacts clean.

The building's gas lights and heaters compounded his problem. New York winters were dark and cold so he had to light and heat the building. But gas left a sooty film over everything, including the paintings. He'd tried cutting down on the heat and light, but people complained that the building was too dark and too cold. Having paid their quarter to get in, people expected the place to be lit like a midsummer picnic and just as warm. For a quarter, no less. How much did they think twenty-five cents bought?

The garbage probably upset him the most. People left things here and there, willy nilly. Why, just this morning he found a banana peel behind a medieval suit of armor. A banana peel!

Louis squinted at the offending peel, which now lay on his desk. He'd meant to throw it away, but then decided to keep it to remind himself to talk to the staff. He leaned back in his chair and thought about putting his feet on the desk and taking a little nap. He'd been on his feet for seven hours today and it was barely lunchtime.

His day started with a pre-dawn pounding on his front door. Louis stumbled downstairs in his robe and opened the door to find a telegram messenger on his doorstep. The museum was in the midst of a crisis. He left Mary sleeping in their cozy bed and went to work.

"It's the thaw, sir," Mr. Ford said. His senior assistant, a Harvard graduate with golden-blond hair that caused the ladies palpitations, was clearly mortified. "The snow is melting."

"And?" Louis barked his question. He hated going to work in dark. He'd done plenty of that in the army and he was done with it.

"The roof's leaking, sir."

"I know that. You sent a telegram, remember? Where? How much?"

Mr. Ford sighed and shook his shock of blond hair out of his eyes. "Everywhere, sir. Water's pouring in all over the place. I haven't had time to check the whole museum, but it seems as if our roof is made of cheesecloth."

In the next few hours, Louis discovered that Mr. Ford had not been exaggerating all that much. He had Ford telegram every employee they had and then mustered the staff to collect every waterproof basin, bucket, and crate possible. He sent his second assistant, an older, dour man, to wake up the night watchman at Stewart's department store. The museum ran an account at the famous department store and their Housewares department would have piles of buckets and garbage cans.

It had been a brutal morning. They had forty-two leaks in the great hall and another thirty-seven in the north gallery. The only good news of the day was that the deluge was confined to those two places.

Still, it was bad enough. Sixty percent of the items in the great hall were from his collection, which meant much of it was fairly impervious to water. Stone and terra-cotta didn't mold or run when they got wet. But there were dozens of Old Masters hung in the hall, and more in the north gallery. He had staff take the paintings down and stack them in the basement, which was, at least for now, still dry. He left a janitor down there to keep an eye on the ceiling and walls just in case. Louis wondered how he could protect the massive art collection, much of it donated by the city's wealthy families, if he couldn't keep the museum dry. He sighed and stood up from his desk. There would be no nap today. He could sit here feeling cranky or he could get back to work. Leaky museums did not fix themselves.

❧

In spite of all the problems at the museum, Louis enjoyed being back in New York. So did Mary. It was even nicer to be back and prestigiously employed. As his fiftieth birthday approached he could finally say that he'd succeeded. He'd transformed himself from a heartbroken second son into an important personage, both in New York and Italy. Two years ago Umberto, the new King of Italy, son of Victor Emmanuelle and grandson of brave Carlos Alberto, recognized Louis's contribution to Italian independence by making him a Knight of Italy. Louis couldn't accept the title because he was an American now, but the honor of it was enough. More than enough really. He might be an American, but he'd always be a Piedmont man. It couldn't be helped.

When they moved back into their New York house Mary immediately set out to modernize and redecorate it. Since the house had been closed up for the better part of a decade, Louis couldn't argue with the need. Also, it made Mary happy and anything that made Mary happy made him happy.

She'd been working on the house for three years. She'd had the kitchen modernized first, which surprised Louis. Ladies generally did their parlors first so they could show off to their friends.

When he asked Mary about it she'd asked, "What friends?"

He'd been caught flat footed by that response. "Surely...."

She shook her head. "I've been gone for eleven years and I wasn't exactly society's darling before we left. No, the kitchen first. If Cook is happy, we'll all be happy."

This answer broke Louis's heart. She'd sacrificed a lot to marry him. Her brother had disavowed her for marrying a Papist and a fortune hunter. He had barred Mary from entering his home and forbidden his wife from visiting Mary in hers. And the society ladies hadn't been much better. Their wedding had been a subdued event because most of society dropped Mary for the same reason her brother did—because her new husband was not one of them. It hadn't improved during the war. Maybe if Louis had become a general, but maybe not. He'd heard it said one couldn't swing a cat without hitting a retired brigadier general.

Lately Mary had taken to calling herself Countess Cesnola. Louis didn't mind, though technically he wasn't a count. Even if his brother didn't have the title, which he did of course, Louis's American citizenship required he disavow his citizenship in Sardinia. A man could be an American or a man could be titled in another nation, but a man could not be both.

Still, he didn't begrudge Mary the use of the title any more than his brother would have. Alerico and Abrielle loved Mary and they wouldn't want her to live as an outcast, not when she could borrow the title and use it to gain a position in society. Louis didn't think any of her new friends were really friends. They were lady collectors, as most society women were, and they collected persons of wealth and influence. And there wasn't anything Americans loved more than a title. Perhaps it came from not having titles of their own, Louis wasn't sure. Society matrons were certainly not immune to the allure of having a countess in their circle. So Mary had friends of a sort. He'd thought about talking with her about her so-called friends, but suspected she knew exactly what they were. Mary was no fool.

The museum trustees tried to get him to use the title, no doubt thinking that having a count running the museum would make it more legitimate in the eyes of its European competitors. Louis couldn't agree. It was one thing for his wife to borrow the title and another for *him* to do it. As a compromise he agreed to be called General Cesnola. His nomination to brigadier general disappeared in the wake of Mr. Lincoln's assassination, so technically he wasn't a general. But he'd earned the title, so he took it for himself. That's what American men did, wasn't it? He became General Cesnola at the museum and his wife became Countess Cesnola among the New York society set.

He smiled at the thought of his wife as he opened the front door to their house. The girls, who'd been reading in the parlor, sprung up to meet him at the door. At seventeen, Gabrielle had turned into a striking young woman. She was the spitting image of Louis's mother: tall, slim, and blue eyed. She was impetuous and headstrong unlike her calm and quiet mother.

At fourteen, Louise was at that awkward stage between childhood and womanhood, all elbows and blushes. She was small, like Mary, but had her father's auburn hair and golden-brown eyes. She'd never be as conventionally beautiful as her sister, but she had a spark of something that Louis thought would make her exceedingly dangerous with the gentlemen one day.

"Papa, Papa, come see," Louise said, tugging him into the parlor. He smiled and followed her.

"What are you two up to?" He took a seat on one of the comfortable parlor chairs. Unlike a lot of ladies, Mary furnished her parlor to be both beautiful and comfortable, so there were none of those stiff, slippery horse-hair sofas and chairs that one generally found in parlors.

"Here," Louise said, handing him a large leather-bound album. "See?"

Gabrielle leaned over his shoulder, the sleeves of her silk gown brushing his cheek, and opened it. "We've been making a Cyprus album. To remind us of home."

He turned the pages, resisting the impulse to correct her. If the girls thought of Cyprus as their home there was nothing he could do about it but wait for time to correct them. They'd collected a number of Mary's photographs, it looked like all the ones that had one or more of the four of them, plus pictures of digs, both houses, and their tent camps and stuck them in the album with drawings and captions.

Louise stood on the other side of him. "And here." She turned some more pages. "Here's our Mustafa page." They'd found two pictures of the old drago man, plus a picture of the wooden train he'd carved for them. One page had drawings of grave goods. Louis had to chuckle. What other New York young ladies would draw sarcophagi in their album?

"Darling, I didn't hear you come in."

Louis looked up to find Mary standing in the double doorway between the parlor and the front hall. She had a handful of fabric in her hand.

"These two commandeered me before I could find you," he explained.

He and Mary shared a fond smile.

"I've been waiting for you, dear," she said as she crossed the room. "I've got some swatches and I'd like your input."

Louis couldn't care less what fabric she used in what room, or what color walls or wallpaper or wood trim would be painted. But he liked that his wife thought he cared.

She handed him the fabric pieces and he pretended to look at them. Really, he looked at her. They'd just celebrated her fiftieth birthday and her face showed it, with small wrinkles at the corners of her eyes and mouth. Her hair was lighter now, its soft brown tempered with silver streaks. The new styles suited her. When he'd met her, ladies had been wearing hoop skirts. The voluminous dresses had engulfed Mary's tiny frame, making her look stouter than she was. Dresses were slimmer now, with the volume moved to the back of the skirt, draped over bustles. Louis thought bustles were stupid, but they were at least preferable to hoops. The draped skirts flattered Mary's small, sturdy body.

When she wasn't working on the house or supervising the girls, Mary volunteered at a local Catholic orphanage, where she taught little ones to read. The Protestant orphanages wouldn't take the Irish and Italian children. Or they would, but only to convert them. Mary didn't really think it mattered which Jesus they worshipped, but she didn't like the way the Protestants taught children that Catholics were the font of all the nation's problems.

"It's too self-hating," she explained to Louis one afternoon. "These children will have enough problems without being ashamed of the people they come from."

While most men of his station had younger, beautiful wives, he had a wife who was two years older than himself and looked like it. He didn't care. They could have their ingénues, he'd take his Mary. She was steady and kind. And she'd done a magnificent job with their daughters. Instead of doing what so many society ladies did, which was to farm out their children to boarding schools for someone else to raise, she'd kept them with her, sent them to day schools, and been there for every girlish confidence and secret. Louis thought that's why his daughters were so much more pleasant than most of the young ladies he met. They were loved and they knew it. A man who had that didn't need a young wife. He didn't need anything.

Except maybe more buckets.

Chapter Eighteen

ONCE MORE INTO THE BREACH

New York—1881–1889

Louis sat his desk, shaking with rage. He held in his hand the August issue of *Art Amateur*. In it was an article by the man who'd once been his French agent, Gaston Feuardent. He pushed his glasses down his nose and held the journal out at an arm's length. The change in view did not change the words.

"To endeavor to increase interest in the collection Mr. Cesnola has altered artifacts and in so doing engaged in profanation of the objects and perpetrated a fraud upon museum officials and the viewing public."

Fraud? Louis could hardly believe what he was reading. Feuardent's main point seemed to be that before Louis sold his collection to New York he'd altered a statuette of the muse Hope to transform it into a much rarer thing, a statuette of Aphrodite.

Nonsense! He'd done no such thing. And Feuardent's argument was ridiculous. His points were thus: that the statue was walking, holding her skirts, and had a flower in her hand. Hope, the French fop contended, was ever thus represented by the Greeks, walking to show she was a fleeting thing and holding a flower as a metaphor for hope. Did he mean to suggest that there were no representations of Aphrodite standing or walking? Did he seriously think that Aphrodite was only shown sitting? And why wouldn't the Goddess of Love hold a flower? Didn't flowers symbolize love?

Worse, Feuardent contended that the tiny mirror in the statuette's other hand had been placed there by Louis. Of course it had been. The tiny bit had been found near the statue. The statue's hand had been empty, but it had clearly once held something so he had reunited the objects. That's what archaeologists did. They reconstructed the wreck that time made of the past.

It was a ridiculous accusation and one that would have died unheard, but for the fact that the fool managed to get it published in a prestigious journal. Oh, how his enemies hated him! Well, he'd been hated before. Men had tried to kill him in three wars on two continents, to no avail. They would see what happened when they attacked him.

Louis regretted the need for the trial. It was embarrassing to himself and his wife and daughters. But it had been nearly unavoidable. The months after Feuardent's initial attack were filled with a series of nasty newspaper interviews in which the gentleman accused Louis of all sorts of malfeasance, from inappropriate antiquity repairs to inappropriate excavation techniques.

The museum undertook its own investigation. They convened a board of inquiry made up of two museum trustees and three outside experts, one of them a respected New York judge. Feuardent made a fuss of course, insisting that the board was ignorant of art and biased towards their director. Both the museum and the New York newspapers dismissed the man's complaints as hysterical and so the inquiry was launched.

In January 1881, Louis appeared before the board to defend himself, a task he undertook with considerable vigor. He pointed out that Feuardent was no art expert, only an out-of-work coin collector, entirely unqualified to judge any archaeological endeavor. He was, in short, a charlatan who was using Louis to attack the museum. He also pointed out that the only restorations ever made to any artifact in his collection had been done by experts at the British Museum, not by himself. He was a writer, a scholar, and an excavator, not a restoration expert. As to his Aphrodite, there were numerous statues like it found all over Cyprus and Greece. There was no reason to make over Hope because Aphrodite figures were far from rare. Lastly, Louis pointed out that Feuardant had once done some contract work for the museum and submitted a bill so inflated and ridiculous that Louis had refused to pay it. The man was simply engaging in cheap and theatrical revenge.

In February, the five-man board cleared Louis of all charges, saying "they have never ceased to entertain the highest confidence in Cesnola's devotion and faithfulness to truth, scholarship and history." But that didn't end it. Both the *Times* and the *Tribune* stayed on the story, probably because a scandal at the museum sold papers. Though both the papers were hostile to Feuardent, their continual rehashing of the controversy kept it alive.

Then in April 1881, the *Art Amateur* attacked again, still alleging that the tiny Aphrodite was a fake. Feuardent followed up with a pamphlet titled, "How Amateur Archaeologists Can Make a Fake Statue." In it he claimed that most of the statues, small and large, in the Cesnola collection were put together like puzzle pieces, with a head from one source, body from another, and so on. And then a poet by the name of Clarence Cook suggested that Louis had fabricated the entire Golgoth dig.

Louis couldn't believe it. *A poet?* How did anyone think the man was qualified to judge any of Louis's excavations? The man had never even been to Cyprus. Why, in his book Louis had written extensively about Golgoth. He had drawings and photographs. Did anyone seriously think he'd fake that? And why? Cyprus had been chock-full of historical sites. He could be digging there still and still finding things. There was simply no need to fake anything

The scandal dragged on for months. Each new accusation was more outlandish than the last. His problem, he concluded, was twofold. Cyprus had been too rich in artifacts and he, an Italian, had been the first American to dig there, not some fifth-generation Protestant New Englander. He'd been too successful for a foreigner. He did the only thing he could think to do: he hired a lawyer and took Mary to Europe for four months.

The trial began in November 1883, over two years after the nightmare had begun. They met in a federal court room in the Old Post Office. One by one the five men on the Museum's board of Inquiry testified, as did a man who had been the superintendent in 1873 when they'd first purchased antiquities from Louis's collections. That part of the trial took over two weeks. The restoration expert from the British Museum testified for four days, well into the trial's third week. Next, the museum's own restoration man testified. Four of the statues were brought in, including the small Aphrodite, and they remained on a side table for the rest of the trial.

The newspapers began to complain about how long the trial was taking. Sensing the trial wasn't going his way, Feuardent's lawyer began attacking not just Louis, but Louis's lawyer too.

Then every disgruntled employee, everyone Louis had ever fired from the Museum for wrongdoing, was dragged through the courtroom to tarnish Louis's reputation. These people had so little to contribute to the case that the jury grew impatient and cranky. Louis watched them file in looking more resentful each day they spent on this nonsensical bit of legal wrangling.

Finally it was Louis's turn to take the stand. He painstakingly described each statue under question, where it had been excavated, when and how it had been cleaned and restored, and by whom. He had paperwork for it all, having learned from a life in the military to keep scrupulous records. He had his book too, which he kept with him on the stand, referring to it as often as he referred to his files.

When that tactic failed, Feuardent's lawyer started in on Louis's title, pestering him about when he'd received his commission, from whom, where he'd served and when. The man made it sound as if Louis had made up his entire military service. Louis kept his temper, but just barely. That this pup, this youngster, would question his military service and everything he'd done for his adopted country, well, it was just too much.

Louis went home that night furious. Mary and the girls were at their country house in upstate New York. Mary and he had argued about it, but he did not want her in the courtroom. She would be a target for both the lawyer and the newspapers. Hobson had retired last winter, but Cook and the two maids went with Mary, so he was all alone. He sat in his dark, cold house and thought. He smoked one cigar and then another. And then he had an idea.

The next day he stopped by the museum and picked up a few tools before he went to court.

He took the stand one last time. As Louis had instructed, his lawyer asked him if the statues were real or fakes. Had they been cobbled together from random bits?

Louis smiled and took a small stone saw and a chisel out of his coat pocket. He laid them on the rail. "I have said, time and time again, that the statues are genuine. Two experts have said they were restored according to accepted practices. But still, Mr. Feuardent and his ilk contend they are not. So I offer this." He waved his hands at the tools. "They may take apart my statues in any way they want. I will reimburse the museum for the cost of the artifacts myself. Surely they will be able to prove they are patchworks then. If these tools do not suffice they may use anything they want."

The gallery erupted. The judge banged his gavel for silence in the courtroom and then looked at Feuardent and his lawyer. "Well?"

Both men declined Louis's offer.

Two days later the jury found in favor of Louis. In their statement they called Feuardent's charges "malicious and unfounded."

Louis walked out of the courtroom feeling oddly flat. He ought to be happy, he ought to be exultant even, but he wasn't. His reputation lay in tatters, no matter the trial's result. And his military service had been cast into doubt.

He walked back to the museum, *his* museum. He stopped on Fifth Avenue, in front of the rear entrance that he always used. He looked up and down the street. Shiny black carriages filled the streets. Ladies in beautiful hats and coats filled the sidewalks, accompanied by men in tailored suits. This was the street where the cream of New York society met. It was the street where he'd met Hiram Hitchcock, not long after his suicide attempt almost thirty years before. He'd come so far, and yet no distance at all. He was still on the outside, using the back door to get in.

"A letter from Mr. Hamlin, dear." Mary tapped the letter that sat next to her and then calmly spread jam on her toast.

Louis held his temper. It wasn't his wife's fault she didn't understand how important this was to him. He picked up the letter, which was ominously thin. Either the news was very bad or very good. "When did it come?" he asked.

She chewed and swallowed, then wiped her mouth with a linen napkin.

"Yesterday, dear. I meant to put it in your study, but Gabrielle came over with the baby and I forgot all about it. Grandchildren are so much more interesting than mail, don't you think?"

"Yesterday," Louis said flatly, trying not to lose his temper and failing. Mary knew very well that he adored his granddaughter and would forgive her, her mother, and her grandmother anything.

"Yes, I'm sorry you missed them, dear. You shouldn't work so late. Not at your age."

Louis snorted. He was sixty-five years old, not a hundred and five.

"Sit down and open your letter, dear." She waved at his chair with one hand as she poured him a cup of coffee with the other, using the silver pot at her elbow.

Louis sat up abruptly, feeling grumpy. He pushed away the cup and used his toast knife to unseal the envelope. He pulled out the letter and opened it. It was bad news.

"Still no luck?" Mary pushed his coffee cup back in front of him. "Drink your coffee, dear. You'll feel better."

He sipped at his cup and handed the letter over to his wife. She scanned it. "Mr. Hamlin says there's nothing more to be done."

Mr. Hamlin was Augustus C. Hamlin, president of the 11th New York Cavalry Corps branch of the Grand Army of the Republic. Louis knew the man had done his best. He'd used members of the veterans group to comb through military and Congressional files for evidence of his appointment to Brigadier General, but they'd had no luck. The Army forwarded his appointment to Congress in March of 1865 just like Louis remembered, but they adjourned without acting on it.

They took the matter to Senator Evarts, hoping he could resurrect the bill, but Evarts explained that the Senate didn't work that way. They required an entirely new bill. And before the bill came to the Senate it would have to be introduced to the House Committee on Military Affairs, pass through that committee, and then pass the House of Representatives. The odds were against him, but Louis had hoped that his current position as the director of the country's most prestigious museum would pave the way for him, even at this late date. It had been a fool's hope.

General George McClellan's son, who was newly elected to Congress, introduced the bill but it died in committee. Hamlin's letter to Louis stated that he had received a letter from the Chairman of Military Affairs saying that neither they nor President McKinley had any authority to commission any retired U.S. Army volunteer as general or anything else. It was done. He'd never get the rank he'd earned in battle. *Never.* The memory of that lawyer questioning his commission and his service in a court of law never went away.

Mary pushed back her chair and walked the two steps to where her husband sat. She wrapped him in a firm embrace.

"You shouldn't care, dear. It's been over and done for thirty, no, thirty-three years. No one can take your accomplishments away from you."

She returned to her seat and tapped the pile of mail again. "There's another letter for you here. Something from the office of the president." She handed it to him. "Oh, and there's a small package."

Louis ignored the package. People were always sending him bits of nonsense for the museum. Most of it was worthless, but the senders always thought they were doing him a great favor by mailing him some family heirloom or other.

"It's probably a condolence letter," Louis said, feeling the slim envelope. He slit the letter open and read it. Then he read it again. Wordlessly, he dropped it on the table.

"What, dear?"

He picked it up and held it out to her, too astounded to speak.

She took it. The letter had the unmistakable navy blue circle with the eagle inside that was the Presidential Seal. Under the seal was the address for the White House. The page contained one elegantly typeset paragraph.

December 3, 1897

On the Authority of the Secretary of War, President William McKinley and the U. S. Congress award Col. Louis P. di Cesnola the Congressional Medal of Honor for distinguished gallantry in action at Aldie, Va., June 17, 1863. Colonel di Cesnola was present, in arrest, when, seeing his regiment fall back, he rallied his men, accompanied them, without arms, in a second charge and in recognition of his gallantry was released from arrest. He continued in the action at the head of his regiment until he was desperately wounded and taken prisoner.

In this action he acted with conspicuous and exceptional personal valor and is awarded the nation's highest honor. A grateful nation thanks him.

Signed
Russell A. Alger, Secretary of War
William McKinley, President of the United States of America

Louis held out his hand to Mary. He noticed it was shaking. "The package, please?"

She held it out to him without a word. Louis looked at her, noticing that he felt as pale as she looked.

The package was small, no larger than two decks of playing cards laid end to end, wrapped in brown paper and tied with plain cotton string. Louis held the small thing in his hand and stared at it. The return address was for the Department of War. He hardly dared open it, fearing that it might be a mistake.

Mary waited, wordless.

Finally he picked up his toast knife one more time and cut the knot on the string. He set it aside and unwrapped the paper. A navy blue box lay in his hand. He opened it. Inside was a medal. The five-pointed gold star was ornately decorated, suspended from a red and white striped ribbon with a bar of blue at the top. An eagle perched on top of the star, on a pair of cannons, with a saber clutched in its talons. An equally ornate gold bar at the top of the ribbon pinned the medal to its red satin bed.

Mary stood again. She leaned over the table and peered at the little box. "Take it out," she whispered in the same voice she used for church.

Louis lifted the medal out and held it out to Mary. As he did he saw the inscription on the back.

The Congress to
Col. Louis P. di Cesnola
For Valor

She gave out a great whoop of excitement and threw herself across the table at him, upsetting both their coffee cups in the process. He jumped up and hugged her, still holding his medal.

She kissed his cheek and then tipped her head back to look at him. "Congratulations!" She hugged him again. "The inquiry into your generalship must have set this in motion. They couldn't give you the promotion you earned but they saw how important you were to the war. How brave you were."

He nodded, his heart too full to speak. It had been the recognition that mattered. He'd been recognized by the King of Italy for his exceedingly paltry contributions to the first of three Wars of Italian Independence, but he'd fought for this country for three years, in the most deadly war in human history. He'd been injured, taken prisoner, and returned to battle. He'd fought and fought and fought. And he'd lived, while all around him men and horses died. Those injured and dying on the battlefield still haunted his dreams and he supposed they always would.

All he ever wanted was to know that his adopted country valued his service.

He'd begun to think this country would never accept him, never acknowledge the part he'd played in making the nation truly free. There were so many men like Pleasanton, men and women who hated immigrants, hated Catholics, and hated anyone not like themselves. This medal was proof that those people were not the real America. He and thousands of other men had all earned a medal of valor for simply fighting in that damn war, for staying and facing the mounting horror it had become. And too many of those men hadn't been born here and were treated badly because of it. And they'd never get a medal. No, the point wasn't that the medal recognized his bravery. It recognized *him*, an Italian Catholic who never felt like he belonged. He looked at the medal again. It was official. He was a real American now.

Mary hugged him again. "Wait until the girls see it. They'll be so proud."

Louis kissed the woman who'd been his wife for almost forty years. "I am a lucky man."

Chapter Nineteen

TAPS

New York—November 22, 1904

From the *New York Times* obituary page:

*General Louis Palma di Cesnola, Director of the Metropolitan
Museum of Art since 1879, died suddenly and after a very short
illness on Sunday night at his residence at Hotel Seymour, 44 West
45th Street, where he has lived since the death of his wife two
years ago. On Friday, after his usual day's work at the museum,
the General attended a reunion dinner of the 11th Corps, with
whom he served in the Civil War. He left the banquet hall in his
usual good health, but on Saturday morning he had an attack of
asthma, probably the result of a cold he caught at the banquet. His
family physician, Dr. Carlo Savini, advised the General to rest in
his room throughout the day. His daughter Miss Louise di Cesnola
summoned her sister, Mrs. Gabrielle Del Cambre and they were
with him until the end came.*

*Gen. di Cesnola's funeral will be held at St. Patrick's Cathedral on
Wednesday, when the Italian Ambassador and members of his staff
will come to this city to attend. The directors of the Metropolitan
Museum will act as pallbearers. The internment will be in the*

Kenisco Cemetery where the General's wife Mary Reid di Cesnola is buried.

General di Cesnola was a native of Rivarola, Piedmont, Italy, where he was born in 1832. When but sixteen years of age he entered the army, serving through the Italian war against Austria and receiving his commission as a Lieutenant on the battlefield of Novara for personal bravery. At the close of the war he completed his education at the Military Academy of Cherasco, after which he served with distinction in the Crimean War.

He came to this country in 1860, and after teaching French and Italian, served this country as an instructor in tactics and cavalry drill. He was appointed Major of the 11th New York Cavalry, serving afterwards as Lieutenant Colonel. He received his commission as Colonel in the 4th New York Cavalry after raising a regiment of immigrants. He served with that regiment for three years, until near the close of the war, save for ten months he spent as prisoner of war in Libby Prison. It was while a prisoner of war that he helped plan a successful attempt at tunneling out of the prison. He also undertook to protect prisoners at the notorious Belle Island prison camp. General di Cesnola was wounded at the battle of Aldie, Va., and in 1897 was awarded the Congressional Medal of Honor for his bravery on that field of battle. At the close of the war, President Lincoln promised him a promotion to Brigadier General and though the commission was never made out, owing to the death of the president, he was always greeted with the title promised to him by those grateful for his service in the nation's time of need.

He was Consul to Larnica, in the island of Cyprus. It was while serving in this capacity from 1865 to 1877 that he undertook an excavation of Cypriot antiquities. The collection he acquired is noted for its size and depth. His book, published in 1877, Cyprus and its Ancient Cities, Tombs and Temples, *led to the establishment of the Cesnola collection, housed in the Metropolitan Museum of Art, a building that is very largely a monument to Gen. di Cesnola.*

Gen. di Cesnola became the Trustee of the Metropolitan Museum of Art in 1877 and its Director two years later. He served as the museum director for twenty-five years, until his death. In the 1880s an attempt was made to secure his removal from the post, but the museum Trustees acquitted him. This led to a suit for libel, brought against him by Gustave Feuardent, the trial of which was the sensation of art circles everywhere. The trial resulted in a positive outcome for General di Cesnola and the General was vindicated.

In addition to the Medal of Honor, the General is the recipient of a gold medal and knightly honor from the King of Italy. He was an active member of various scientific and archaeological societies and the author of several pamphlets dealing with art subjects.

His daughters ask that donations be made in his name to the Sisters of Charity, Home for Catholic Children, an institution much favored by he and his wife.

Postscript

REAL AND NOT-SO-REAL THINGS

As I began research on Louis Palma di Cesnola I found that much of what has been written about him was based on what can only be termed careless research. Also, many of the events in Louis's life are so astounding they are difficult to believe. Thus I began this file to document what is based in fact and what is fiction in this novel.

A word about naming. When Cesnola came to America he changed his name from Luigi to Louis (pronounced "Lewis"). I honor his choice by calling him Luigi until the 1860, then Louis afterwards.

The Italian, Crimean, and American Civil War battles, as well as the regiments, brigades, and divisions mentioned in this novel are historically accurate. I made up Louis's feelings, but not the actual battles.

Cesnola did leave home when he was fourteen years old, first for military school before enlisting in the Sardinian Army. He was in his first battle when he was sixteen. In a letter to his wife-to-be, written years later and partially transcribed in Chapter Eight of this novel, Louis writes that he had a great love affair and heartbreak when he was fourteen. That much is true. The rest

I made up, the sources being utterly silent on the identity of his lady love and all other details. Thus, Abrielle is a figment of my imagination.

There is little information available about the Military Academy at Cherasco, so I modeled it on the Military Academy of Modena. The Italian Military Academy in Cherasco is South of Turin so it makes sense that Louis attended that military school, but I cannot be sure as the sources are exceedingly unreliable.

Louis was promoted from Under-Corporal to Corporal during the first campaign of the First War for Italian Independence. Again, there are no details about why he received this promotion, except to say he did something noteworthy, so I made them up. One source said that Louis contracted malaria at some point in his service to the Sardinian Army. Since malaria generally causes lifelong bouts of intermittent fever, and since there is no report that he ever suffered the consequences of a malaria infection, I switched his ailment to typhus, or typhoid fever, which was exceedingly common among armies in the nineteenth century.

General Giorgio Ansaldi was a Major General with the 17th Regiment of the Sardinian Army and he did serve in both the First War of Italian Independence and the Crimean War. Enrico Fardella served in the Kingdom of Two Sicilies army (Sicily and Naples). He also served in the Crimea with the British Army and in the United States Army during the American Civil War. King Carlo Alberto (Charles Albert) did lead the Sardinian Army into battle in both interludes of the First Italian War of Independence and he was nicknamed "the Hesitant." The loss at Navarro was disastrous and in an effort to forestall a revolution by the Piedmontese he abdicated in favor of his son.

The Sardinian army was driven back to the Alps by Radetsky's Austrian Army after Navarra.

At least two biographical sources say Louis attended the Cavalry School at Pinralo. There is no such place. There was an Italian Cavalry School at Pinerolo, just west of Turin, established in 1823. In 1868 the school was moved to Modena. The ride I described is taken from the description written by a student several decades later. Italian riding techniques were different from English riding, much as Chapter Four describes.

I entirely invented Luigi's affair with a senior officer's wife, but there is evidence that something like what I described took place. He was summarily dismissed from the Sardinian Army when he was twenty. There are two competing theories about this: that he got himself into some kind of debt or that he had an illicit affair. Most sources go with the debt story, but it doesn't make much sense. Louis's family had money and he had a life-long horror of falling into debt. Moreover, in his letter to Mary Reid he admits to a love affair when he was fourteen and another when he was twenty, the latter of which broke his heart and made him incapable of ever loving again. Aha! But, like Abrielle, I invented Carolina.

Louis was friends with Fardella and Fardella did come from a small town on the west coast of Sicily. I invented Louis's trip there, having no sources for what he did with the time between when he was dismissed from the army and when he left for the Crimea.

The 1855 letter from Ansaldi in the novel is a fabrication. There is considerable disagreement in the sources about who Louis fought for in the Crimea. One source said the British Foreign Legion, but strictly speaking, such an entity did not exist and the British regiments made up of foreigners did not deploy to the Crimea until the war was nearly over. Another source says he enlisted in the Osmanli Irregular Cavalry, a unit in the British Army, 15th Hussars as General Ansaldi's aide-de-camp, but Ansaldi belonged to the Sardinian Army, not the British Army. Other sources said he joined the Italian Army, but no such army existed, there being no nation of Italy in the 1850s. Several sources say Louis was aide-de-camp to General Ansaldi, but I couldn't find Ansaldi on the rolls of the Sardinian Expeditionary Corps, the "Italian" force that went to the Crimea in 1855–56. The Sardinian Expeditionary Corps (SEC), made up partially of Sardinian Army regiments and partially of volunteer regiments, was related to but separate from the regular Sardinian Army. It turns out Ansaldi led the Reserve Brigade of the SEC for only a few months, dying in the Crimean cholera epidemic only two months after the SEC arrived in Balaclava. He was replaced by Major General Di Cavero, who is listed as the general for that brigade in almost all the sources, which explains why I couldn't find Ansaldi in any rosters.

Thus, I guessed that Louis served in the Reserve Brigade of the SEC, under first Ansaldi and then Di Cavero, as a volunteer and aide-de-camp. This means every source that says Louis was present at the Battle of Balaclava and the Charge of the Light Brigade is incorrect because that military engagement happened a year before the SEC arrived in the Crimea. Louis's letters agree. He wrote about the Siege of Sevastopol, not Balaclava. Thus I invented a letter where Ansaldi asks Luigi to join him on the expedition.

George McClellan, who would become the Army of the Potomac's first commander, did visit the Crimea with the Delafield Commission. He and Cesnola met there. This would support the theory that Louis was an aide to a general like Ansaldi. A random twenty-three-year-old cavalry lieutenant would not have had occasion to meet with an important American delegation, but the aide to a major-general would.

Secondary sources are unclear about who exactly put Cesnola under arrest on the eve of the Battle of Aldie and who gave him the borrowed sword. Different sources cite different names, from generals who did not exist to generals who were not at that battle. Louis's Medal of Honor file, held at the National Archives, says Gen. Gregg stripped him of his sword and then Kilpatrick restored it by ordering Estes to give his sword to Louis. The military file seemed the best source.

A word on Civil War military organization. Colonels commanded regiments. Brigades, made up of two to four regiments, were commanded by Brigadier Generals. Thus in late 1862–early 1863, Cesnola merited a promotion to Brigadier General because at that time he had command of multiple regiments. After his February 1863 disgrace he commanded only the 4th New York, as would befit the rank of Colonel. This oversight has its roots in two problems, the refusal of the Union Army high command to treat cavalry officers like infantry officers and in the fact that Louis was Italian. General Pleasanton, commander of the Union Cavalry Corps, was unquestionably a rabid xenophobe who believed that no "foreigner" should be allowed in the Union Army. Louis did lose his brigade command. General David M. Gregg's brother, Colonel John I. Gregg replaced Louis.

The letter to Mary in Chapter Eight is an excerpted transcription of a real letter Louis wrote, shortened for brevity. The letter to George McClellan in Chapter Nine is a transcription of Louis's words as well, also excerpted. The same can be said of the letters in Chapter Ten. The letter to Stanton is a combination of two letters, one to Stanton and one to his Assistant Secretary of

War. General Order Number 50 in Chapter Ten is an excerpt from the real General Order, taken from Army records.

Irishman Thomas Morley enlisted in the British Army, 17th Lancers in 1849 and was with the regiment in the Crimea where he must have met Cesnola. Morley came to the United States in 1861 and enlisted in the 12th Pennsylvania Cavalry as a 2nd Lieutenant. The Confederates captured him in 1862, but he was released in a prisoner exchange less than a month later. He was recaptured June 15, two days before Louis fell and was captured at the Battle of Aldie. The two did meet in Staunton (Louis's biographer identifies their first prison camp at Winchester, but the Official Record and Morley himself say they met in Staunton). The two men were in Libby Prison together until March 1863, when Morley was paroled. After the war, Morley returned to England and the British Army. He named his second daughter Cesnolia.

Louis published a ten-page pamphlet about his experiences as a prisoner-of-war titled *Ten Months in Libby Prison*. I took details from his time in Libby and at Belle Island from that work. Frederico Cavala was in Libby Prison, but his balloon was shot down during the Battle of Gettysburg, so I have him in the prison about a month too soon. In 1864, he was released and wrote a book about his Libby Prison experience that was helpful for this book. Thus, I thought it only fair he make an appearance. Elizabeth Van Lew, along with her mother Eliza and a number of black servants (ex-slaves she'd secretly freed) played in an important role in the pro-Union, Richmond underground. She often visited Libby Prison carrying both legal and secret goods in and out of the place.

Post-traumatic stress disorder, as we now call it, was not a well-recognized problem during the Civil War. Nineteenth-century medical professionals recognized syndromes they called "Soldier's Heart" and "Nostalgia," that included panic attacks, depression, insomnia, suicidal thoughts, and more. Doctors did indeed recommend a return to battle as a cure. Most antebellum Americans were deeply suspicious of any man claiming psychological problems as a result of the war. These poor men were generally accused of malingering or being weak and unmanly.

General Grant really did tell Meade to let Sheridan fight Stuart after the Battle of the Wilderness, in pretty much the exact words I have used in this book. The Union Army did not put much faith in its cavalry for the first two years of the war.

The United States has a long and enthusiastic history of nativism and anti-Catholicism. In 1834, a mob set fire to a convent in Charlestown, Massachusetts. Anti-Catholic and anti-immigrant sentiment found wholesale expression in the 1840s Know-Nothing or American Party. That party was absorbed by the Republican Party in the 1850s. Though the pre-Civil War Republican Party differed from the current party of that name in a great many instances (the party of Lincoln being considerably more pro-woman and more liberal) they do share a common embrace of nativist ideologies.

Louis's biographers say that Abraham Lincoln offered him the post at Cyprus, but there is nothing in Lincoln's papers or federal records to suggest this was so. There is a letter from Louis to Hiram Hitchcock, dated July 6 (well after Lincoln's murder), in which Louis reports that he is in Washington waiting to see Seward about the post. I took all the details about the Cesnolas' arrival at Larnaca and the confrontation with the Turkish authorities from Louis's book about his life and excavations in

Cyprus. He may have been an unreliable narrator but I thought he deserved to have his story told the way he told it.

I entirely invented Octavia Thompson, but she is modeled on British novelist and amateur archaeologist Amelia Edwards. One of the great nineteenth-century lady excavators, Edwards went to Egypt in the 1870s. Like the fictional Octavia, Edwards lived and traveled with her companion Ellen Braysher. Edwards is also the inspiration for Barbara Mertz's (aka Elisabeth Peters) nineteen Amelia Peabody novels.

Though Heinrich Schliemann was once considered a lion among archaeologists, by the 1970s members of the discipline condemned him for being everything from a poor excavator to a dangerous con man. Other critics point out that his excavations destroyed as much as they uncovered and that his record-keeping was at best inadequate. Other archaeologists point out that it is deeply unfair to judge Schliemann against twentieth-century excavating techniques. He was, they say, no better or worse than everyone else in the field. In fact, he may have been the best excavator of his time. Much the same thing might be said about Louis Cesnola's excavations on Cyprus. One of his biographers seems to have written about him only to excoriate him and his techniques, calling him disrespectful to ancient civilizations and accusing him of devastating Cypriot historic sites, pillaging them for his own personal gain. From a twentieth- or twenty-first-century perspective that may very well be true, but Cesnola was behaving no differently than the pack of European and American archaeologists working in Egypt and the Middle East. That he, along with every other field archaeologist, was a tool of European imperialism cannot be disputed, but this was the normative state of things in the last decades of the nineteenth century and it is all too easy to blame individuals for cultural norms we may now find repugnant. Hindsight is a tricky beast.

French archaeologist Jane Dieulafoy and her husband made a number of important discoveries in Susa, in what is now Iran. She did indeed dress as a man, from her suits to her haircut, a practice she began when she followed her husband to war in 1870.

The Medal of Honor described in Chapter Eighteen is the medal as it looked before 1896. It has been redesigned several times since then.

The obituary in the last chapter is a partial, but not entire reproduction of Louis's *New York Times* obituary. I cleaned up the awkward (for modern readers) English usage and removed several egregious errors of fact.

Lastly, I discovered that nearly everyone who wrote about Cesnola disliked him (to put it mildly). I thought there must be good reason so I began this project worried about how much of a scoundrel I would find him to be. But the more I learned about Louis the more I liked him. Yes, he was ambitious and proud, but Americans generally admire those traits (at least in men). Louis had more reason than most Union Army officers to be self-assured (or what his biographers call arrogant) and if he was impatient with his commanding officers he was not the only one. The Union Army had more than the usual comple-ment of incompetents and fools in its ranks. In Cyprus he was a good consul, more understanding of the locals than many con-suls were. He dug up antiquities with little regard for modern archaeology techniques (they having not yet been invented), but that was the way archaeologists worked at that time. Muse-ums existed to display the power of one culture to treat another culture's artifacts like objects of entertainment. Museums were, and to a great extent still are, tools of the imperialist impulse. This does not make them bad or unworthy of a visit, no more than the early Metropolitan Museum of Art's collection makes Louis a reprehensible character. In the end I was forced to conclude that the nearly unanimously negative writing about Louis Cesnola could be attributed, at least in part, to this nation's long history of anti-immigrant, anti-Catholic, and anti-Italian biases. There are hundreds of books cataloging the nativist impulse in America so I will not recount that history here. Suffice it to say, Louis Cesnola was no worse than many of his fellow and sister citizens and in many cases he was a great deal better. How many American men sat out the war, or made money from it? Not Louis. He fought for the Union when he did not have to and he led a regiment made up of immigrant men who were doing the same. He fought when he could have quit and gone home. So did the "foreigners" he fought with. He was brave, intelligent, and independent. He never gave up and never stopped reinventing himself. He worked hard all his life and he took every job seriously. In those qualities, like so many immigrants, he embodies the best of what it means to be an American.

About the Author

Peg A. Lamphier lives in the mountains of Southern California with five dogs, seven tortoises, a huge cat, two canaries, one husband, one daughter, and a collection of vintage ukuleles. When she's not writing fiction or otherwise fooling around she's a professor at California State Polytechnic, Pomona, and Mount San Antonio Community College. For more information and to sign up for her newsletter see www.peglamphier.com.

Also by Peg A. Lamphier

Kate Chase and William Sprague: Politics and Gender in a Civil War Marriage

Spur Up Your Pegasus: Family Letters of Salmon, Kate and Nettie Chase, 1844-73 (with James P. McClure and Erika M. Kreger)

Women in American History: A Social, Political and Cultural Encyclopedia with Document Collection [4 volumes] (with Rosanne Welch)

The Lincoln Special: Kate Warne Civil War Spy Series

Christopher Columbus: His Life and Discoveries
by Mario Di Giovanni

Dark Labyrinth
A Novel Based on the Life of Galileo Galilei
by Peter David Myers

Defying Danger
A Novel Based on the Life of Father Matteo Ricci
by Nicole Gregory

The Divine Proportions of Luca Pacioli
A Novel Based on the Life of Luca Pacioli
by W.A.W. Parker

Dreams of Discovery
A Novel Based on the Life of the Explorer John Cabot
by Jule Selbo

The Faithful
A Novel Based on the Life of Giuseppe Verdi
by Collin Mitchell

Fermi's Gifts
A Novel Based on the Life of Enrico Fermi
by Kate Fuglei

First Among Equals
A Novel Based on the Life of Cosimo de' Medici
by Francesco Massaccesi

God's Messenger
A Novel Based on the Life of Mother Frances X. Cabrini
by Nicole Gregory

Grace Notes
A Novel Based on the Life of Henry Mancini
by Stacia Raymond

Harvesting the American Dream
A Novel Based on the Life of Ernest Gallo
by Karen Richardson

Humble Servant of Truth
A Novel Based on the Life of Thomas Aquinas
by Margaret O'Reilly

Leonardo's Secret
A Novel Based on the Life of Leonardo da Vinci
by Peter David Myers

Little by Little We Won
A Novel Based on the Life of Angela Bambace
by Peg A. Lamphier, PhD

The Making of a Prince
A Novel Based on the Life of Niccolò Machiavelli
by Maurizio Marmorstein

A Man of Action Saving Liberty
A Novel Based on the Life of Giuseppe Garibaldi
by Rosanne Welch, PhD

Marconi and His Muses
A Novel Based on the Life of Guglielmo Marconi
by Pamela Winfrey

No Person Above the Law
A Novel Based on the Life of Judge John J. Sirica
by Cynthia Cooper

Relentless Visionary: Alessandro Volta
by Michael Berick

Ride Into the Sun
A Novel Based on the Life of Scipio Africanus
by Patric Verrone

The Soul of a Child
A Novel Based on the Life of Maria Montessori
by Kate Fuglei

What a Woman Can Do
A Novel Based on the Life of Artemisia Gentileschi
by Peg A. Lamphier, PhD

FUTURE TITLES FROM THE MENTORIS PROJECT

A Biography about Rita Levi-Montalcini
and
Novels Based on the Lives of:
Amerigo Vespucci
Andrea Doria
Antonin Scalia
Antonio Meucci
Buzzie Bavasi
Cesare Beccaria
Father Eusebio Francisco Kino
Federico Fellini
Frank Capra
Guido d'Arezzo
Harry Warren
Leonardo Fibonacci
Maria Gaetana Agnesi
Mario Andretti
Peter Rodino
Pietro Belluschi
Saint Augustine of Hippo
Saint Francis of Assisi
Vince Lombardi

For more information on these titles and
the Mentoris Project, please visit
www.mentorisproject.org